DARK MIRAGE

By

Geoff Loftus

Saugatuck
Books

Dark Mirage

© 2016 by Geoff Loftus

All rights reserved. No portion of this book may be reproduced, stored in a retrieval system, or transmitted in any form by any means — electronic, mechanical, photocopy, recording, scanning, or other — except for brief quotations in critical reviews or articles, without the prior written permission of the publisher. For information, please contact info@geoffloftus.com.

Dark Mirage is a work of fiction. Any resemblance to actual people is unintentional and coincidental. A serious attempt has been made to portray the details and geography of the New York metropolitan area accurately, but the needs of the story may have driven me to exercise poetic license, even with some actual places and buildings. I hope the reader will excuse this.

Cover design by Tom Galligan, Green Thumb Graphics.

Published by Saugatuck Books.

For Stephen Pitts,
An everyday hero—I'm humbled to be your friend

1

NIGHT – MANHATTAN: CENTRAL PARK WEST

MARISSA CARVAJAL WOKE UP SOAKED IN BLOOD. Her head was pounding, her throat was raw, and she was still drunk even as she slowly regained consciousness directly into a hangover. It was impossible to think or feel anything except for the pain in her skull, but she gradually became aware that everything was wet: the sheets, the pillows, her naked body.

She forced her eyes open. The bedroom was almost pitch black, with a tiny sliver of light seeping from a thin crack between a door and its frame. Marissa didn't know where she was. Didn't know how she had gotten there. There was a vague, quick flash of memory: She had climbed into a taxi with a man. A tall man with a chiseled chin and sandy hair. But that was all she remembered. Was that earlier this evening? Or earlier this week? She was too drunk to locate the memory accurately.

She rolled over, twisting in a puddle in the middle of the bed. With a start, she realized the wetness had awakened her. She pulled her hand up and looked at it in the thin shaft of light from the crack at the door—her hand, her entire arm, was covered in blood. She glanced down at her breasts and stomach and the sheets—everything was soaked in glistening blood.

Marissa gasped—the chiseled-chin man from the taxi was on his back next to her, naked, his eyes open and unblinking, blood covering his chest, throat, arms, and face.

Marissa staggered to her feet and backed away from the bed, whispering, "Oh my God . . . oh my God. Please, God, no. . . ."

She left bloody footprints on the carpet as she backed toward the light. She was panicked. Where was she? She knew that she had never been here before. She pushed through a door into the bathroom and locked it behind her as if that would keep her safe from the horror of the dead man.

She was gasping, panting for breath. Marissa caught her reflection in the mirror: she was bloody from head to foot. She stepped toward the door, considering returning to the bedroom, then turned back toward the mirror and glimpsed the marble shower stall in the reflection. She turned on the water, and as soon as it was hot, stepped inside and washed herself clean. As the water coursed over her, she wondered if she and the man had had sex, but she couldn't remember. After soaping—Marissa recognized the citrus-piney scent of Penhaligon soap, very expensive but wonderful—and rinsing off twice, she turned off the water, pushed open the glass shower door, grabbed a thick, Egyptian-cotton towel, and dried off. She dropped the used towel in a hamper to one side of the bathroom, wrapped herself in a dry towel, and walked back into the bedroom.

Only as she crossed the room did it occur to her that the dead man could not have cared less if she was naked.

Marissa had left the bathroom door wide open, allowing light from the bathroom to spill into the bedroom. She was relieved: her dress was draped over a leather chair in front of a large, high-def TV. Her bra and panties were on the floor. She had another brief flash of memory: She was kissing the chiseled-chin man as they staggered drunkenly toward the bed. He pulled her clothes off, dropping them randomly on the floor and the chair in a path from the door to the bed. There was a quick cut in her memory: She was naked on the bed, and the man stood by the bedside, took off his clothes, tossed them at a chair near the window, and lay down beside her. She snapped out of the memory and checked: his clothes were in a heap over the chair. The blood hadn't splattered to that side of the very large room. She dressed rapidly, found her heels on the floor inside the bedroom door, stepped into them, glanced around the room to make certain she was leaving nothing behind, and walked out.

She went down a hallway, through an enormous living room toward what she guessed was the front door. She paused to glance through the wall-to-wall windows of the living room. The apartment was probably on a floor in the twenties, with a spectacular eastward view over Central Park. Marissa saw the entrance to the park's 86th Street Transverse only two or three blocks north on Central Park West. One of those grand, pre-war buildings with twenty-four-hour doormen. And a security camera in the lobby. Maybe even one in the elevator. She turned back toward the bedroom. *Oh my God, did I kill him? I couldn't have . . . could I? Why did I kill him? Why? And how, how could I do that . . . God, please no, please. . . .*

But she was alone in the apartment with a murdered man. She was hit with a wave of nausea as she realized that she would certainly appear guilty to the police. She was breathing hard as if she'd just run a marathon, trying to figure out what to do next.

You have to get out, she told herself. *Now.*

The front door had a security peephole at about her eye level. At a right angle on the wall next to the front door was another door with no peephole—a closet. Her coat was hanging next to a man's overcoat with a scarf draped over the hangar's hook. She grabbed her coat, the man's scarf, then reached up to pull a black, wide-brimmed fedora from the shelf. She slid into the coat, wrapped the scarf around the lower part of her face, pulled the hat down low over her eyes, dug her gloves out of her coat pockets, and pulled them on. As she was about to pull open the front door, Marissa noticed a small, lacquered table with a stack of mail on it. She searched through the bills; all were addressed to Jackson McGill.

Marissa dropped the mail and slumped back against the wall. Jackson McGill. New York's answer to Richard Branson. Wealthy beyond counting, successful at everything he put his hand to (including women), and covered as often by the celebrity press as by business journalists. She realized that the dead man matched the news pictures of Jackson McGill.

Marissa whispered, "Oh my God." She took a deep breath, straightened up, grabbed the front doorknob, opened the door, and stepped into the small hallway.

There was only the one apartment on the floor. Marissa pressed the call button for the elevator and it arrived with a quiet metallic thunk. The doors slid open. She tugged the hat even lower over her eyes and walked onto the elevator.

As she crossed the building's lobby, Marissa didn't look at or say anything to the doorman. She stepped out onto Central Park West and turned south. That was not the direction of her apartment, but she was taking no chances that McGill's doorman noticed which way she headed.

She walked quickly, unaware of the December chill in the dark, early morning air. The Christmas decorations on the front of many of the apartment buildings made no impression on her. She couldn't remember a thing from the evening before except for the vague flash of getting into the taxi with McGill, getting into bed with him, nothing else. Did I kill him? I must have . . . I must have . . . but I couldn't kill him. Could I? I didn't stab him to death. . . .

Marissa stopped completely still in the middle of the sidewalk. The weapon—she hadn't seen it anywhere. It was probably still there, lying in the bloody sheets or fallen under the bed.

Her fingerprints might be all over it. She took a few stumbling steps back toward McGill's building, stopped, turned back again. She couldn't go back. She gasped and began walking, almost running, eager to escape. She reached a corner and had to stop as a car turned off Central Park West into a side street. She checked her watch: It was 5:38 A.M.

2

In the early morning of December 13th, with the digital clock on my bedside table reading 5:38 A.M., I woke up without knowing why. I didn't have to go the bathroom (I'm not that old, yet); I didn't have a splitting headache from too much to drink; and my late wife Maggie was not calling me to wake up. More's the pity.

I lay in bed, awake and alert, listening. But there was nothing. What the hell, I thought, might as well make some use of this moment. I got out of bed, went into the bathroom, used the facilities, and put the toilet seat down when I was finished—Maggie had gotten me into the habit. I checked the dark apartment in case someone was there. Nobody. I stood still in the middle of the living room and listened intently. Nothing. In my bedroom, I checked and listened again. Nothing. I couldn't figure out what had summoned me from a deep sleep.

"Maggie?" I whispered. I didn't expect an answer. My wife had passed away more than five years ago. Which didn't stop me from calling to her. "Maggie?"

There was no answer. I went back to bed, laid down, and stared up through my dark room at the ceiling.

Once upon a time, my wife was murdered on the front steps of the Manhattan brownstone where we lived. I was shot, too. Four times to be precise. Lots of blood. And pain. But I survived. Maggie was dead within seconds of the bullets ripping into her.

I had been a U.S. Marshal and taken a bribe. I wish there was a way to whitewash that evil fact, but there isn't. I was a criminal with a badge, taking money from some very bad people to do a bad thing—sell out witnesses in the Witness Protection program. Since I didn't actually possess the information regarding witnesses and, therefore, couldn't deliver it to the folks who'd bribed me, I had rationalized that what I did was a stupid idea but not a terrible, immoral act.

That was bullshit. Taking a bribe was wrong no matter what. No matter how I tried to rationalize it or minimize it, it was wrong.

Even worse, the ugly types bribing me had no sense of humor when it came to my failing to deliver what they had paid for. So they put four bullets in me. Three more bullets hit Maggie. She died on the spot, on the stoop of our brownstone on the Upper West Side. After her death, most nights I lay on my bed in the dark, staring at the ceiling, drunk and exhausted, unable to sleep. Barely able to breathe because my guilt over my wife's killing was immense.

For five years after Maggie's murder, most nights I had passed out drunk. Sometimes I had passed out on the couch and managed not to roll off. Other nights, well . . . I had ended up on the living room floor or the kitchen floor or the bathroom floor. Even when I had woken in the bathroom, it didn't mean I had brushed my teeth or even gone to the bathroom before passing out. Almost no matter where or when I woke up, my mouth had felt as if it were stuffed full of musty, dusty carpeting. Some nights my pants had been dry; other nights they had been soaked from my urinating in my unconscious state.

On the June night of the fifth anniversary of my wife's murder, I had enjoyed the good fortune of passing out on the couch and not wetting myself. Maggie had woken me, appearing to me in the middle of the night and saved my life. Yes, that's right: she had appeared to me, like Marley's ghost in *A Christmas Carol*.

I heard her softly calling my name. My eyelids were so heavy I could barely open them. I blinked, expecting to see an empty apartment, believing that her voice was a dream. But she was standing a few feet away from me.

"Jack," she whispered, "I need to talk to you."

She was in the same light-yellow T-shirt and khaki shorts she had died in, but there was no blood. And she was surrounded by a warm glow, almost as if her body were in a halo.

"Jack, are you awake?"

"Maggie?"

"I'm here."

"You can't be. It's just not possible. Not. Possible. NOT." I pushed myself off the couch and took a half-step toward her. She stepped back the same distance, her halo

moving with her. "Are you . . . are you . . . I'm sorry, but you're . . . dead. Is this a dream?"

"No. I'm really here. We're really talking."

I shook my head—a truly terrible idea when you've had as much to drink as I had in the last twenty-four hours. "I've been drunk before . . . even had some hallucinations, but this . . . this is the worst. No, best—it's good to see you, to talk to you, even if you're not real. I've missed you so much."

"I miss you, too."

I didn't know what to say. Should I offer her a drink or a seat? Ask her how she was? "I, uh . . . well . . . I . . ."

She cut me off, "I hate what you've become. You're more than this."

"Sorry, but I'm not trying to impress a hallucination—"

"Stop that," *she interrupted me.* "You're throwing your life away. You're capable of more."

"Says the ghost. Or the hallucination. Take your pick."

"You're drunk, but I am not a hallucination. I'm here to help you become what you're supposed to be."

I collapsed back onto the couch. "Oh, geez. I don't think I need my drunken subconscious delivering a self-help lecture. Forget it. Not interested. Get lost."

Maggie paced a few steps toward the bay window overlooking 76th Street then came back to face me. "Please don't drink for the next twenty-four hours."

"Why? What difference will twenty-four hours make?"

"Please? I'll come back tomorrow night, come back when you're capable of understanding that I'm really here and not an alcoholic hallucination."

"You are the damnedest dream I've ever had."

"If you love me, don't drink, and I'll return tomorrow."

And she was gone.

Maggie didn't fade away, and she didn't pop invisibly out of sight. She just . . . disappeared.

"Holy shit," I muttered. "That was a doozy."

. . . I had spent the next day avoiding a drink because the ghost of my murdered wife had requested that I be sober for our next meeting. Despite the lack of booze, I hadn't been jittery or hungover—I had been in a state of anxious, yet happy, anticipation that Maggie was coming to see me that night. And she did. . . .

"You didn't drink today."

"I wanted to see you again." I sat up.

"You believe in me now. I'm not just a drunken dream?"

"Maybe you're a symptom of some kind of mental break, I don't know." I found it impossible to believe she was really there, standing in my living room in her halo, but I was incredibly happy to see her. "I'm glad you're here, whatever you are. I've missed you."

"I know, but the man I loved was someone I wanted to have a family with—now you're a . . . " her voice faded, unable to finish.

"A bum? A guy who drinks too much? Who's throwing his life away running errands for people on the wrong side of the law?"

"Yes."

I took a deep breath and confessed, "That started before you died."

"You took a bribe."

"Yes."

"Why? Why would you do such a thing?"

"I've asked myself that a thousand times, and I still don't have a good answer." I paused to swallow and then take a deep breath. *"I . . . I saw too many awful things in Afghanistan. Maybe I was suffering from PTSD, I don't know. And . . . I was angry that we had fertility problems, . . . I was ticked off with my bosses, I hated the mob guys I was escorting into witness protection. And since I had no intention of passing on the info the bribe was paying for, I didn't feel like it was as horrible as it was."*

"That's all rationalizing," she said gently.

I nodded. "I was angry and felt sorry for myself because of the war, and because of our issues, and my work . . . my drinking . . . I acted out. It was an angry, terrible thing to do. It was an incredibly stupid thing to do—I'm . . . sorry." I paused, trying to collect myself. *"I got you killed, I never . . ."* I swallowed hard a couple of times. *"I'm so sorry,"* I muttered through my tears.

Maggie took a step closer but stopped short of touching me. *"You didn't kill me. You are not the evil person who murdered me. You made a very bad choice, but someone else killed me."*

I wiped the tears from my cheeks.

"You volunteered to serve your country, and you served well. You won a Silver Star and a Purple Heart. But those medals weren't enough when you came home and needed help to adjust. You buried your feelings and joined the Marshals and that meant you could continue to serve. But you never got any help. When we met and fell for each other, it was wonderful for both of us. I saw how funny you are, how caring. But the happiness of early romance masked a lot of your issues. Eventually, even with our love, your problems were still there. Because we were close, I couldn't see what you needed and do anything to help you. And, since you didn't get help, you acted out. You made a horrible choice. But you're not a bad man, and you didn't kill me. Do you hear me?" she asked.

"Yes."

"I still love you. That's why I'm here. I love you too much to watch you waste your life. I interceded on your behalf and got you a chance to turn your life around."

"What the hell are you talking about?"

She smiled again. "Hell has nothing to do with it. I'm talking about a second chance. Do you want it? Do you want to redeem yourself?"

. . . Snapping out of my memories, I thought: Who didn't want to redeem himself? But her visit had been so . . . *bizarre*. I had to have been lost in a drunken delusion. As if I were some kind of weird, modern Ebenezer Scrooge and Maggie was a tantalizingly appealing version of Jacob Marley's ghost in *A Christmas Carol*. But it hadn't feel like a delusion. It had felt real. . . .

"Do you want to redeem yourself?"

"What do I have to do?"

"Help others. Make things right for them. You've been wallowing in self-pity for five years when you could have been focused on helping others."

"Geez, don't hold back."

"It's true, and that is your fault."

I took a deep breath. "Okay, you're right. Whom do I help and how do I help them?"

"Harry will tell you what to do."

"Harry? Who is Harry? Maybe I should ask, what is Harry?"

"He'll be your . . . ," Maggie hesitated, searching for the right word, ". . . guide. He'll explain what you need to do for your second chance."

"Oh." I was afraid to ask what I had to ask, "What about you? Will I see you again?"

She whispered, "I don't know."

"Please, please come again."

"I will if I can."

And she was gone. I sat on the couch, put my head in my hands, and wept.

Maggie's ghost had intervened on my behalf, the same way Marley's ghost helped Scrooge. She had found an opportunity for me to right the wrongs in the lives of other people. I was to employ the many skills given me by the U.S. Army Special Forces and the Marshals Service to do good for others. Like Scrooge, I would be redeemed by my own good, selfless acts. My wonderful Maggie had arranged for me to meet Harry . . .

Without any understanding of how I arrived there, I found myself on a beach, the waves breaking and rushing up the sand toward my bare feet but stopping inches short of my toes. The sun was setting and the sky was red with a beautiful, end-of-day glow. It made me think of the old adage: Red sky at night—sailor's delight. Looking around, I realized two things: I didn't know where I was and I didn't know the black man standing next to me. He was tall, slender, and wearing a well-cut, light-gray suit and a dark blue tie. His dark skin was without wrinkles and stretched smoothly from his cheekbones to his solid jawline. He could have been anywhere from twenty-five to forty years old.

"Do I know you?" I asked.

"I'm Harry," he said. His voice was deep and firm. "Your wife told you I was coming."

"I'm—"

He interrupted me, saying, "Jack Tyrrell. I know almost everything about you."

"Really?" I packed as much sarcasm into the short word as was possible.

"Yes. For example: I know when, where, and how you were shot and how Maggie died."

"Are you serious? Did you witness her killing?"

"Yes, in a way," Harry said quietly.

"What does that mean?" I repeated in shock.

"It means, 'Yes,' I am completely aware how she was killed, how you almost died in the same incident, and your feelings of guilt."

His calm demeanor made me angry. Or maybe it was his pronouncement that he knew about Maggie's death and my guilt. I gazed out to sea and watched the ocean toss wave after wave onto the sand. How could I be on the beach? How could I hear the surf and smell the salty air? How could I be here? I was struck by a thought so overpowering I couldn't believe it.

"Are you . . ." it was impossible to say the words, but I tried again, "are you . . . ?"

"No. But I work for Him."

"Are you taking me somewhere?"

"No, I'm going to send you somewhere."

"Where?"

"Wherever the Chairman wants you to go."

"The Chairman . . . ? Is he . . . ?" I couldn't phrase my question. Instead, I timidly pointed toward the sky.

"Yes." Harry nodded. "I work for Him. I'm your Supervisor."

I found it hard to breathe. I walked around in a small circle, ignoring the tide line and the surf coming over my feet. "You work for . . . Him? And . . . I work for you?"

"We—you and I—both work for the Chairman. I'll be the one conveying His plan to you."

"Do I get to meet the Chairman at some point?"

"Everyone meets the Chairman eventually."

"Could I . . . could you tell me what His plan for me is?"

"You're going to right wrongs."

"Now my job in this business is to right wrongs?"

"Yes. Maggie interceded with the Chairman to give you this chance before you die."

"Why didn't the Chairman give me this chance before taking Maggie?"

"He did."

I stopped walking in a circle. "What the hell does that mean? Are you saying I had this chance and I blew it?"

Harry replied evenly, "The Chairman has given you many chances."

"Have you come to me before?"

"No. But some of my colleagues have. The Chairman doesn't give up easily—even when dealing with someone as obstinate as you."

"Why didn't He make me see the light?"

"That's not how it works. We all have free will; we all choose how we live. You chose not to recognize my colleagues, and you chose not to listen to their messages."

I sighed, staring at the ocean's dark horizon against the less-dark night sky. Finally, I said, "Okay, what does this righting wrongs job involve?"

Harry said, "Your experience will be put to use in helping people—victims—that the law enforcement community isn't able to assist."

"How the hell am I going to accomplish what the NYPD or the FBI or any other agency can't? I'm not Superman."

"You will receive direction from me, something the police and federal agents don't get. The Chairman will make sure you have the resources you need to solve cases and help people."

"Why doesn't the Chairman help these folks directly? Couldn't He do it quick and easy?"

"He could, but then you wouldn't have the opportunity to help them."

I said, "The opportunity to help them—are you telling me we're all supposed to take care of each other?"

His large, dark eyes met mine. "Yes."

. . . Now you know how I met Harry Mitchum. One instant I was asleep, and the next, I was on a beach talking with Harry. Despite his friendly name, the mere idea of Harry was terrifying. Why? Well, I had come to believe that Harry was . . . well . . . an angel. I know the word "angel" makes me sound nuts. The possibility that I am completely and absolutely out of my mind is very real. I'm not asking you to understand how this angelic presence works, because there is no way I can adequately explain it. I'm not asking you to believe. But this is the only story I have to tell. You don't need to understand because I don't understand Maggie's intervention or Harry's presence in my life. You don't have to believe.

But *my* story is that I believe that Maggie did intervene and that Harry is active in my life. I believe that Harry and I teamed up, saved a couple of veterans suffering from PTSD, and wiped out the New York operations of a very nasty Russian Mafia boss, who also got wiped out. (A note of clarification: I did the wiping out. Harry is not an *avenging* angel; he does not engage in that kind of activity.)

Helping others by taking on the Russian mafia—one of its New York City chapters, anyway—was crazy, frightening, and sad. Apparently the Chairman felt that my talents, honed by the U.S. Army's Special Forces and the U.S. Marshals Service, made me capable of helping in this kind of situation. And, I have to admit, that once all the death and fear had passed, once my goodbyes had been said to the people I helped, I felt good for the first time in five years.

When all of my dealings with the Russians were complete, when every last detail had been settled, I had asked Harry if I would ever see my wife again, and he had replied, "I don't know."

To be completely honest, I'm not sure if Harry really didn't know or if it was against the rules for him to tell me what he did know. Maybe I shouldn't call them rules, maybe they were guidelines. Incredibly strict guidelines. You probably need to understand the rules or guidelines I operate under when I'm working with Harry.

I must do good for others, with no thought of myself. I can't right the wrongs of my past—that especially means avenging Maggie's death. The people I help will not remember me after I accomplish whatever mission Harry gives me. The whole process is about me giving to others. There's nothing in it for me. If that sounds like baloney to you, well, . . . it did to me, too. But frustrating as it is to be forgotten by people you've come to care for, selflessly doing right by others is stupendously satisfying.

Now, every night when I go to sleep (and I *go to sleep*, I do not *pass out*), I hope Maggie's soft voice will wake me again, and I'll see her one last time. Then I would be truly lucky.

No, not lucky. I would be blessed.

3

I woke up for the second time that morning at 7:10 and glanced at the empty space in bed next to me. Well, Tyrrell, you can mope because you're all alone or you can get up, shower, shave, make breakfast, and read *The New York Times* while sipping your java. I chose the shower, shave, breakfast path over moping. Once I was settled with my breakfast, I confess that I skipped past the news stories and the political commentary—and went straight to the sports pages. Many New York sports fans will tell you that you must read the *Post* or the *Daily News*. Each paper has fans who insist that the *real* deal is to be found in its sports pages. I enjoy both, but I've always preferred the *Times*. I grew up on the Old Gray Lady's sports section. When I was seven-years old, my father had helped me read my way through Red Smith's column. Even at that young age, I loved Smith's writing. (And loved the time with my father.) Red Smith and my father were both long gone, but I saw no reason to change my allegiance to another newspaper. Maggie would have said that was because I never really grew up.

I read the paper (I thought of it as a newspaper even though I read the digital version on my laptop) but without giving it my full attention. I was restless and couldn't begin to figure the reason. Ever since my 5:38 A.M. wakeup, I felt as if I was being called to a mission. But that was a figment of my imagination. (Or, as my friends and I had said when we were kids, a fig newton of my imagination.) I finished the sports section, drank the last of my coffee, rinsed the plate of the vestiges of eggs and toast, wandered into my living room, and gazed out the windows, waiting. I cannot begin to tell you what I was waiting for, but I had a very definite sense that something was about to happen. . . .

I was on a beach, with waves crashing up the sand, stopping short of my bare toes. I was dressed in the same long-sleeve T-shirt and gray sweat pants I'd been wearing at breakfast. There were gray clouds in the sky, but sunlight flashed in breaks between the clouds, creating towers of light over the ocean. I didn't know where this beach was, but I recognized it. This was the beach where Harry had held his first consultations with me. Where he had given me my first mission to right wrongs for other people.

Still looking out to sea, I said, "Hello, Harry."

"Hello, Jack." As usual, Harry was well dressed—navy-blue pinstriped suit (not the gangster pinstripes you might see on *Boardwalk Empire* or *The Sopranos*, but a subtle, Ralph Lauren suit). His dark skin was unwrinkled and made him looker younger than my weathered, white skin. He had close-cropped dark hair, while I had wavy, light-brown hair that was long enough to go over my ears and collar. His eyes were brown and mine were blue. I liked to think I had nicer eyes than Harry, but it was probably a matter of taste.

"You look well," he said.

"That's an awfully formal locution. But thanks, I am well. And you?"

The tiniest of smiles flashed briefly across his face. "We don't . . . *live* the way you do. We don't *feel* the way you do. Your question isn't really germane. But thank you for asking."

"Was that angel-speak for 'mind your own business'?"

"No."

I didn't respond to that and continued to enjoy the waves and the play of sunlight through clouds onto the ocean surface.

"Would you like to know why you're here?" Harry asked.

"You'll tell me when you're ready to."

"I *am* ready." His face was serious. At least, I think it was serious. From what I could tell, Harry really only had two expressions: serious and *very* serious. If he was puzzled by something, he appeared to be serious. If he was serious, he appeared to be *very* serious. In rare moments, if I was watching closely, I might catch a glimpse of a microscopic smile or scowl. An eyebrow might creep up his forehead by an infinitesimal amount. This wasn't to say that Harry didn't have emotions. I was pretty sure he did. But he seemed unable to express them the way you or I would.

"Who am I helping?" I asked.

"Don't you want to hear what her problem is before you agree to help?"

"Is that really part of our deal?"

"I wasn't aware we had a deal."

"Our situation, our process, the thing that we do, or maybe I should say: the thing that I do. You tell me, and I go help."

"No, the Chairman sends me to talk to you, I explain the problem, and you choose to help."

"Please, no speeches about the Chairman and free will. I surrender—I will choose to help."

"Or not."

"Or not," I agreed. "Who needs me?"

"Marissa Carvajal. She woke up in bed with Jackson McGill, in his apartment. She was naked and covered in blood. He was dead."

"Holy shit."

"Not how I would have phrased it, but . . . yes."

"Do the police have her?"

"She left the apartment at 5:38 A.M. As yet, the police are unaware of the crime."

I raised my eyebrows. "My early morning wakeup was a call to action, wasn't it?"

"If you think so."

"Does the Chairman want me to prove her innocent? Or . . . ?"

"The Chairman wants you to discern the truth of the situation and then do what you can to help whomever needs your help."

The waves rushed farther up the sand. The tide was coming in. I was going to have to step back or get soaked. Take action or get wet.

"I don't suppose I could see McGill's apartment?"

A second later, we were on Central Park West, on the park side of the street, with a grand, pre-war building opposite us. I said "a second later" but that sounds as if I was aware of a tiny sliver of time passing or of transferring from the beach to Manhattan. I wasn't aware of anything at all. In one moment, I was on the beach, thinking about stepping back to keep my feet dry, and the next moment—*with no sensation of time passing or distance traveled*—I was on Central Park West. I was also appropriately dressed for a cold December morning in Manhattan, in a heavy, warm parka courtesy of L.L. Bean, gray wool sweater and blue, oxford shirt underneath, blue jeans, and suede ankle boots. I patted myself down with my gloved hands: my wallet was in the inside pocket of the parka, where I usually kept it, my apartment keys were in a zipped outer pocket. Harry had miraculously decked me out with only one thing missing: my Ruger pistol in a shoulder holster. I hoped that meant there was no gunplay in my immediate future.

"You gotta teach me how to do that," I said appreciatively.

"Do what?"

I nodded sagely, as if I had anything to be sage about. "Got it. It's an angel thing."

Harry shook his head, an extremely minimalist shake, and pointed across the street. There were three police cruisers and a couple of unmarked cars parked in front of the building. "That's McGill's building. He has a penthouse on the twenty-fifth floor."

"Nice neighborhood." I scanned the building from top to bottom. "Could we go in through the lobby, take the elevator, and check out the apartment? Invisibly?"

Harry's face was like stone. "No one will be aware of us."

We crossed the street in the middle of the block, and since we were jaywalking (like all good New Yorkers do), I checked the traffic in both directions. The traffic wasn't a problem, but something pinged my internal radar: A dark, metallic-gray E350 Mercedes sedan was parked a half a block away on the Central Park side of the street. Two Asian men in dark suits, white shirts, dark ties, and sunglasses sat inside. The sun was in the eastern sky, and the Mercedes was in the shade of the park's trees. I had a strong feeling that the two men were wearing the glasses to obscure their looks, not to aid their eyesight. If these two weren't staking out McGill's building, I was sadly mistaken. By mistaken, I mean thinking "MySpace would be more successful than Facebook" mistaken. Another item I was 99.9% certain about: these two were not police. Not FBI, DEA, or ATF. It was faintly possible they were CIA, but then again, the CIA is not supposed to be operating domestically. My guess: these guys were Chinese intelligence. Jackson McGill had done a ton of business with Chinese entities; he was one of the first Americans to invest in China in a huge way. All of which led me to believe that the Asians in the Mercedes were Chinese. Maybe government, maybe corporate—in China the lines could get very blurry.

I plucked at Harry's sleeve as we crossed the street and gestured toward the Mercedes, "Do I need to worry about those guys?"

He paused for a fraction of a second in mid-step, examined the car, resumed his step, and said, "Possibly."

"Very helpful. Who are they?"

"They are Chinese. But you already guessed that."

"McGill's company, Cú Chulainn Enterprises, is invested up the wazoo in a bunch of Chinese firms, and I would bet my last yuan that those two stake-out artists are from China."

Harry didn't bother to respond to my theory of a connection between McGill and the Chinese.

We crossed the street and threaded our way through the parked police cars and into McGill's lobby. I ignored the uniformed police officers and the on-duty doorman instead taking time to inspect the lobby. There were two cameras, one high up inside the front door, and another at the back of the lobby. No one could walk into this building and escape unobserved. Unless they happened to be with my buddy

Harry. As we stepped toward the elevator, I took in the lobby's décor: marble floors, a marble-topped service desk for the doorman, and what looked (to my untrained eye) like extremely expensive wallpaper.

Harry said, "It's imported from France."

"Cost a kazillion bucks a yard, right?"

"That is not a real number."

"Spoil sport."

We stepped into the elevator, which I assume Harry had magically summoned. More expensive wallpaper and polished brass for the elevator buttons. A small, cushioned bench backed up to the far wall of the elevator. I guessed the bench was for the building's rich old ladies—they could sit as they rode up. Rest their tired feet after a morning of shopping at Tiffany's. Or Cartier's. Or Bendel's. Or someplace much more chic—some exulted place far beyond my humble station. How humble? Well, that small bench cost more than my living room couch. Probably more than all of my living room furniture put together. Sheesh.

As we stepped out of the elevator onto the twenty-fifth floor, I said, "What's with the Chinese on Central Park West? Why are they interested in McGill's building?"

Harry shrugged, like all of his gestures it was subtle to the point of being barely perceptible. "I have no idea."

We stood in a small foyer with two doors. One had a security peephole and a brass number plate that read "25" and was wide open. I pointed to the other door.

"Service entrance?"

Harry nodded and waved me past a uniformed cop and into the apartment. He led the way through a gigantic, opulent living room with a magnificent view of the park down a hall and into the master bedroom. The room was so big it made the king bed look small. There was a large wooden desk to one side of the room with an upholstered, swivel desk chair. In another corner, there was a small sitting area with leather chairs and love seat in front of a 50-inch high-definition TV.

The bedroom was full of police. Plainclothes detectives examined the crime scene. Uniformed cops were helping a couple of crime-scene techs carry bagged evidence away. A female photographer snapped photos from every possible angle. Another woman was lifting fingerprints from every surface in the room: the crystal glasses on the night tables on each side of the bed, all of the furniture, doorknobs, windows and sills, and the light-switch plates near the doors.

Two detectives were focused on the body. Jackson McGill. Billionaire philanthropist and playboy. A bloody mess at the moment. He lay on his back, his arms crossed over his abdomen as if he had been holding onto his belly. His eyes were wide open; savage wounds covered most of his naked body. Blood everywhere.

I whispered to Harry, "Whoever cut up McGill was an amateur. Or wanted him to suffer. There's too much blood for a quick death, which is how a pro would have done it. Quickly."

"You don't have to whisper. They don't know we're here."

"Can't help myself."

I stepped closer to the body and listened to a gray-haired man from the Medical Examiner's Office point out to the detectives a particularly ugly wound on McGill's neck: "See this? I think that's the fatal wound. The others are slashing cuts. This one's deep stab—then a sawing motion to make sure it was lethal."

Harry pointed at a whipcord-thin woman detective and said, "Renee Luker." Then he gestured toward her partner, a short Hispanic and said, "Miguel Islas."

A crime scene tech handed Luker a plastic evidence bag containing a very bloody, very slender blade with an ornate handle. The tech said, "Looks like a Renaissance stiletto. Not sure if it's Italian or French. If it's a genuine antique, it probably costs about two thousand bucks. There's tons of Renaissance era silverware on shelves in the living room, and an empty knife stand."

"Two thousand bucks? For one ancient knife?" Islas asked.

"Antique," Luker corrected. She looked at the guy from the Medical Examiner's office, "Could the killer have used this to cut through the carotid?"

"Definitely. Death would have been quick after that. The bleeding stopped when the heart stopped. If I'm right, this was the last wound. All of the others were to make the victim suffer."

The detective waved her hand at the rumpled, blood-soaked bedding, "What do you think, Miguel? Maybe an unsatisfied lover? Could someone get that pissed off over a Viagra malfunction?"

Islas asked as if genuinely interested, "Is Viagra the one with the people in bath tubs on TV?"

"No, that's Cialis," Luker replied.

"Renee, you are a font of useless info. What the hell are the bathtubs for? And why are the man and woman in separate tubs? Isn't the point of the drug to make sure you can get it on when you get it together?"

"Who knows?" Luker pointed at the sheets again, "Do you think McGill's lover could have done this?"

The medical examiner shook his head, "Hard to tell. McGill was a big, healthy, active man. Hard to imagine a woman could inflict this much pain and still pin him down. On the other hand, if he had enough alcohol and/or drugs in his system, the killer would have had an easy time of it."

"If he was drunk or drugged, why are the eyes open?"

"Maybe the pain from the early cuts brought him to consciousness—just in time to have his carotid cut."

"Charming," said Islas. He glanced at his partner, "There were no signs of forced entry, no signs anyone was here besides McGill and his lover, right?"

"Right. No live-in staff. Before I came up here, I reviewed the security tapes for this evening. McGill walked in with a brunette a few minutes after midnight. The woman was five foot three or four, thick, dark hair to her shoulders. Couldn't tell the color of the eyes; couldn't see any distinguishing marks. But a very curvy lady—exactly who you'd expect given McGill's reputation."

I shifted my attention to Harry and raised my eyebrows in a question. He nodded.

Islas asked, "Anyone else come up here?"

"There's no video of anyone else being here. But a woman in a wide-brimmed hat left around the probably time of death. Couldn't see her face, but approximately the same height and similar coat as the woman who entered with McGill."

"Interesting. How good is the security set-up? Could someone else have slipped in and out?"

"Damn near impossible," Luker said. "There are two security cameras covering the lobby from different angles. Then there's another in the elevator. There are cameras on the outside and inside of the service entrance on the southern edge of the building. The service entrance is a plain steel door, hinges on the inside, opens to the inside but there are anti-pry plates on top and sides. Four sliding bars lock the door: top, bottom, and both sides. The freight elevator, which is inside the service entrance to the building, also has a camera. All the cameras feed into a computer at the lobby desk and simultaneously from there to a private security service called Celtic Dragon, which is jointly owned venture of McGill's company, Cú Chulainn and a Chinese firm called SHK Dragon. There are also sensors on the front and service doors—all entrances and exits are logged into the same system and synched with the video. The entrance logs also go to Celtic Dragon. It's damn close to air-tight."

"What about the roof? Any access there?"

Luker shook her head, "This building is taller than its neighbors; you can't climb down to the roof. And there are more cameras up there, and the log for the roof shows no one going through the door in the last seventy-two hours. Before you ask, yes, McGill's apartment is also secure. There are two cameras covering the twenty-fifth floor foyer—those cameras also feed direct to Celtic Dragon. Both the front and service doors are steel; both have sliding bars to lock from the inside. Once Mr. McGill was inside, he was a safe guy."

"Unless he brought his killer with him."

"Yeah, well, it's always something."

*   *   *

We returned to Central Park West, directly in front of McGill's building via one of Harry's whooshes or teleportations or whatever the hell they were. One moment we were standing by the bed of the murdered man, then I nodded to indicate I was done, and without the tiniest awareness of time I found myself standing on the sidewalk.

The Chinese pair were still on watch in their Mercedes.

"When I asked you if I should worry about those gentlemen," I jerked my thumb at their car, "you said, 'possibly.' Should I go eavesdrop on them in invisible mode? Or maybe we could go visible and ask a few questions."

"We are now visible," he wasn't amused by my suggestion.

We crossed the street to the passenger side of the Mercedes. Neither head turned to follow our approach. If they were watching us, they were doing it out of the corner of their eyes. I rapped on the window with my knuckles.

The men sat completely still, giving no indication that they were aware I was knocking on their window. I turned my fist sideways and pounded on the window with the outer, fleshy edge of my hand. It made for a nice series of deep thumping noises. But there was no reaction from inside.

"Okay," I said to Harry. "Not the cooperative types."

His only response was his expressionless face.

I shrugged, walked to the back of the car, crouched near the rear tire on the passenger side, unscrewed the cap on the tire valve, and used my apartment key to depress the valve's pin. There was a sharp hissing noise and the tire began to deflate. Not enough so it would be a problem at first, but if one of the gents didn't get out of the car and stop me, it was going to require a can of compressed air to inflate it pretty darn soon.

The guy on the passenger side tilted his head to look at me in the side view mirror. His shoulder moved and the door opened. I pocketed my keys and stood up straight. I was four or five inches taller than he was. My height seemed to intimidate him; he stopped in the open car door when he realized what he was facing. He ducked down to check with the driver, who also now opened his door and stepped out of the car into the uptown lane of Central Park West.

The guy nearest me said in the slightest of accents, "Why did you deflate our tire?"

"I want to ask you some questions."

"No." He turned his back on me and began to get back into the car.

"I'll deflate the damn thing until the tire rim is sitting on the ground," I said with force.

He stopped, twisted back up to an upright position, and slid his right hand under his suit coat—exactly where a gun would be holstered if he had a gun.

I held my left hand up with the palm facing him in a stop motion and said, "Don't do that, or I'll kill you right here."

He froze. I could only see his partner out of the corner of my eye, but he seemed to have frozen, too.

My guy smiled after a long moment. "Are you so fast you can kill me before I kill you?"

"You're welcome to find out."

His hand hovered out of sight under the jacket for what seemed to be a half-century. Maybe it was only a quarter-century, but the seconds crawled by as he made up his mind. Finally, in slow motion, his right hand dropped down to his side. Empty.

The driver also relaxed his posture. How nice. No gunplay on Manhattan's scenic Upper West Side.

"Why are you outside this building?" I asked. When there was no answer, I followed up with: "Are you staking out Jackson McGill?"

Both of them smiled but kept silent.

"He's dead," I said.

"Oh?" the passenger side man, the one closest to me, replied.

"Didn't you know?"

"How could we know?"

"Nothing personal you understand, but maybe, just maybe, you assisted his departure from this world."

"Nothing personal." The smile intensified.

"How's this for personal—I'm suggesting you killed him."

Passenger-side man grunted. I couldn't tell if he was grunting in amusement or annoyance. Given the usual reaction people had to me, I guessed amused annoyance. He climbed back into the front seat of the car, as did the driver. The window rolled down, and he turned to me. "Interesting suggestion."

The engine started, the window glided up, and the Mercedes pulled away. The car turned at the first westbound side street.

"Did you scare them off?" Harry asked. "Or were they waiting for confirmation of McGill's death? Or something else?"

"Something else, I think. Not sure."

"Would you really have killed him if he reached for his gun?"

I shrugged.

"*Could* you have killed him? Are you that fast?"

"Probably not. Besides, I don't happen to have a gun on me."

"You lied."

"I bluffed."

"What's the difference?"

"Strategy."

He considered me for a long moment. "I have to admit I don't fully understand you."

"That's okay. I don't get you either."

"What did you accomplish by confronting those men?"

"Personal satisfaction."

"Is that all?"

"Isn't it enough?" Harry frowned—at least, I thought the tiny, momentary expression was a frown—and I continued, "I established that a pair of violently inclined men are very interested in Jackson McGill. I'm almost certain they are interested because they are paid to be interested. And I suspect that they might even be involved in his murder."

The wheels in Harry's mind turned for a second, then he said, "In other words, you have no proof of anything."

"But I have a strong feeling."

*   *   *

Harry whooshed me to the front of another pre-war building. We had crossed Central Park effortlessly and were now on the corner of 87th Street and Madison Avenue. Christmas music wafted up the slight slope from 86th Street, courtesy of Salvation Army volunteers who played Christmas carols and pop songs on a boom box and rang hand bells in time with the music. At the moment, their selection was "Frosty the Snowman."

This part of the Upper East Side was a nice neighborhood. Upscale boutiques sold clothing and jewelry next to gourmet food stores, bakeries, and restaurants. All of which had Christmas decorations in their windows and throughout their stores. And, of course, there was a Greek coffee shop halfway down the block, because no neighborhood in Manhattan can survive without a Greek coffee shop.

I pointed at the building's 87th Street entrance, "Is this where my new client lives?"

"Yes. Have you already decided to take the case?"

"We discussed this. You know I'm going to help. The Chairman knows it. Let's not have another discussion about free will. Okay?"

"But it's important that you understand that you are making that choice. No matter how inevitable you want to make it sound."

"Fine. I'm making my totally free, completely inevitable choice. Can we go meet my client?"

Harry took a deep breath, exhaled, and gestured for me to proceed him into the building.

4

The lobby of Marissa Carvajal's apartment building wasn't quite as overwhelming as McGill's—I guessed that approximately a ton less marble had been used in Marissa's lobby—but the effect was still impressive as all get-out. A uniformed doorman greeted us, and Harry informed him that we were there to see Ms. Carvajal. The doorman picked up a house phone to announce us, as I surreptitiously inspected the surroundings. Small, barely noticeable cameras were mounted below the crown molding and scanned the entire lobby.

"You can go up," the doorman said. "Fourteen A."

Harry thanked him, and we stepped into the elevator. There was another camera mounted in the elevator's ceiling.

"Is this building as secure as McGill's?" I asked and pointed to the camera above us. "It sure has the same number of entryway cameras."

Harry pressed the button for fourteen and said, "As you no doubt noticed, this building is a tiny bit less grand than McGill's. And it's a little bit less of a fortress."

"You said this woman woke up in bed next to a dead Jackson McGill."

"That's right."

"I'm guessing she hasn't told anyone about it."

"That's right."

"Then why is she expecting you?"

Harry's mouth flicked up at the right corner—like most of Harry's facial expressions, it was so brief and so tiny I almost thought I imagined it. "Marissa has no idea why she's expecting us. But she won't question our being here."

"Do I detect the Chairman's light touch?"

Harry shrugged. "Detect whatever you like."

The elevator settled smoothly at fourteen, the doors rolled open, and we stepped out. McGill's apartment had occupied an entire floor. Marissa Carvajal's only occupied half. Her door, A, was to our left. It swung open as we stepped toward it.

A dazzlingly sexy brunette stood in the doorway. She was about five foot four, with thick, dark shoulder-length hair. She had large brown eyes, dull at the moment, but I had a feeling that they were energetic and hypnotic under less-strained circumstances. And, as one of the detectives had said: a very curvy lady. A woman so good-looking that even a legendary playboy like McGill would have found her impossible to resist. On my last case with Harry, I had reacted to every woman I met as if she were the most desirable female on the planet. While each of them was very pretty and sexy, not one of them was quite as perfect as I had thought. But when you're a widower drowning your sorrows for five years and then waking up to the fact that the world is full of attractive women, well, you tend to overreact to the ones you meet. Given my recent overreactions, it was nice to know that the cops and McGill had the same impression of this woman that I had.

"Mr. Mitchum?" she asked in a husky, strained voice.

"Yes," Harry offered his hand. They shook hands, then he gestured toward me, "This is Jack Tyrrell."

"Mr. Tyrrell."

"Please, call me Jack."

We shook hands. Hers were soft, manicured. She wore a light-gray cashmere sweater and black slacks, which subtly showed off her physical attributes. Jackson McGill had been a lucky man to take her home. Lucky until he was murdered, of course. Marissa wasn't wearing any rings, bracelets, or earrings. It was my experience that women this affluent always wore a bit of jewelry—at least they wore earrings when they had pierced ears as Marissa had. I figured the lack of jewelry was a sign of the stress she was under.

"Why don't you come in?" she didn't wait for an answer but led us to her living room. By the standards of a normal Manhattan apartment, say mine, her living room was huge. But it was maybe half the size of McGill's. Her view was onto Madison Avenue—quite pleasing. McGill's view had been overlooking Central Park—incomparable. Her furnishings had none of the heavy masculinity of McGill's. Much more Louis XIV with rounded forms and curved edges. And gilt all over. (At least I thought it was Louis XIV. Maybe it was Louis the XVI? Those Roman-numeral French kings confused me.)

Marissa showed us to a couch and sat opposite in an armchair. "Would you like something to drink? Coffee? Tea? Water?"

Harry said, "No, thank you," while I shook my head.

Her offer of beverages was the last thing anyone said for what seemed like an eternity. After a moment or two, Harry nodded at me. Marissa was looking at her hands, folded in her lap.

"Excuse me, Ms. Carvajal, but how can we help you?" I asked.

"I . . . ," she took a deep breath and went on, "I, uh . . . I . . . woke up with . . . ," tears ran down her cheeks, and she shook her head, sobbing, "I woke up next to a dead man this morning. Jackson McGill."

Marissa pulled some tissue from her pants pocket and dabbed at her tears. I let her cry for a moment. When her crying subsided a bit, I asked, "Did you know McGill?"

"No. I never met him before. I must have met him at . . . some point last night."

"You don't remember actually meeting him?"

"No."

"Where were you last night?"

"I was attending a benefit at Lincoln Center, the Philharmonic."

"Maybe you met him there?"

"No, I don't think so . . . " her voice trailed off as she struggled to recall the night before. "Wait. I *did* meet him there. I was getting a drink at intermission on the balcony overlooking the fountain in the plaza, and . . . he came up to me as I was waiting on line at the bar. He introduced himself and asked if he could buy me a drink."

"Did you have a drink before you went to the benefit?"

"Why do you ask?" She was startled. And angry.

"Well, I'm guessing you had a drink, maybe two, while you dressed and did your makeup. That you were already feeling no pain at intermission, which is why it's taken you so long to remember meeting McGill. No judgment on you, just trying to figure out what happened."

The tears were flowing freely again. "I did . . . have a couple of drinks while dressing. And one in the bar before the concert began."

Why would a woman this beautiful feel the need to fortify herself with alcohol before an evening on the town? I felt sorry for her and wished there were a way to comfort her. Geez, Tyrrell, you need to snap out of it.

"Okay, you met him at intermission. Did you meet him again as you were leaving the concert?"

"It was a benefit. There was a big reception afterward for all the benefactors. Not that I'm in Jackson's class as a benefactor. Anyway, there were hors d'oeuvre and drinks."

"You saw him again at the reception?"

"Yes, actually, at intermission we agreed to meet afterward."

"More drinks at the reception and then back to his place?"

"No," she paused, thinking, "we went to Enthousiaste in Hell's Kitchen for a late night supper."

"After that?"

"I'm not sure . . . we must have gone to his place . . . I don't remember anything after Enthousiaste except getting into a taxi." She paused, "Oh, and . . . and going to bed with him."

"Nothing after that?"

"No."

"The next thing you knew, you woke up in his apartment, right?"

"Yes."

"You said you never met McGill before, but did you know him by reputation? Did you recognize him?"

"Of course, I recognized him. He's too familiar from business news and celebrity gossip for me not to know him. Besides, I'm in real estate, very high-end, Manhattan real estate. I sell co-ops that list for millions. I recognize anyone and everyone who's a potential client."

"Okay," I glanced at Harry and got no reaction of any kind from him and proceeded to more intimate questions. "I don't mean to embarrass you, but did you know of McGill's reputation as a . . . ladies' man?"

She gave me a bitter smile, "My, how delicate you are. Yes, I knew of his reputation. It probably added to his attractiveness, but to be honest, I don't remember what my initial reaction was when I met him."

"Are you . . . I'm sorry to have to ask," I really was sorry to ask. Years of law-enforcement work should have made me a little tougher when asking personal questions, but at least in this instance, with this woman, my work experience was not helping at all. "But I *do* have to ask: are you like McGill? A player?"

She sighed, "Sometimes. I'm not . . . proud of it."

"Do you usually go home with a man you've just met?"

"Why are you asking me this?" She stood up and paced back and forth next to the living room window. Watching her was stimulating all kinds of thoughts in me—not one of which was useful or germane to the problem at hand. Get a grip, Tyrrell. Now.

"What the hell is this about?" she demanded. Before I could answer, she spun angrily on Harry, "What were you thinking bringing this man—he's supposed to help me?"

"Jack will help you," Harry said quietly. "He's very good at this kind of thing. Trust him, and he'll help you."

"Trust him? While he digs through my life and insults me?"

I said, "I'm not trying to hurt you. I'm not judging you. But I need to know you and your patterns. I'm learning about McGill, too. See if I can make the pieces fit and figure out what happened to him last night."

"Why do you need to know about my sexual behavior? About my drinking?"

"You never know what piece is going to finish the puzzle. I'm making sure I have all the pieces."

She paced in silence for a few moments. I glanced at Harry, but his stone face gave away absolutely nothing. As usual in uncomfortable conversations, he was next to no help at all.

"Marissa?"

She stopped pacing and faced me.

"Would you please sit down?"

She did, dumping her well-dressed and well-shaped body into the chair as if it were a sack of dirty laundry. She was collapsing emotionally; waking in bed next to a dead man was overwhelming her. As much as she wanted to throw me out—she was far from the first person to feel that way about me—she needed help too much to toss away what looked like her only option. Her shoulders slumped. She stared blankly at the floor.

I took a deep breath, leaned forward over the coffee table, and reached for her hand with my left. At my touch, she flinched but didn't withdraw her hand. "I want to help you," I said. If I was completely honest with myself, I wanted to do more than that. Focus, Tyrrell. Focus. "I wish I didn't have to ask you these things. But asking lots of questions is the only way I know to look into a . . . situation like yours. It's the only way I know to help you."

"All right," her voice a barely audible whisper. She brushed her long hair back from her face and said, "You wanted to know about my drinking and my sexual acting out?"

"Yes."

"I got divorced a few years ago. Ever since then, I've been drinking too much, partying too hard, sleeping around too often. My therapist says I'm running away from the pain of my divorce."

"But that's not all you're running from, is it?"

Her hand clutched mine tightly. "What do you mean?"

"You're running from the chance you'll get hurt again."

Marissa slowly released my hand and nodded. Fresh tears coursed down her cheeks. I waited for her to wipe them away before asking my next question.

"Is there any business overlap between you and McGill? Anything at all? Maybe you arranged for office space for one of his companies? Or one of his New York-based charities?"

"No, no, nothing. We can check my records in case I had a client that was connected to Jackson without my knowing it, but I'm pretty sure that there's no connection between us. The Philharmonic is probably the only thing in common."

I stood; it was my turn to take a few turns on the rug. "Well, it looks like this was a random, social encounter."

"Yes."

"I know you said you only have brief bits of memory—getting in the cab, going to bed—but I need to ask you about McGill's apartment. Are you all right with that?"

She stared at the floor and nodded.

"Do you remember getting out of the cab? Going into the building? Did you see anyone as you went in?"

"I think there was a doorman. But maybe I'm remembering that from when I left."

"Did the doorman greet McGill as you entered?"

She replied slowly, "I don't remember."

"What about the elevator? Or going into his apartment?"

Marissa shook her head.

"Okay, don't worry about it. We'll figure something out."

Her head snapped up, "What will we figure out? How will we figure it out?"

"Uh, well . . ." I hesitated, looking at Harry. He said, "Ms. Carvajal, you should have faith in Jack. He can figure out anything."

My eyebrows shot up. I realized that Marissa probably wouldn't find my expression reassuring; I relaxed my face and let my brows drop to a normal level. But she was fixed on Harry and had missed my facial contortions.

"How? How can he do that?"

"He's very good at this sort of thing. And, he has resources you can't imagine. He can help you."

At that moment in time, I didn't have a clue how I was going to help her. I was thrashing about, asking questions, hoping I got lucky with one of her answers. If Harry was certain I'd figure this out, he must mean that he and the Chairman were going to do the heavy lifting on her problems.

She turned from him to me. "Go ahead, ask what you need to."

I wished I knew what I needed to ask. Instead, I blundered ahead with more questions that probably wouldn't help me or her. "Once you were in the apartment, did you see anyone? Did you see signs of anyone else—maybe domestic help? Or a girlfriend's lingerie? Anything?"

"Nothing. What little I remember is mostly from my dashing out of the place. But it was spotless, except for poor . . . for Jackson. . . ."

"Besides the doorman, whom you're not sure about, you didn't see anyone?"

"Not that I remember."

"What about you and McGill becoming physically involved? Do you remember any of that? For instance, where did you take off your clothes?"

She closed her eyes and took a moment to recollect whatever thoughts and memories she could. "What little I remember all happened in the bedroom. We were drunk, laughing . . . undressing, dropping our clothes as we headed toward the bed . . . " she paused to take a deep breath and went on, "kissing and touching and then we went to bed . . . and then nothing until I woke up."

Marissa wiped more tears from her cheeks. I wanted to reach out and hold her hand, give her comfort, but physical contact seemed like a very bad idea given the conversation.

"About the sex, do you remember anything about it? Was McGill tender and thoughtful? Was he into anything kinky? Anything that might have made you uncomfortable? Were you uncomfortable in anyway?"

"I . . . don't think so . . . if I had been frightened or hurt, don't you think I'd remember it?"

"Probably. Maybe. I'm not sure, I don't know how—"

"—how drunk I was?" The tears had stopped. She was angry again.

"Yes."

"Is everything you ask me going to come back to my drinking?"

"Yes," I said. I hoped my tone was firm yet gentle. "You got into some awful trouble because you were drinking. You can't remember exactly what happened or how much trouble you got into because you were drinking. I'm sorry, but yeah, we're going to keep coming back to that."

Her head dropped in shame. She was crying again.

I stood next to her and stroked her arm. "I'm sorry, Marissa. I'm on your side, really."

She nodded but didn't look up.

"Marissa? Could I please see your hands?"

She was puzzled but stretched out her hands.

I examined them one by one. Her hand were well manicured with soft-pink nail polish. No bruises, nicks, or cuts. "Would you mind pushing your sleeves up past your elbows?"

Still puzzled, she did as I asked. No wounds on her forearms.

"Thanks," I said. "You can pull the sleeves down."

"What was that all about?" she asked.

"Defensive wounds. You don't have any, which probably indicates that you didn't feel the need to protect yourself with McGill."

"Or I was too drunk to realize I needed to," she replied bitterly.

"Do you feel sore anywhere? Any bruises or cuts that you can't explain? Any kind of pain anywhere?"

She sat still for a moment, then stood, walked out of the living room into a small hallway and through a door and out of sight.

Harry watched her depart and said, "I'm wondering if my confidence in you was misplaced."

"Right now, I have to admit I'm wondering the same thing."

We waited for a few minutes. No sign of Marissa. "Okay," I said. "Guess I blew this one."

Harry stood, looked at me, then down the hall, and back to me. "I'm very disappointed in you."

"Is that you speaking, or am I in trouble with the Chairman, too?"

"Just me speaking."

"I guess we should let ourselves out." I took a step when I heard a door click and footsteps come down the hall toward us.

Marissa stopped as she entered the living room. "Are you leaving?"

"Uh, well, uh . . ." I sat back down. "No."

Harry also sat. She walked over and joined us.

"I took off all my clothes and checked my entire body in a full-length mirror. I found nothing. And before you ask," she said, glaring at me, "no, I'm not sore in the vaginal area."

"Thank you," I said. "That pretty much rules out rough sex."

"And what does that mean?"

"It means you probably didn't kill him in self-defense."

She stared at me for a long time, and then her face went tight with anger and fear, "But it doesn't prove I didn't kill him for any other reason."

"No, it doesn't."

She turned to Harry, "Are you sure he can help me? Right now, I have no confidence whatsoever that he can help me."

Harry forced a smile. It wasn't a bad smile for someone who almost never attempted that particular facial expression. "We haven't been working your problem for very long. We're just starting."

I wasn't sure that working her problem longer was going to be of any use to her. At that moment, I agreed with Marissa. I had no confidence that I could do anything to get her out of this homicidal mess: She had gone into Jackson McGill's building with a live, billionaire playboy. She remembered their engaging in foreplay, and she had woken up naked in his bed, making it highly likely that she had had sex with him. And given that she had woken up covered in his blood, it was highly likely that she had been there when he was killed . . . so, it wasn't hard to figure her as McGill's killer. She didn't seem to have a motive, but she was very drunk and couldn't remember anything he had said or done. She was so drunk, it was hard to know what she was capable of in the moment or why she felt she had to act in whatever way she had.

The only way out that I could see: someone else had entered the apartment and killed McGill while she lay next to him in a drunken stupor. But the building video security system seemed to rule out the possibility that anyone else entered the building.

Maybe I wasn't supposed to prove her innocent of murder. Maybe the Chairman wanted me to help her deal with what she had done. Trying to support a beautiful woman as she coped with her guilt from what appeared to be a drunken *Twilight Zone* episode knotted my stomach.

"Jack," Harry said, his voice a bit louder and edgier than usual. I realized he'd already said my name twice without any response from me, hence the harder tone. As I focused on him, he said, "Marissa would like to know what we're going to do next?"

I had no idea. I squinted, hoping that my contorted face would imply deep thought. "Well, we have a . . . contact inside the police department. We'll, uh, ask a few careful questions there." Marissa's eyes went wide with fear at the mention of the police department. "No, don't worry," I said. "We'll be discreet."

Harry agreed, "Please, don't worry. We'll be able to get information from the police without revealing anything."

Marissa glanced back and forth at the two of us. She desperately wanted to believe us. If she had only known Harry's background . . .

"Marissa," I said, "have you ever been fingerprinted? Ever had a DNA sample taken? Is there any way you could be identified by physical evidence in McGill's apartment?"

"No, nothing. Nothing like that."

"Okay. That means they can't tie you to the crime scene. But you're going to need to go into hiding."

"What?" Marissa shot to her feet, her face pale and eyes wide. "What? Why?"

I stood, took her hand, and gently pulled her back to her seat. I crouched next to her, still holding her hand. Despite the stress of our conversation and the fact that I had only met her a few minutes earlier—and the other, truly ugly fact that she was the odds-on favorite to be convicted for Jackson McGill's murder—having her hand in mine was very exciting. Tyrrell, please. Put a lid on it.

"The police will reconstruct McGill's evening," I said. "They'll figure out that you left the Philharmonic together and went to Enthousiaste; they'll get a description of you and match it to the security video for later that night . . ."

"Oh my God . . ." she began crying. "I'm going to be arrested."

"That's why you should go into hiding. Gives us more time."

"I guess I could check into a hotel—"

"No . . . sorry. That's a really bad idea."

She was frozen in her chair. Her breathing sped up, and her tears flowed more freely. "I'm going to be arrested," she murmured. "I'm going to spend the rest of my life in prison . . ."

"Let's not leap to any conclusions. Harry and I need to work your case."

"Why? What's the point? I must have . . . killed him. There's no other explanation, is there?"

"Marissa!" I said sharply to snap her out of her guilty reverie. She focused on me and wiped away her tears. "Marissa," I said more gently and gestured at Harry and me, "we need to figure this out. And that means you need to hide so the police can't find you after they reconstruct McGill's evening."

She sniffled and nodded her head. "Where do I go?"

I turned to Harry and said, "Is there someone in your . . . uh, network who could hide her for a while?"

Harry gazed up and then at me. "Yes." To Marissa he said, "You should pack a few things right now. We'll leave as soon as you're finished."

"And," I said firmly to grab her attention, "do *not* tell anyone where you're going."

"But—"

"No." I stretched the "o" sound for emphasis. "No way. No one. No how."

She pursed her lips, stood up, and walked down the hall into what I guessed was her bedroom. I watched her every step. She was definitely worth watching. I caught myself longing for her and sighed in frustration.

"Is it always going to be this way?" I asked Harry.

"What way?"

"The way where I want the woman I'm helping. Is this some kind of perverse test from the Chairman?"

"Marissa needs your help. The fact that you are attracted to her is your problem. Not hers. Not the Chairman's."

"You're a real comfort."

"Thank you."

"I was insincere."

"I was ignoring your lack of sincerity."

"Nicely played," I replied and got no reaction whatsoever from him. "Where are we taking Marissa?"

"Rye."

"Rye? In Westchester? I suppose you're tucking her safely away in a gorgeous mansion overlooking Long Island Sound?"

"You would probably describe it as a mansion. And yes, it overlooks the Sound."

"Where the hell do you come up with a place like that?"

"Certainly not from hell."

We had a staring contest, which I lost. After years of serving in combat and then as a deputy U.S. Marshal, I can tell you that I have developed one helluva withering stare. Harry was completely and utterly impervious to my best effort. It bounced off of him like bullets off Superman.

I walked to the window and looked down. "I wonder if we're alone."

"What do you mean?"

"The Chinese outside McGill's. Maybe they're outside here, too."

"How would they know to be here?"

I faced him. "They could have followed her last night."

Harry's eyebrows rose a millimeter then settled back into their normal place. It was an outburst by his standards. "Why do you think that's a possibility?"

I looked down the hallway to make sure Marissa wasn't about to appear and overhear our conversation. "All the evidence, circumstantial though it is, points to Marissa. The police are going to develop a lot of witnesses who saw Marissa and McGill at the Philharmonic, then more witnesses who saw them at Enthousiaste. McGill's building's security video places her at the crime scene at the right time. They'll collect all kinds of DNA and fingerprint evidence in his apartment. They'll have the doorman's testimony and the video showing a woman in a hat leaving shortly after the time of death. There is no video of anyone else coming into or out of the building near the time of death.

"Once the police establish Marissa as McGill's guest, they check her prints and DNA against what they collect at McGill's apartment, and the only thing left for her will be a plea arrangement. Probably manslaughter and at least ten years in prison."

"I already know that—why do you think all that evidence makes it likely that the Chinese are waiting outside her apartment?"

"Because maybe, just maybe, she's innocent."

Harry's eyebrows shot up this time and took longer to settle down. "How could you possibly know that?"

"Because the Chairman wants me to help her. If she's guilty she doesn't need me, she needs a really good lawyer. But the Chairman didn't send a lawyer, he sent me. Which means . . . she's innocent."

"That might be true, but you're way too quick to jump to conclusions."

"Okay, *maybe* it's true. Let's assume, for the sake of argument, that she's innocent. In that case, someone else killed McGill. Someone with a motive and the ability to get past the security. Someone who had been staking out McGill and waiting for an opportunity. Along came Marissa, gorgeous, sexy, distracting beyond belief, and very drunk. An innocent person in the wrong place at the wrong time."

"You think she could have been framed?"

"Absolutely. Someone seized the opportunity created by her presence, murdered McGill, and set her up. If I'm right, that someone followed her out of McGill's apartment to this building. And if I were that someone, I'd keep an eye on her until and when the police show up."

"That way the real killer can confirm that the patsy has been arrested?"

"Exactly."

Harry stood next to me at the window. "This is all conjecture."

"Yup. Could be complete fantasy. But if she's innocent, then it's probably what happened."

"And you're going to proceed as if she is innocent?"

"I'm pretty sure that's what the Chairman wanted."

Harry's Mona Lisa smile flitted across his face. "How are you going to get Marissa past the Chinese—if they're outside?"

"That could be a problem . . ."

Marissa's footsteps approached down the hall toward us. She had an overnight suitcase on rollers and a ballistic-nylon, black backpack with leather trim. Pretty fancy for a backpack. "I'm ready to go. I guess."

"Would you, by chance, have access to the building superintendent's workshop?" I asked.

She was completely bewildered. "I'm sorry . . . what?"

"I need a can of paint. Or two."

Her mouth gaped, and she turned to Harry. He shrugged and raised his hands palms up in a gesture that I took to mean: I don't know what's the matter with Tyrrell.

"Don't worry," I said, "there's a method in my madness."

"I hope so," she replied.

5

I exited Marissa's building onto East 87th Street, carrying two cans of paint in a plain brown-paper bag cradled in my arms. I stopped on the sidewalk directly outside the front door, scanned the street in both directions, made a huge show of checking my watch, then scanned the street again. I hoped that anyone watching the building would guess that I was waiting to be picked up. Instead of what I was really doing, working to foil the efforts of a surreptitious stakeout team watching Marissa's building.

Most of the cars parked along the street were exactly what you would expect them to be this late in the morning of a business day: motors off, empty, no one sitting inside. There was a large, white panel truck double-parked directly across the street, and about 20 feet behind it, a forest-green Ford Transit; both clearly delivery vehicles.

And then there was a black Chevy Tahoe with tinted windows and New York plates that set off my instinctual alarm system. It was parked at a meter across 87th Street from me near the corner of Madison Avenue. The engine on—exhaust smoke rose from the tail pipe. The motor was running because the people inside probably wanted to keep the heat on. Sitting in a parked car in Manhattan in

December can be a chilling way to spend time. A woman sat behind the wheel, a man in the passenger seat, both white, both wearing sunglasses. It was hard to tell through the tinted glass, but they both seemed to have dark hair. His was short. Hers was shoulder-length.

Walking west, I turned onto Fifth Avenue, headed downtown, and stopped as soon as I was out of sight of the Tahoe's side and rear view mirrors. I waited for five minutes, walked back to 87th Street, and headed east toward the parked vehicle at the corner of Madison Avenue. As I closed in on my target, I wondered if there was any significance to the fact that the folks who had staked out Marissa's building, unlike the gentlemen watching McGill's building, were definitely not Chinese. Were two groups behind McGill's murder? Working together? Or working at cross-purposes? Would they fight each other to profit from his death? Were both groups framing Marissa? The thought of having to deal with two groups capable of circumventing the security at McGill's building and deploying teams to stakeout the victim and the patsy made me very anxious. I was only one guy, after all. A very capable guy with the incredible resources of the Chairman behind him, but I knew from experience that I would have to do the heavy lifting when it came to aiding Marissa. I also knew that the Chairman was not guaranteeing my safety or success. I had to put out the effort, but the results were out of my hands. As Harry had told me in a number of ways: no guarantees meant I had to have faith. And faith was achieved by a conscious choice on my part.

Like I didn't have enough problems dealing with the bad guys, Harry also expected me to be spiritually enlightened. Ugh.

I approached the Tahoe from behind. I wished I had a gun—it would have made my life easier and safer at that moment. But my weapons (every last one of my weapons, actually) were back in my apartment, where they were safe and sound instead of keeping me that way. If I had a gun, I wouldn't be lugging two, mostly full, one-gallon paint cans.

The Tahoe was parked on the south side of the street, the passenger side next to the curb. Given that the people inside were staking out a building to their left, I hoped their attention would be out the side windows and away from the path of my approach. Also, the odds were good that neither of them would be checking out the sideview mirror to keep track of the pedestrian traffic on the sidewalk behind the SUV. I knelt on the sidewalk immediately behind the Tahoe and pulled the paint cans out of the paper bag, one paint-can handle in each hand. I stepped up to the rear of the SUV and swung the can in my left hand at the taillights. The glass shattered on impact, and there was a deep thump as the can crushed through the taillight assembly and hit metal.

The passenger side door opened quickly, and a man's said, "What the fu—"

I was already rushing forward as he spoke, swinging the can in my right hand, and I caught him full on the jaw as he stepped out of the Tahoe. The paint can slammed into his face, his body slammed into the open door, and he dropped to the sidewalk. I leaned over and yanked a Beretta M9 pistol from his under-the-shoulder holster beneath his coat. The woman behind the steering wheel was still pulling out her own pistol as I slid into the passenger seat and pressed the Beretta's barrel into her side, above her waist.

"Don't," I said. She froze. "Now, be cooperative and—extremely slowly—lift your weapon from its holster. Only use your fingers."

She did exactly as she was told and held the weapon, another Beretta M9, the official handgun of the U.S. Army, out to me. I took it and slid it into my parka's pocket. One of the things I love about parkas: they usually have pockets with more than enough room for temporary pistol storage.

"Okay, you're going to get out of the car, walk around to this side and help me get your friend into the back. And don't even think about making a run for it. I won't hesitate to use this if you give me a reason."

She had large brown eyes, which were trying to burn a hole through me, a pug nose, and a square jaw that was tight with tension. She was wearing a black pant suit that was all business. She grunted assent and climbed out of the vehicle. I stepped out at the same time she did and arrived next to her fallen comrade the instant she did. He was no lightweight. Shorter than I was by a few inches, but much broader in the shoulders and deeper chested. I'm six feet two and nobody's idea of slender, but this guy was heavier than I. Probably equal amounts of muscle and beer belly. With a fair amount of huffing and puffing, we managed to flop him into the cargo space behind the rear seats. We had to bend his legs to tuck him inside.

An old lady walking a tiny, gray-haired terrier stopped and said, "Is your friend all right? Do you want me to call someone?"

"No, thank you," I smiled at her. "He has fainting spells." I jerked my thumb over my shoulder, "This way he can stretch out. He'll be fine in a few minutes."

"Well . . . if you're sure . . ."

"Yes, thank you." I grinned appreciatively at her. However, I was keenly aware of the absurdity of a tiny, old woman offering to assist me in the loading of an unconscious slab of man into the back of an SUV. The old lady tottered away, talking to her terrier. I checked to see if my "friend" was all right. He appeared very comfy. I noticed a pair of cases tucked next to the wheel well on either side of the cargo space. One was a black tool box with steel latches on it. The other had a white lid that fit over a red bottom: a first aid kit. I checked to make sure the woman was still standing on the sidewalk, behaving herself, and I pulled the tool box close. It didn't have the Chevrolet brand on it, which meant it wasn't tools for changing tires. Inside were all kinds of security goodies: audio surveillance bugs, GPS trackers, a pair of walkie talkies, a flare pistol with three flares, a set of lock-pick tools, and plasticuffs (also known as plastic handcuffs, riot cuffs, wrist ties—you put someone's hands through the plastic loops, zip the loops tight around the wrists, and your prisoner is trussed like a turkey at Thanksgiving).

I pulled the man's arms behind him, grabbed a pair of plasticuffs, and cuffed the his wrists. Then I patted down his pockets and slipped his wallet, phone, and ammo clip into my pocket. I did all this while glancing back and forth from my unconscious friend to the woman. She looked like a kid about to go to the dentist to get her first cavity filled.

Because I'm a thorough kind of guy, I checked out the first aid kit, but it was exactly what it appeared to be: a first aid kit. Bandages, topical disinfectant, topical anesthetic, medical adhesive tape, gauze pads, scissors, and a choice of over-the-counter painkillers: aspirin, acetaminophen, and ibuprofen.

"Turn around," I said to the woman. I checked the sidewalk to see if anyone was noticing us, but no one seemed interested. Feeling safe from observation, I cuffed her hands behind her back. "I hope you don't mind, but I think I might find a use for all of this stuff in these two convenient cases. I'm going to take it along with me."

"Knock yourself out, you ass—"

"Shut up." I enjoy a little profanity myself once in a while, but this woman and her partner were boringly inept at it. "Go. Get in the middle seat, passenger side."

She didn't move, clearly considering whether to shout for help.

"Please get in," I said. "I really don't want to dump your unconscious body into the back with your partner."

She gave me the once over, decided I meant business, walked to the passenger side door, and waited for me to open it. I had to help her climb into the seat—it's not easy clambering into an SUV with your hands cuffed behind you.

Once she was settled, I said in a calm, measured tone guaranteed to be missed by any passers-by, "Take off your belt."

"What the—?"

"Shut up and give me your belt." I raised the pistol in my right hand to remind her what a serious individual I was. She did as she was told, but with a string of profanities that were as imaginative as they were ugly.

"Shut up," I repeated. "Lean forward."

She followed instructions, and I looped her belt around her elbows, pulling her arms together and binding them tightly.

"You prick," she hissed.

"I love you, too." I closed her door, picked up the paint cans, dumped them on the floor in front of the passenger seat, and put the tool box and first aid kit on the seat. Then I walked around the front of the Tahoe and got in behind the steering wheel. I locked all the doors and smiled at the woman in the rearview mirror.

Bells were ringing nearby. And music was playing. To my right, Madison Avenue sloped down gently to the corner at 86th Street. The Salvation Army volunteers were still ringing their bells in time to "All I Want for Christmas."

They were executing some very basic dance steps; the people gathered around them were all smiles.

"Who is your employer?" I asked the woman.

"Like I'm going to tell you."

I reached into the glove compartment and found the registration and insurance card for the Tahoe. The vehicle was owned by Cú Chulainn Enterprises, Inc.—Jackson McGill's corporation.

"Do you work for Cú Chulainn Enterprises?" I asked.

No reply.

"Private security?"

Still no reply.

I leaned past the steering wheel, found her purse on the floor under the front edge of the seat, and grabbed it. A quick search of the simple black-leather bag produced a cell phone, wallet, and another pistol. A brown-leather cosmetic bag held lipstick, blush, and a hairbrush. The purse had enough room for brass knuckles in addition to everything else, and given the woman's demeanor, brass knuckles would have been less surprising than makeup. Her driver's license identified her as Susan Bouchard. There was an employee ID card in her wallet—what a surprise: she did work for Cú Chulainn Enterprises.

It seemed logical to discover the identity of Ms. Bouchard's partner, so I pulled the man's wallet from my pocket. In the rearview mirror, Ms. Bouchard was giving me the most hostile Evil Eye she was capable of, but I've had fanatical terrorists give me the Evil Eye so I was utterly impervious to her effort. My unconscious friend's driver's license said he was Michael Flynn, and he also had an employee ID for Cú Chulainn.

"Why are a pair of Cú Chulainn employees staking out an Upper East Side apartment building?"

Ms. Bouchard chose to reply with silence and continued reliance on her Evil Eye.

"You ex-military? Maybe MPs?"

She reluctantly answered, "How did you know?"

"I usually recognize another vet. Are you working security for Cú Chulainn now?"

"Yeah, so?"

"Just asking. I'm guessing that's better than the Army."

"Better pay, better clothes, better hours."

"What's not to like?"

She grunted, clearly uninterested in continuing the conversation.

"Don't you ever worry about what your company asks you to do?" I asked.

"What do you mean?"

"Well, like staking out an apartment building. Why were you doing that? It's not like you're in law enforcement. Why the hell is private security staking someone out? Doesn't that worry you?"

"No." Bouchard shifted in the middle seat; it must have been very uncomfortable to have her arms bound behind her back. She muttered, "Shit," and threw another Evil Eye at me. This one had as much success as the others had. "I'm not telling you anything else, so what the hell are you going to do now?"

I'd been asking myself the same question. Did I need more information? How far was I willing to go to get more? Was I willing to torture her?

When I'd been in Afghanistan, I'd seen some pretty awful things. Done some awful things, too. But traumatized as I was by the grim violence and loss of life, I didn't feel guilty about it. I had believed in what I was doing: I was making sure I didn't let down the guys in my unit. When I had been a Deputy Marshal, I had occasionally done what needed to be done, no matter how ugly it was.

Unfortunately, in the five years immediately after Maggie died and my leaving the Marshals Service, I had been a complete sleazebag. I worked for scummy people, I did things that I would never have considered doing in the Army or in the Marshals Service, and I drank myself into a walking stupor to forget my shame.

Now, thanks to Maggie, I worked for the Chairman with Harry Mitchum as my case manager, and my mission was to help people.

When Harry first explained how my job would work, he had led me to understand that mankind was my business. I helped people without any kind of reward for me. Given what I understood as my charter, it seemed highly unlikely that the Chairman or Harry would countenance my torturing someone. Whether Marissa had killed Jackson McGill, or if she was a fall guy for someone else, she needed help. To help her, I needed to find out everything I could about the players involved in McGill's murders. That meant discovering Bouchard and Flynn's reason for staking out Marissa's apartment. Unfortunately, they were unlikely to give me any usable information if I asked politely.

On the other hand, as Tevye says in *Fiddler on the Roof*, Bouchard and Flynn might know if Marissa was McGill's killer or if she was being framed for murder. It was possible they could clear Marissa. Maybe a little torture . . .

I checked in the rearview mirror. The Salvation Army volunteers were dancing hard to "God Rest Ye Merry, Gentlemen." I couldn't really hear the words of the carol over the traffic noises, but I didn't need to: "God rest ye merry, gentlemen / let nothing you dismay." I sighed. Let nothing you dismay. Okay, no torture. I would have to bluff and hope. I stepped out of the car, walked around the front, and climbed into the middle seat, next to Bouchard, leaned over the seat, grabbed Flynn by the arm, and shook him. "Nap time is over."

He groaned. I shook him again, with more intensity. "Wake up."

There were more guttural noises; more shaking by me. A minute passed, still more shaking, and he woke up. His eyes rolled around as he tried to focus.

"What the fu—"

"Quiet," I said. "You and Bouchard are my prisoners. Cooperate, and you'll be fine. Try anything stupid, and you won't be. Understand?"

He cursed in response. Pretty prosaic profanity given the quantity of obscenities.

I considered my situation: I had two Cú Chulainn Enterprises security people in one of their corporate vehicles that was probably decked out with all kinds of technology and equipment specifically for security purposes. I would have laid a substantial bet that there was a GPS tracking system as well. Moving the Tahoe anywhere—without reporting in—was likely to alert someone in the bowels of Cú Chulainn security that something was wrong.

"Are you supposed to check in at intervals?"

Flynn cursed again and bloody spittle dribbled down his chin. Violent contact with a paint can will do that to you. Bouchard was content to let her partner reply for both of them. I leaned over the seat and cracked Flynn across his shin with his own pistol. He grunted in pain but was much more quiet otherwise. Maybe a teeny weeny bit of torture was okay. However, I hope that would be the last time I resorted to that tactic.

Instead, I asked Bouchard, "Do you need to check in?"

Flynn was still groaning. I jerked a thumb in his direction and said, "Please, I don't want to hit him again. Answer the question."

"Yes, at 11:30." In three minutes.

I dug her phone out of her purse. She told me the code to unlock it and what phone number to call. "Any password when you check in?" I asked.

"Grow up," she snarled. "What do you think this is, James Bond?"

I dialed the number, put the phone on speaker, and held it near her.

"Security," a no-nonsense female voice answered.

"It's Bouchard. Still nothing."

"Fine. Call in again in half an hour."

"Will do."

I disconnected fast. Didn't want Bouchard getting creative.

As I tucked the phone back in her purse, I said, "Thank you for your cooperation."

Bouchard grimaced. Flynn, predictably, let out another string of profanity, urging me to do something that was anatomically impossible.

"Shut up," I said tiredly. "If you were any good at cursing, it might be entertaining. But your use of profanity is utterly without style or imagination."

Flynn's eyes flared like a rat's does when you catch it full beam with your flashlight. He was in pain and angry, wishing he could get his hands on me. On the other hand, I had a feeling that reason might work with Bouchard. She was tough but had at least a smidge of brains. "I'm not going to waste your time by pretending that I'm going to torture you," I said. "It takes too long, and when it finally works, the victim will say anything. Which means it doesn't really work."

Bouchard smirked. "So, you're going to threaten to kill us instead?"

"Come off it. I'm going to commit murder to get a few scraps of almost worthless information? As long as you don't do something stupid, you'll be fine."

"We won't do anything stupid."

"I didn't think so. You probably know next to nothing. You were assigned a stakeout, and you did what you were told. You probably have no idea why someone wanted that apartment watched."

She grunted and shook her head, as if dismissing me for my stupidity. Flynn seemed to be struggling to understand what was going on. I guess a paint can to the jaw will do bad things for your comprehension.

"You weren't just staking out the building, were you? You were supposed to follow someone, right?"

This time her reply was another shake of the head.

I went back into her purse and dug out her smart phone, searched through the phone's photos, and found Marissa Carvajal.

"Hmm," I said, "You were staking out Marissa Carvajal's building. You were supposed to follow her if she left the building. Right?"

"So what?"

"It's been fun talking to you," I replied and dropped her phone back into her purse. "Be a good girl and sit tight."

"You stupid pri—"

I interrupted her, "Please don't. I have a much higher opinion of you than Flynn. Don't ruin it by cursing with as little zest as he does."

Leaning over the center console to the front seat, I grabbed the first aid kit and pulled some gauze out of it. Then I tore off a piece of surgical adhesive and taped the gauze over her eyes. "Open your mouth," I said.

"Screw you," she hissed through clenched teeth.

"Okay," I replied. "We'll do this the hard way." I hit her in the stomach, not hard enough to hurt her but enough to make her gasp. The instant her lips parted, I shoved a wadded piece of gauze into her mouth. Her gasp turned to an angry shout, but a muffled shout.

A quick check of the sidewalk and traffic on 87th Street showed that my little exercise in domination was drawing no special attention. I leaned over the seat into the cargo area and said to Flynn, "Open your mouth."

No argument, no cursing—he must have finally absorbed his reality: He *was* going to end up complying with my wishes. He allowed me to gag and blindfold him.

Working on the theory that it can be a very good thing to have a direct line of communications with your enemy, I pulled out both of their phones and copied a half-dozen numbers, including each of theirs, from their contacts into my phone. Then I stuffed their guns and phones into Bouchard's purse, tucked her bag under the driver's seat, grabbed the keys out of the ignition, and shut the door. I used the key fob to lock the Tahoe, dropped the keys on the pavement, and casually kicked them under the vehicle. Carrying the tool case in one hand and the first aid kit in the other, I crossed 87th Street. When I reached the sidewalk in front of Marissa's building, I looked back at the Tahoe. Thanks to the dark-tinted windows, no one would know that two people were prisoners inside. I went into the lobby and asked the doorman to call Ms. Carvajal's apartment and inform her that I was ready. In less than five minutes, Marissa, Harry, and I were walking out the front door.

"Were you correct in surmising that there was a stakeout team?" Harry asked.

"Of course."

"What did you do to them?"

"I'm not sure I like your tone." I pointed across the street at the Tahoe. "They are sitting exactly where I found them. Are you implying that I might have damaged them?"

"You have been known to . . . play rough."

I sighed. "They're fine."

"But you immobilized them and blindfolded them?"

Marissa was struggling to appear calm, but talk of immobilizing and blinding was more than a bit frightening.

"Yes," I said to Harry, then to Marissa, "Don't worry, they're tied up and blindfolded. They'll survive."

"Why were they watching my building?"

"I don't know. But I'm going to find out."

* * *

DAY – MANHATTAN: Cú Chulainn Tower

CÚ CHULAINN ENTERPRISES WAS HEADQUARTERED in a dark-gray granite and black-glass skyscraper on Seventh Avenue and 55th Street. The building tapered as it rose above Manhattan. An atrium rose the full height of the building. On the sixty-fourth floor, a woman sat in a black-leather armchair opposite a man at a long glass-topped conference table.

The woman was Savannah Faringer, Jackson McGill's Chief Operating Officer at Cú Chulainn. Her eyes were a cool blue, and she had long, straight blonde hair. She wore a charcoal-gray pant suit, which showed off her tall, slender body.

The man was extraordinarily big, more than six feet six. He had broad shoulders and hands like cinderblocks. Brown hair, brown eyes, straight nose, and a jawline like the prow of a ship. He wore a leather jacket over his white button-down shirt, but he was muscled up to such a degree that his clothing barely contained him. Altogether a formidable physical specimen. Faringer could not have been less impressed.

She was absorbed watching the video feed on a large wall monitor behind the man. The camera was pointed at the doorman's desk in the lobby of Marissa Carvajal's building. Harry Mitchum and Jack Tyrrell were talking to the doorman. Faringer used a remote to fast forward as Mitchum and Tyrrell disappeared, and seconds later, as Tyrell, Mitchum, and Marissa Carvajal exited the building.

Faringer pointed at the monitor, "This is the last time that Marissa Carvajal was seen going in or out of the building. Our camera at the service entrance picked up the other man leaving the building a few minutes before these two. Then he returned through the front door and waited for them in the lobby. During the interval between his departure and return, we lost contact with our surveillance team parked outside."

"Quite the coincidence. You want me to find Carvajal and/or the men?"

"Yes. We're running the faces through facial-recognition software now."

"The white guy looked like a cop. Or ex-military."

"In which case we're almost certain to identify him. We can log into every Federal and NYPD database. We also have access to hundreds of security cameras in the New York City area, and we have dozens of people looking for these three. If they leave Manhattan via train, tunnel, or bridge, or it they try to go to ground in Manhattan, we have a good chance of finding them."

"With all of this hardware at your disposal and all of the people behind it—what do you want from me?"

"As good as our security team is—and it's very good because we hire former law enforcement and veterans—none of them has your experience. Or your credentials. Or, equally important, Mr. Reznik, your special freelance status. Which allows us to pay you cash and leave no connection between you and us."

"My face has probably been captured by a half-dozen security cameras since I walked into this building, but you can doctor the security feeds and eliminate all traces of me, right?"

"Of course."

His reply was a feral grin. He pointed at the monitor frozen on Marissa Carvajal, "What do I do with these people when I find them?"

"You arrange to turn the woman over to the police. I don't care how, as long as she's in one piece and there is no blowback for us."

"And the men?"

"Mr. Reznik, I leave that to you."

6

We rented a black Chrysler 200 at an Avis location a few blocks from Marissa's apartment, and I drove us out of the city, using a torturously winding route. Our destination was Rye, which is northeast of the city. Instead of going in that direction, I headed west, up the west side of Manhattan, taking the George Washington Bridge into New Jersey and then the Palisades Parkway north.

"I thought we were going to Rye," Marissa said from the back seat. "Is there a problem?"

"No," I replied. "I want to be sure the folks we left in front of your apartment didn't have company on their stake out."

"You're making sure we're not followed?"

"Yes."

"Mr. Mitchum," she said, "are you sure he's good at this?"

"Why do you ask?" Harry responded.

"I'm not sure if he's making this up as he goes along or really knows what he's doing."

Harry glanced at me then twisted in his seat to look at her. His smile was genuine and reassuring. "He's as good as it gets. Believe me."

I kept my mouth shut, but I could see in the rearview mirror that Marissa was looking back and forth from Harry to me. "Are we being followed?"

"No," I said.

"I'm going to be safe?"

"At least for the next few days."

"What then?"

In my head, my response was: Then you go to jail, unless I figure something out. What I said out loud was: "By then, I hope to have found Jackson McGill's killer."

"And you'll deliver the killer to the police, and I live happily ever after, is that it?"

"The happily ever after part is up to you."

Her eyes flared at me in the rearview mirror then softened. "I guess it is," she spoke so quietly I could barely hear her.

I exited the Palisades Parkway onto Interstate 287 and drove east across the Tappan Zee Bridge all the way through Westchester County toward Rye. I sped up, slowed down, changed lanes without signaling, and when I exited the highway in Rye, crisscrossed local streets for 20 minutes. It would have taken the magical powers of Voldemort to follow us.

"Harry, I think we're ready to go to Marissa's hiding place. Could you direct me, please?"

"We're going to Manursing Island."

"Oh my," I muttered appreciatively. "Are we talking gated community?"

"Yes."

He gave me instructions. We arrived at the gate, a no-nonsense affair of steel set in stone pillars, with walls extending out of sight in either direction. A lean man in the charcoal-gray uniform of a private security outfit stepped out of the guard house, peered at our license plate and then a clipboard he was carrying, and leaned back inside the small house. The gate swung open, and he waved us through.

"Did you use a Jedi mind trick to get us in?" I asked.

Marissa chuckled over that remark. A small but definite chuckle. Harry shook his head and replied, "Did you notice the security cameras at the gate?"

"Of course."

"Steel-and-stone gateway, security cameras, private security—it would take a small army to get in here," Harry said firmly.

"I could get in here," I responded.

"Yes," he smiled microscopically. "But you're you."

Harry directed me to North Island Drive and onto a very long driveway in front of a cream-white Colonial. Trees filled the yard, and we could catch a glimpse of the Long Island Sound just beyond the house. I parked to one side of the drive, turned the motor off, and pointed at the house, "I'm guessing 6,000-square feet. Seven bedrooms, six baths. In-ground pool in the back, overlooking a couple hundred feet of waterfront property on Long Island Sound. Right?"

"Yes."

"Want to give us the lowdown on who lives here?"

"Andrew and Barbara Selkirk. He's the founder of a hedge fund. There's also a live-in housekeeper and her husband who handles the gardening and handyman jobs and acts as a driver."

"I knew I should have gone into hedge funds . . . ," I climbed out of the car, and the others followed suit.

"Do the Selkirks know about me?" she asked.

"No," Harry said. "I was able to provide some assistance to them in the past, the way Jack and I are assisting you. They won't ask any questions and won't tell anyone you're here."

She nodded and slowly turned around. The tension in her shoulders eased visibly as she absorbed her surroundings. "Thank God," she said softly.

"Sounds about right," I said, lifting her bags from the trunk.

Harry led the way up three steps and knocked on the front door, a massive, carved wood portal with a brass knocker in a roaring lion's head that was in the center of a very large Christmas wreath. Without waiting for the door to be opened, he led us into the evergreen-garlanded, marble-floored, two-story high foyer where we were greeted by a small, thin woman with mousy brown hair drawn back in a tight bun.

"I'm Frieta," she said in a German accent. "I'm the Selkirks' housekeeper." A small, thin man with mousy brown hair and steel-rimmed glasses walked into the foyer.

"This is my husband Otto. He'll take your bags up to your room."

Otto said nothing, picked up Marissa's two bags, and glided up the stairs with them. He was older than I was and considerably smaller, but there was a wiry strength in his body; he climbed the stairs smoothly and easily.

Harry made quick introductions, giving Marissa's name last. Frieta smiled, took Marissa's hand and said, "You'll like it here. It's very nice." Then she showed us into the living room.

It wasn't quite an acre of floor space, but it seemed vast to me. Room enough for the 18th green at Augusta National or a display of the fossilized skeleton of a triceratops. Oriental rugs were strategically scattered on the floor in the spaces around the contemporary furniture. The were tall French doors overlooking the back yard and the Long Island Sound. The walls were filled by large abstract paintings. The room screamed money, but it screamed money and taste. At one end of the room was a very large Christmas tree, probably twelve-feet high. Nutcracker Kings of all sorts and sizes were spread throughout the room on end tables. A choral group was singing Christmas carols, but it was impossible to spot the music system or the speakers.

A man and a woman had been sitting on one of the couches and stood as we entered. Both close to fifty years old, trim, and fit. The man was about my height. Both had gray in their medium-brown hair, but only enough to give them mature sex appeal.

"I'm Andrew Selkirk," he said and shook hands with each of us. His handshake was a bit firmer than necessary, as if he was proving that he was a big tough guy, too. "This is my wife, Barbara."

As we said hello, I noticed that despite Barbara's tamped down, WASPy appearance, she was a very—Stop it! Tyrrell. Please. Get a grip.

After everyone had said hello, Andrew addressed me and Harry: "I want you to know that Ms. Carvajal will be safe here. No one will know anything about her."

"I'm sure she's happy to hear that," I replied.

He smiled uncomfortably and nodded at her. She nodded back. Geez, I thought, I'm stuck in auditions for bobble-head dolls.

"Would you mind if Harry and I went outside for a quick word?" I asked.

"No, no, of course not."

"Thanks," I led the way out the French doors at the end of the living room, the side that faced the water. We walked across the vast lawn, with the pool to one side, then huddled deep inside our coats atop a stone wall at the edge of the Sound. The wall was about six feet higher than the current tide level. Near the southern end of the wall, there were steps that led down to a floating wooden pier. Nothing was moored there—at this time of year, many people took their boats out of the water.

"What did you need to discuss?" Harry asked.

"How trustworthy are the Selkirks?"

"They work for the Chairman. Just like you."

"So . . . trustworthy? Or should I check them out?"

Harry didn't deign to give me an answer, instead he looked at the heavy gray clouds.

"Is this another free will thing? I have to make a choice as to whether to check them out or not?"

"Maybe it's a faith thing," he replied with a flat tone, his eyes still on the sky.

"Is it going to snow?" I asked.

"I am not a prophet. You know that."

"Will the Selkirks remember me or Marissa?"

"No."

"Why not?"

"There's no need for them to remember."

"But I remember everything that happened with the Russian mafia six months ago. Shoot ups in Brooklyn and Bedford."

"Yes."

"And I'm guessing I'll remember everything from this . . . uh, case."

"Yes."

"Why?"

"You need to remember."

I considered that for a long moment. "It's part of my becoming a man for others, huh?"

"Exactly."

"Aren't the Selkirks on a similar mission?"

"The mission of others is not your concern. Everyone is different."

"Was that a nice way of telling me to mind my own business."

"It was a way of telling you to stay focused on your mission. What is your next step?"

"I have no idea."

"Marissa would find that very reassuring."

"You're a comfort." I had a theory that, once upon a time, Harry had been the model for the Sphinx. "What should I do next? I don't know who the Chinese guys were, I can't dig into their backgrounds and look for a reason for their involvement. I could try to dig up something on Cú Chulainn Enterprises, but that's a massive organization with its own security force. Not to mention that they sell all kinds of security systems and hardware. Which will make it next to impossible to get inside and find out what they were doing at Marissa's building."

I closed my eyes and took a deep breath, inhaling the salt-water air. "Could you get me inside the NYPD? To the detectives working the McGill homicide?"

"Now?"

"Not quite. Could you ask Marissa to come out here? I want to talk to her for a minute, then you and I will get out of here."

"As you wish." He walked inside.

Snow flakes drifted gently down. Very pretty, but it made me feel even colder. I gazed south across the Sound toward Long Island. I wasn't sure what part of the island I was facing. Maybe Oyster Bay, where Teddy Roosevelt had his home at Sagamore Hill.

"Why did you want to talk to me?" Marissa asked. Her voice wasn't hostile, but it wasn't warm, either. Maybe she was cold despite the forest-green down coat she was wearing. Maybe she didn't like snow. Then again, maybe she didn't like me.

"We got off to a bad start, and that was my fault."

"Yes, it was."

I ignored the verbal slap in the face and said calmly, "I know what it's like to hurt inside and lose yourself in alcohol. I was in the Special Forces, the Green Berets, in Afghanistan. When I came home, well . . ." I stopped, took a breath, exhaled forcefully, and resumed speaking in a hoarse whisper, "I had a very hard time adjusting. I drank way too much. Even though I managed to join the Marshals, I was a mess."

"PTSD?" she asked. Her voice was much softer.

"Yes. I couldn't bring myself to get help."

"Sometimes it's incredibly hard to do that."

"Incredibly hard. And, in my case, bitterly ironic. My wife was a therapist."

"She couldn't do anything for you?"

"She wanted to, but I wouldn't let her. Too busy hiding in booze."

Marissa examined my face for a moment then she turned toward the water. "You said 'was' a therapist. Is she . . . gone?"

"Yes, she was killed." My voice was so low it was hard to believe Marissa heard me. But it was all I could manage. "My wife's death . . . was my fault. I made a deal with some mob guys, and they objected violently when I reneged."

I had to pause and take a very long breath. It never seemed to be easy to talk about Maggie. "But . . . my wife pulled me out of my . . . darkness. I mean, the memory of her led me to help people like you. To be a better man."

"Why . . . why are you telling me this?"

I sighed, "I asked you to be honest with me about some pretty painful stuff, and it seemed that I should be honest with you to earn your trust."

She stood patiently in the falling snow, mulling over what I'd said for what felt like a very long time. Finally, she said, "Thank you."

* * *

Harry whooshed me into the detective squad room at the 20th Precinct. The room was exactly the way TV squad rooms look. Dull paint on the walls, the color could have been a faint olive green or maybe a dusty beige. Gray filing cabinets were tucked in between desks and lining some of the walls. All of the desks and chairs appeared to have come from a catalog selling furniture that was functional but too ugly even for the federal government. A few garlands of fake holly hung here and there, and in one corner a three-foot, artificial Christmas tree sat next to the coffee pot. The Christmas decorations didn't add to the décor at all.

One wall of the room was a floor-to-ceiling partition, about two-thirds glass. Behind the partition, the two detectives from the McGill crime scene were briefing their lieutenant, a short, thick Asian man with a tight mouth and unfriendly eyes. The nameplate on his desk read: Lt. James Han. Detectives Luker and Islas were laying out the case for him.

Islas was speaking, "There were shallow cuts all over McGill's body. Not defensive wounds, either."

"Torture?" Han asked.

"Maybe. Maybe the killer really wanted McGill to suffer. Slashed him a bunch of times, then went for the kill. It was personal. Angry, you know? Then again, maybe it was a professional covering his tracks by making it look that way."

"What about the murder weapon?"

"A genuine Renaissance stiletto, Italian, *very* expensive. Lots more expensive Renaissance stuff all over McGill's place, so the stiletto was probably a weapon of opportunity."

"The killer just grabbed it." Han nodded. "Any DNA or fingerprints?"

"Nothing yet," Luker said. "The place was pretty clean, so we checked—the cleaning lady had been there the day before. It won't be surprising if all of the prints we pulled belong to McGill and his lady friend."

"And if her prints or DNA aren't in the system, we have zip on her," Islas added.

"What about the security video?" Han asked.

"Not much," Luker replied. "We pulled the best shot we found of the woman, and we're showing it around, hoping someone recognizes her."

"Who are you showing it to?" Han asked.

"McGill was at some fundraising event at Lincoln Center, which means we're lucky—because it was a fundraiser, they have most of the guests' names. We work our way through the guest list, showing the lady's picture and hope for a name."

"That could take forever," Han said.

"We don't think so," Luker said. "Since the crime scene didn't give us much, we decided to reconstruct McGill's evening. We've got some detectives canvassing last night's guests. A couple of them said that he left with a woman matching his late-night guest. Sooner or later one of them will have a name or recognize the photo."

I looked at Harry and whispered, "They are going to find her. It's a matter of time."

"You'll have to work fast."

"Thanks for your wisdom."

Han nodded to his detectives, an unconscious gesture while he pondered what they had said. His face relaxed as he thought; he seemed a lot less harsh to me. "Okay, assuming we get a name, we collect the lady in question, you'll talk to her," he pointed at Luker as he said it, "and hopefully she confesses to everything, right?"

"Oh, sure, that always happens," Luker responded.

Han grinned, shook his head, and said, "Just playing devil's advocate: if you don't find the woman, are you developing any other possibilities? Any motive or opportunity for anyone else?"

Islas shrugged and grunted, "Come on, Loo, digging into a guy like McGill takes manpower. He's got more businesses, money, and women than Tony Stark."

"Tony Stark?"

"You know: Iron Man's real identity," Luker answered. "Billionaire playboy, scientist, arms manufacturer, blah, blah blah."

I spoke to Harry, "Nice reference: Jackson McGill to Tony Stark."

"Shouldn't you be paying attention?"

"I'm multitasking. I'm annoying you while I pay attention to the detectives."

"Very mature."

"Just trying to lighten the mood."

Lieutenant Han said, "I don't care which superhero McGill was. Dig into him. There could be plenty of people who might have wanted to kill him."

"But we're pretty sure the woman was there," Islas pointed out stubbornly.

"But we're not absolutely damn sure," Han said. "Maybe she was in the wrong place at the wrong time. You told me that the way McGill was cut up looked personal, a crime of passion, maybe. But it also could have been a pro disguising what he did. Or did I forget something?"

"No."

"I'll give you a couple of detectives to dig through McGill's background, see if we can develop some possibilities there."

"Yes, sir," Luker said. Islas echoed his partner, and they walked out of the lieutenant's office.

"I'm done here," I said to Harry.

"Where to now?"

"My apartment."

"You can walk from here."

"What no whooshing? I bet it's still snowing outside—"

He didn't answer me. He did whoosh me, all by my lonesome, to the sidewalk in front of the modern, fortresslike 20th Precinct on West 82nd Street in between Columbus and Amsterdam Avenues. It was still snowing. Harry had never sent me on a solo whoosh before.

"Okay," I said under my breath, "I'll walk."

It was a short walk, maybe a whole 10 minutes if I strolled really slowly, which is exactly what I did. Snow was beginning to accumulate on the sidewalks and streets. It was late on a December afternoon, and with the snowy weather, it was getting dark. I savored my walk, enjoying the snowfall and the Christmas decorations in store windows.

Approximately eleven minutes after departing the 20th Precinct, I turned onto West 76th Street, heading toward the brownstone where I lived. The place Maggie and I had called home. As I got closer, I made a list in my head of the things I needed: cash, clean clothes in a backpack—and my gun. Having my own gun was probably a very good idea given some of the folks I had run into earlier that day.

But right at that moment, having my gun was an absolute necessity. Parked across the street but directly in front of my brownstone was a dark-maroon Chevrolet Impala with two people inside. The car was pinging my instinctual radar like crazy. More Chinese? Or another pair of security types from Cú Chulainn Enterprises? I didn't want to find out. At least, not until I had a gun in my hand. After what I had done this morning, whoever these folks were, they'd be ready for me.

I stood on the sidewalk on the southern side, my side, of the street, fifty feet behind the Impala, which was parked on the northern side. The snow, the growing darkness, and a tree gave me cover while I considered my situation. Who were they? What did they want? And how the hell did they get here, anyway? How did they know who I was and that I was involved with Marissa? Since I couldn't answer any of those questions, I ignored them. I had to find the answer to a much more immediate and urgent question:

How was I going to get into my apartment, get what I wanted, and then disappear without these guys jumping me?

Like many streets on the Upper West Side, 76th consisted of a long row of brownstones running side-by-side on both sides of the street. When I say side-by-side, I mean the buildings were tight—one brownstone's side was built into the next's. The steps to the front door of my brownstone were about fifty feet away—like the Impala sedan. There were parked cars on both sides of the street. Crouching low, I crept from behind one car to the next, slowly moving toward my home. Looking through the windows of the parked cars, I made sure no one was getting out of the Chevy. As I got closer to my home and to their car, I crawled from car to car on my hands and knees on the snowy sidewalk. I was wet and cold.

After what seemed like a couple of miles of crawling—not easy when you have to get around parking signs, the occasional tree and a fire hydrant—I was directly opposite the front stoop of my building. I slowly rose until I could barely see through the window of the Toyota Camry I was hiding behind. The Impala team wasn't moving. Now all I had to do was climb a long set of stone steps to get inside and somehow do this without being noticed. As I was trying to figure out a way of accomplishing this, fate stepped in. Or maybe it was the Chairman.

A delivery van was coming down the street toward me. Coming slowly. There were a couple of cars double-parked—not an uncommon occurrence in Manhattan—and the van had to maneuver carefully around them. The vehicle was big enough and slow enough to screen my climb up the steps if I was quick. As the van's nose went by me, I was on my feet and dashing up two and three steps at a time, key in my hand sliding into the lock, swinging the outer front door open, and plunging into the tiny foyer. I looked out the window in the top half of the outer door to check on the Impala. Two men were clambering out of the sedan.

"Shit!" I hissed. I turned and stepped to the inner door, key ready, and saw what had given me away: Someone had duct-taped a smart-phone sized camera to the wall, pointed at the outer door. It wasn't pretty, but it was effective. No one could enter the building without the people on the other end of the camera knowing it. I slid inside the inner door and ran up the stairs to my apartment. I heard the brownstone's outer front door open and close. There was a bang as the inner front door was broken open. I stepped through my door and slammed the dead bolts—half-inch thick steel rods—into the steel door frame. Battering down my front door would require a major effort. I figured I had two or three minutes. I went to my bedroom closet, lifted a steel case with my gun off the shelf, slipped into my shoulder holster, pulled my Ruger SR9 with a 17-round magazine out of the case and put it in the holster. On the floor of the closet was a small backpack with a few hundred dollars in cash, an untraceable "burn" phone, some underwear, socks, a rugby shirt, and a flannel shirt. The backpack was my Quick Exit Kit, put together for just such occasions. One minute gone. I stood still and listened. No loud thumping sounds at my door. I tiptoed out to the living room to within a few feet of the apartment's front door. There was the whisper of metal rasping from the far side of the door—they were picking the lock.

I smiled. Once they had picked the lock, they'd still have to get past the steel dead bolts, and that would not be easy. I had a bit more time than I first thought. I went through the bedroom, unlocked the window, climbed out on the fire escape, and closed the window behind me. Then I went up the escape as quickly and quietly as possible. I was leaving footprints in the snow on the steps, which meant that if the guys breaking into my apartment bothered to check the window, they'd know where I'd gone.

But I made it to the roof without seeing anyone leaning out my window to check the fire escape. Must have still been struggling with the door. I clambered from the rooftop of one brownstone to another, moving west, trying to get as far from my own building as possible. When I reached the third to last brownstone, I tried the door of the small shack on the roof that housed the top of the stairwell. Locked. Next roof, same thing. Finally, on the last roof, I found the door unlocked and quickly descended through the brownstone's interior to the first floor. I let myself out the front door and stood on the top of the stoop, looking east toward the Impala. I could see the car through the snow, but I couldn't tell if the guys had given up on my door and returned to the car.

Maybe they had gotten through the door and were following my footsteps over the rooftops and toward me right now. Maybe they had called for backup. Dallying at the top of the stoop seemed like a very bad idea. I hustled down the steps and turned left, to the west. I hadn't gone more than ten feet when I heard a car accelerating behind me. The Impala was reversing the wrong way on the one way 76th Street at high speed, coming toward me.

Tires screeched from the other direction. I twisted to look west, and my Chinese friends in the Mercedes were barreling toward me from the other end of the block. It appeared that backup had been summoned. Were there more coming? Could the folks in either car see me or were they playing the odds to trap me in between? No time to find out. I dashed back up the stoop I had just come down. The front door was locked. I pulled out my gun, smashed the glass, and reached in to open the door. As I stepped through, I could hear cars jerking to a stop and doors slamming. The inside door of the brownstone had a wire mesh over the windowed part. There was no way to reach through and unlock the door. I peered through the glass—no one inside. I aimed my Ruger in a downward angle at the lock and fired. The bullet went through the lock and into the floor beyond. I kicked the door open and ran for the stairs, pounding footsteps right behind me. I was halfway up the first flight of stairs when I heard the *thwipp*! *thwipp*! of a silenced pistol and felt something sting the back of my right shoulder. I ran a few more steps and reached the second floor, but I was overwhelmed with dizziness. I managed to climb most of the next flight of stairs but had to stop and clutch the railing. Blurry figures were rushing up the stairs toward me. My knees buckled, and I toppled forward onto the third floor.

7

I woke up with my arms and legs duct-taped to the armrests and legs of a wooden chair. I was in a large, unfinished space with bare cement floors and semi-transparent plastic drop cloths hanging like curtains from floor to unfinished ceiling throughout. The plastic swayed in a light breeze. The only light was from an uncovered bulb hanging by its cord from a metal pipe jutting from the exposed concrete of the ceiling. The bulb was twenty feet away and dim, maybe 60 watts. The space was lonely and gloomy, probably waiting to become offices for a law firm or a digital-age ad agency. There was a soft sound of traffic from way below.

My coat was off; my holster was still tucked under my left armpit, empty. I couldn't see my coat or gun or backpack. My mouth felt as if it had been washed out with vinegar. I guessed that was an after-affect of whatever drug they had shot me up with. I peered as far into the dark space as I could, but saw nothing but the single light bulb, hanging plastic, unfinished ceiling and bare floor. The chair was not secured to the floor, but since I was very securely taped up, the only way I could move the chair would be to push off with my toes and tip backward. Probably concussing myself when I hit the floor. No thanks.

Several sets of footsteps came from behind me. There was nothing hurried about their movement. It was deliberate. And slow. I had the ugly feeling I wasn't going to enjoy what was about to happen.

"Harry?" I said softly.

Michael Flynn, the Cú Chulainn Enterprises security guy I'd hammered with a partially full gallon paint can on Madison Avenue this morning, stepped in front of me. "No, not Harry," Flynn said with a smile. Then he hit me with a right cross, with his feet planted and the full force of the punch driving through my jaw.

My head snapped back, the chair fell over, and I slammed down on the floor. I felt the back of my skull bounce off the cement and lost consciousness for a few seconds. The next thing I was aware of was several hands pulling me upright, still in the chair.

"How do you feel?" Flynn asked, still smiling.

"I've been worse. You hit like a girl." The second I uttered it, I knew it was a mistake. His right fist caught me full on the cheekbone, sending me crashing to the floor, where the cement knocked me out.

The lovely ammoniated aroma of smelling salts brought me back to consciousness. I was upright again. It took me a few seconds—I think it was seconds, maybe it was minutes—to focus. Standing around me in a half-circle were the two Chinese men from the Mercedes on my right and Flynn and Bouchard on my left. About five feet directly in front of me stood a small digital video camera and microphone on a metal tripod. A small red light was on, which I guessed meant there was a live feed going someplace.

The left side of my face, where Flynn had connected twice, felt raw and swollen. The back of my skull throbbed with pain. In the future, I would really have to think twice about mouthing off to a goon like Flynn when I was completely powerless.

"Mr. Tyrrell?" Bouchard asked. "Are you awake? Do you understand me?"

"Yes. I guess so."

"Where's Marissa Carvajal?"

"How do you know who I am? How'd you find me?"

Bouchard looked from me to the Chinese men. All three smiled. Not nice smiles. Self-satisfied, smug smiles.

"How?" I repeated. I wanted to ask them questions to keep them from asking me. I was going to have to stonewall them. In my experience, not answering questions in a situation like this would eventually lead to extremely unpleasant repercussions for me.

"Our company manufactures all kinds of security devices. Including the cameras at Marissa Carvajal's apartment building. We jacked the feed from those cameras, ran it through facial recognition—" she smiled her unappetizing, self-satisfied smile, "the facial-recognition software is fantastic. Bing, bang, boom—we had your name, address, and personal history."

"Lucky me." Harry had whisked me past all the security in McGill's building, but we had entered Marissa's like normal people.

"Well, you have quite a record." Bouchard raised her hand to her ear, as if adjusting an earbud. She spoke softly, "Okay." Focusing back on me, she said, "Now, tell us where you took Marissa Carvajal."

"Can we negotiate about this?"

"Negotiate?" one of the Chinese asked. He was taller and better groomed than his Chinese comrade. His accent was barely perceptible; his English impeccable. He spoke the way someone does when he's been very well trained in English as a second language. "What do we have to negotiate?"

"Well, you tell me why you want Marissa, and then maybe I'll tell you where to find her."

"We don't have to negotiate," he said. He reached over and tugged at my arm, which didn't budge thanks to a masterful duct-taping job. "Tell us or suffer."

"She's out of the country," I said. "Flew to Canada."

"I doubt it."

"Wait a minute, you're right. She didn't go to Canada. Who goes north at this time of year? She took Amtrak to Florida."

Flynn lunged at me, fist flying. I twisted my face to the side—the result: I was hit hard enough for it to sting, but not hard enough to smash me to the floor again. "Let's stop fucking around," Flynn said.

"Do you plan on continuing to hit him?" the Chinese asked.

"No," Flynn grinned and rubbed his knuckles. "I got a better idea." He walked out of sight. I could hear him rummaging through what I guessed were tools. I was secured to a wooden chair in a construction site. I didn't want to imagine the selection of tools Flynn was choosing from and what he would do to me. His footsteps came closer, and he said, "This ought to come in handy."

He stopped directly in front of me, holding an oxyacetylene torch in his right hand and a striker to light the torch in his left. The shorter Chinese, whom I thought of as Silent Sam, rolled the fuel tanks behind Flynn.

I've seen and felt many awful things and been wounded in combat. I'd like to say that I'm tougher than nails. But in that moment, as Flynn lingered near me with that torch, I was almost overwhelmed with nauseous fear. I've smelt burnt flesh, and it's horrifying. The idea that I was going to smell my own burnt flesh and feel the searing pain made my heart pound extremely hard and fast. I forced myself to take a deep breath. And then another.

Flynn noticed my deep breaths and my eyes locked on the torch in his hand. He stepped very close to me and waved the unlit torch inches from my face.

"The fingertips have a large number of nerve endings," the taller Chinese man said. "I would suggest you burn one fingertip at a time until Tyrrell tells us what we want to know."

"That sounds good," Flynn replied.

Mr. Impeccable English pointed at my arms, "If you don't mind a suggestion . . . ?"

"Sure, what?"

"Undo his tape, turn the arm over, re-tape it to the armrest. Then the hands will be palms up and the fingertips will be easily accessed."

Flynn nodded, and Silent Sam stepped forward and began to undo the duct tape around my right arm. Bouchard, who had been farther away on the left, walked closer and aimed a gun, my own Ruger, at me.

When Harry and I had worked our last case, he told me that I would get whatever help I needed to do what the Chairman hoped I would do. That was very reassuring until I realized that my definition of need and Harry's—maybe it was the Chairman's definition—were quite different.

As Silent Sam freed my right arm and began to twist it so my palm faced up, Flynn used the striker to light the torch. It hissed with flame, pink at the outer end, blue in near the nozzle. At this moment, it was an absolute, imperative *need* that Harry or the Chairman intervene, to save me from torture. I wasn't tough enough not to tell them where Marissa was after they used the torch on me. No one was that tough.

Silent Sam pulled a long strand of duct tape loose to roll around my arm and the chair's armrest.

"Harry," I muttered, chin down toward the floor, "I really need your intervention here. Really."

Flynn smirked, "Who the hell is Harry?"

Our eyes locked. "He's my guardian angel."

Silent Sam fastened the tape to the bottom of the armrest and began to pull it around. Flynn asked, "Want to tell me where Marissa Carvajal is?"

"No."

"I'm going to enjoy this—" and the light bulb went out. Only the glow of the torch's flame provided any illumination. There was a half-second of shock and surprise among all of them. A half-second would have to do.

I jerked my right arm hard across the front of my body, pulling Silent Sam with me. He staggered into Bouchard, who fired. The bullet whizzed past my head and pinged off a wall as it ricocheted into the distance. I yanked my partially taped arm down as hard as I could, forcing Sam into a forward fall, which knocked Bouchard off her feet into Flynn. Stretching toward the floor, I reached under Sam's jacket, found his holster, and yanked out his Beretta. I whacked him across the head with his own gun, knocking him unconscious. I straightened up and aiming the Beretta at Mr. Impeccable English, who was pointing his weapon at me, too.

Bouchard struggled to her feet and brought my Ruger pistol to bear on me. Flynn carefully set the still-burning torch on the floor and drew his gun.

"Everybody hold still," I said loudly and firmly.

"Yeah right," Flynn said, aiming at me. "Get fu—"

I shot him in the right shoulder. He toppled backward, and his gun clattered across the cement floor. I swung my weapon toward Bouchard and Mr. Impeccable English. "Hold still."

Flynn was groaning, "Oh, God . . . you shot me you—"

"You were going to burn my fingertips off, you prick," I grunted to Flynn, never taking my eyes off Bouchard or Mr. Impeccable English. "Put your guns down," I said.

"Are you so fast you can kill me before I kill you?" Mr. Impeccable said, a repeat of what he'd asked me this morning as we faced off on Central Park West. "So fast you can kill me before Ms. Bouchard kills you?"

"Probably," I said. "After all, about 30 seconds ago, I was helpless, unarmed, and secured to this chair. Now I've got a gun, and two of the four of you are out of commission. Do you really want to find out?"

He looked at Bouchard, and she shrugged.

"Put your weapons down," I said.

They did as they were told, gently laying the weapons on the floor.

"Kick them to your left, my right."

The guns were sent skittering into the dark beyond the glow of the torch.

"Now, you," I pointed at Mr. Impeccable, "lie down next to Flynn." He did as he was instructed. To Bouchard, I said, "Come here, kneel down by the chair, and free my left arm. Hey!" I said sharply as she took a long, quick step toward me, "Don't get any ideas. Get down where you are and crawl over here."

She knelt and crawled as if we were playing Simon Says. When she was within a foot of the chair I twisted forward and pressed the gun barrel to her left temple. "You do anything beside free my arm, and I will blow you away."

"Got it," she said. It took her a minute to tug and pull the tape off, but she succeeded and I was free.

"Okay, back off. Go lie down next to your buddy Flynn."

As soon as she was next to her groaning colleague, I fumbled around with my left hand to free my right leg, all while keeping a steady gaze and my gun on the four of them. It would have been much easier if I could look at the tape, but it would also have been much easier for them to gain the upper hand if I concentrated on the tape and not them. It took me a few minutes, but I finally freed my legs.

"Harry? Light please?" I said. The light bulb snapped back on. Under my breath: "I knew that was you." The bulb didn't offer glorious illumination, but it was much better than the torch. "Bouchard, turn off the torch. Don't stand. Crawl over to it."

She was surly but compliant, crawling over to the torch's fuel tank and closing the valve. The flame hissed out. "Go back."

Once Bouchard had returned to her spot on the cement next to Flynn, I inspected my surroundings. A few feet behind the chair I had been secured to were a couple of tables made from four- by eight-foot, half-inch plywood sitting atop saw horses. One table, to my right, was piled with all kinds of tools. The table to my left had some building plans unfurled on top of it and was surrounded by five wooden armchairs exactly like the one I had been tied to. My coat was flung over the back of one chair, with my pack back on the chair's seat. I dragged the chair with my things over to the table with the tools.

"What's your name?" I asked Mr. Impeccable English.

"Wei."

"Okay, Mr. Wei, you and Ms. Bouchard help Mr. Flynn to one of these chairs. Empty his pockets onto the table. Then use the duct tape to secure him to the chair the way you secured me."

Flynn cursed as unimaginatively as he had earlier but with a lot more oomph. Pain will do that to a person's cursing. He was especially displeased with the way they dumped him into a chair, after pulling everything out of his pockets.

"Mr. Wei, please get the tape. Ms. Bouchard, please take a step back. But just a step."

She did as she was told and stayed where it was easy for me to cover her. Wei fetched a roll of tape and did a very nice job of tightly wrapping Flynn's arms and legs to the chair.

"Don't forget his mouth," I said.

Flynn's cursing escalated, and I have to admit I was surprised at the quantity and the quality of the profanity, and then Wei silenced him with a piece of tape. I gestured with the pistol for Wei to step away, and once he was out of reach, I leaned over to inspect the job on Flynn.

To Flynn: "Yeah, you're not going anywhere." To Wei and Bouchard: "If you'd do the same for Mr. Wei's colleague."

When they finished, Silent Sam, ike Flynn, was tight like Thanksgiving leftovers in plastic wrap.

"Ladies first," I said to Bouchard.

"Fuck you," she hissed.

"Aw, you never talk dirty to me like you mean it."

"Fu—"

I stopped her continuing by touching the barrel of the pistol to her lips. Her eyes blazed at me over the gun. "Empty your pockets then sit down," I said.

She pulled each item from her pockets slowly, angrily slapping them onto the plywood tabletop. Keys, cell phone, magnetic ID card, a small Swiss Army knife.

"Sit down," I said, waving the pistol at her. "If you please, Mr. Wei."

He did as thorough a job on her as the others, and then, without being asked, he emptied his pockets onto the table and sat in the last empty chair. I stepped behind him, grasped the roll of tape roll, pulled a long strip loose, looped it around him, and taped him around his chest, biceps, his back, and the chair. I taped his right wrist to the armrest and then, walking behind him again—no point in offering him the temptation to kick me—I secured his left wrist. I did each of his legs from the side, again offering no opportunity to lash out with his feet. While I was crouched over, I took off Wei's shoes, and then did the same for the other three. Being a construction site, the space was unheated, and the cement floor felt like the bottom shelf of a refrigerator.

When you've been a U.S. Marshal, you're used to having to paw through people's stuff from time to time. Most everyone—even criminals—has boring stuff. Some—especially criminals—have disgusting stuff. Blood on clothes, handkerchiefs, tissues, icepicks, knives, forks, spoons, screwdrivers, chisels . . . you get the idea, right? But when you're in law enforcement, you have to inspect this boring and sometimes disgusting stuff, because you learn things when you do.

I didn't bother to go through either Bouchard or Flynn's wallets, I'd been through them both that morning. But Wei's and Silent Sam's, whose name was Liào, revealed things I did not know. For instance, according to their business cards, they worked for SHK Dragon Technology, headquartered in Shanghai and Hong Kong. However, both Mr. Wei and Mr. Liào had phone numbers and office addresses in Hong Kong *and* New York.

"Does SHK Dragon Technology do business with Cú Chulainn Enterprises?" I asked Wei.

He didn't answer.

"What kind of technology does SHK Dragon make?"

No answer.

"For crying out loud, I can Google it. Just tell me."

"Software and hardware."

"Security products?"

"Among others. We are heavily involved in the medical, travel, inventory, sales and distribution . . ."

"Okay, I get it. Now that you and I are having a nice conversation, let me ask you again: Are you in business with Cú Chulainn Enterprises?"

Silence. Again.

"Maybe your company owns a chunk of Cú Chulainn? Or they own a piece of you?"

More silence.

"What do you want with Marissa Carvajal?"

Even more silence, but now, instead of staring off at a gently flapping piece of plastic in the dim space, he smiled.

"Thanks for your cooperation." I duct-taped his mouth shut. Where's your smile now, Wei?

I stepped in front of Bouchard, considered her for a minute, then moved over to Flynn. "You're going to tell me what I want to know. If you don't, I'm going to do to you what you threatened to do to me."

His eyes went wide, and he made angry noises behind the piece of tape over his mouth.

"Not going to talk, huh?" I picked up the oxyacetylene torch and striker, grabbed the handle of the roller the fuel tank sat on, and brought everything close to Flynn. I slowly waved the unlit torch a couple of inches from his face. "Karma's a bitch, huh, Flynn?"

He was screaming behind the tape. I couldn't begin to understand what he was saying, but he was clearly a very unhappy, very frightened camper. He rocked backward, and the chair wobbled but didn't go over. I made an elaborate show of opening the fuel valve, picking up the striker, and clicking it. Hissing blue flame sprouted from the torch. I leaned over until my eyes were level with his. I knew he could feel the heat of the torch below his chin, because I could feel it, too.

"Flynn, please remember: I'm the guy who shot you. The guy who's still pissed that you were going to burn off his fingertips. Keep that in mind when you decide whether or not to answer me."

I moved the torch a tiny bit closer to him. He squirmed and moaned. I moved it farther away, reached up and roughly pulled the tape off of his mouth.

"Why do you want Marissa Carvajal? What are you going to to with her?"

"No, no, please . . . I can't . . . I can't . . ."

"Have it your way," I said and moved the flame close to the fingers of his right hand. The flesh wasn't burning—and I confess, I hoped he would break before I had to burn him—but the heat was probably pretty damn uncomfortable.

"Why do you want Marissa Carvajal?"

Sweat poured down his face, and his mouth was open in a rictus of fear. It made me nauseous to think I could be deliberately inflicting this kind of anguish. Not to mention the horror I felt at the thought of burning his flesh. Could this really be what the Chairman wanted me to do? To treat another human being like this? Did the end—protecting Marissa—justify the means? I thought: Please let him break before I have to do this . . .

Flynn panted desperately, "We're supposed to turn her over to the police!"

"Oh?" I withdrew the torch. "For what?"

He was crying now. "McGill's murder."

"Did she kill McGill? Or are you people setting her up? Is she being framed?"

"I don't know."

"Why don't I believe you?" I moved the torch close enough so the heat was painful.

He sobbed, "I don't know, I don't . . . I'd tell you . . . please."

Given how terrified I had been when facing this torture, I was pretty darn sure that I was getting the truth out of Flynn. I checked the expressions on the other's faces: All were were wide-eyed and pale. Torturing me would have been fine as a spectator sport. Seeing one of their own be tortured this way, and knowing either of them could be next, well, that was completely and terrifyingly different.

Flynn was telling the truth. The whole truth. Nothing but the truth.

Time to go, I thought. Maybe past time . . . "Do you have backup?" I barked at Flynn. "Are you supposed to check-in with someone?"

Flynn gasped, "Yes!"

I grabbed the nearest phone off of the table and checked the time, "It's almost 8:00. When are you supposed to check-in?"

"Now, at 8:00." He was panting with fear, the words spilling out. "They'll be on their way within minutes if we don't check-in."

"How many?"

"Four, four, I swear to God, four . . ."

Oh dear, I thought. Backup would be here within a couple of minutes. The flame snapped out as I closed the valve on the fuel tank. I retaped Flynn's mouth. Found a canvas drop cloth, gathered all their shoes, weapons, phones, everything I had taken from them, and dumped it all in the cloth. It was like Santa's Christmas gift sack, only some of the toys were lethal. I checked my Ruger's magazine, put the safety on, and slid it into my holster. I grabbed my wallet and phone off the table, put on my coat and backpack, slung the Santa bundle over my shoulder, and hurried around the floor until I found the emergency stairs. I pulled the door open and saw from stenciled lettering painted on the cement wall that I was on the 53rd floor. I jogged down the stairs to the 47th floor. There was a sign on the door that said: "Re-entry on this floor." I pushed open the door, whipped the Santa sack off my shoulder and through the door into the glow of the 47th floor emergency-lights. Back inside the emergency stairwell, I moved quickly down to the 38th floor, where a sign said I could re-enter on that floor. I stepped into a hallway and walked to the elevators. I heard an elevator rising in the shaft. It sounded as if it was above me. I hoped that was the backup security team.

I pressed the button and heard machinery whir. Unless my hearing was completely messed up, the elevator I had summoned was coming from below. I took no chances—when the doors rolled open, I was in a combat crouch with my Ruger pointed at the elevator, ready to provide a warm welcome to anyone who happened to be in the elevator. No one was there. I stepped inside, the doors shut, and the elevator descended to the lobby. It occurred to me I had no idea where I was. Probably Manhattan. But midtown or downtown? Not a clue.

The elevator settled, the doors rolled open, and a couple of men in polyester, Navy-blue blazers looked up from the monitors at the security desk. The desk was near a plexiglass railing. The lobby was actually a mezzanine above the building's ground floor. The walls were a tan marble. I took the escalator down to the ground floor and saw a gigantic wall of glass at one end of the lobby. I smiled in recognition—I was in the MetLife Building, formerly the

Pan Am Building, which sits atop Grand Central Terminal. Even if the bad guys' backup was only a minute or two behind me, Grand Central provided me with a plethora of escape routes.

Turned out I didn't have a minute or two. A man and woman, both African Americans, were waiting inside the revolving doors on the street side of the lobby. They were pretending to chat but broke off their conversation and focused on me like laser beams as I stepped off the escalator. I pulled a U-turn at the bottom of the escalator and rushed toward Grand Central. A glance over my shoulder showed that the couple were following quickly, and the woman was speaking into a mobile phone. Which meant someone else was here to help them. And hurt me.

I reached the escalators that descended into the main concourse of Grand Central. The concourse floor was enormous, almost three hundred feet long, one hundred twenty feet wide. Tan-colored marble covered the floors and walls. In the middle of the concourse was an information booth with an ornate brass clock atop it. The far wall of the concourse was lined with ticket booths, most of which were closed at this hour, and above them large digital displays showing the times of departures on the three lines of the railroad that served Grand Central. Above it all, the blue-green ceiling arched more than one hundred feet above the floor. On the ceiling were constellations—the stars were shiny, bright lights, and the zodiac figures such as Taurus, Gemini, and Orion the Hunter painted in gold on the ceiling itself. I've been in and out of Grand Central hundreds, maybe thousands, of times in my life. But never with a bunch of potentially lethal people chasing me, so I didn't stop for any sightseeing.

Descending the escalator, I had only traveled ten feet when I saw the welcoming committee at the bottom: two more Chinese men. Given the large number of police officers and National Guardsmen in the station, it was unlikely that they would pull a gun. But they could stab me with a knife or inject me with a needle full of sleepy-time medicine. It looked impossible to get past them.

The escalator step had almost reached the bottom when I leapt forward, planted both hands on the metal divider between escalators like a gymnast on a pommel horse, and vaulted feet first toward the nearest Chinese. Both feet caught him full in the chest and sent him spinning backward, tumbling over the floor. As I landed, I rolled to an awkward crouch on my hands and toes and lunged out of my ungainly stance into a full body tackle, taking the second man down. I chopped him hard in the neck, reached under his jacket, pulled out his automatic pistol, and with a tiny flick of my wrist sent it clattering across the marble floor. Then I was on my feet and running hard for the southwest corner of the concourse, toward the Times Square shuttle.

There was a lot of shouting behind me, which I guessed was the police. Hopefully at least a few of them were paying attention to the Chinese and the loose gun on the floor. But I could also hear feet pounding after me. Cops were chasing me and probably radioing other units in the terminal to cut me off. If the black couple were following—and they had probably remained discreetly out of the fray with the Chinese—they'd be right behind any pursuing cops and also calling for more help to track me down. All of which meant I had to get out of Grand Central before law enforcement or the bad guys caught up with me.

I burst through the wood-and-glass doors to the subway. To my left, the passageway stretched east toward the Lexington Avenue line. To my right, the Time Square Shuttle platform was very close at hand. I decided against the obviousness of the shuttle, turned left and ran as fast as I could toward Lexington Avenue. About halfway to that platform, I heard shouting behind me. The hot pursuit was still hot.

"Harry, you want to whoosh me out of here?" I panted under my breath. "Harry?"

There was no whooshing to safety. But as I hustled into the Lexington Avenue subway station, I heard the deep rumbling of an approaching subway train. I glanced down the stairway to the downtown platform: no train. I raced to the stairs for the uptown platform, ran down to the platform, and slid between closing doors on the uptown express. A couple of police officers reached the platform just as we were pulling out. They probably hadn't seen me enter the train, but I was sure they'd play the percentages and have the train met at the next stop, 59th Street.

Rocking side to side with the motion of the subway, I walked back to the very last car and positioned myself in front of the last set of doors. The train pulled into 59th Street, and a crowd of the passengers turned left as they got off the train, heading for the station exit. I crouched down to minimize my height and turned right as I exited. I walked to the end of the platform and climbed down a small ladder into the darkness of the tunnel. I stumbled as I hit the ground but didn't lose my footing completely. I turned to look back up at the platform. There were no police officers in sight, and the crowd was dense enough to have screened me from the sight of any cops who were standing close to the station exit.

The train pulled out of the station, moving north toward its next stop at 86th Street. I ducked under the edge of the platform and waited. And waited. And waited. Another express train came in, dumped its passengers and picked up new ones, and departed. More waiting. Another train.

When the second train left the station, I checked my watch and saw that it had been thirty minutes. The dark, damp, dirty space under a subway platform is not a spiffy place to hang out. But at least no rats had come out to make my acquaintance. I leaned out from under the edge of the platform and checked the station. No cops anywhere to be seen. A minute later I was up on the platform and making my way out of the station. I went up into Bloomingdale's, which like all stores during the Christmas season, was open late. I walked the aisles, pretending to shop for jewelry, taking in the Christmas decorations, and listening to Josh

Groban and Diana Krall sing Christmas carols over the store's sound system. Leaning over display cases to get a close look at the merchandise is a great way to scope out your surroundings without being obvious about it. No one can tell if you're closely examining a bracelet or if your eyes are darting all over to make sure you're not being followed. However more than one person stared at my face, making me wonder what the hell was going on—until I realized the effects of Flynn's punches must be showing on my cheek. I found the nearest men's room, washed the dirt off my face—amazing how filthy you get when someone pummels you into the floor—and ran wet fingers through my hair. My appearance was a wee bit less wild. My cheekbone was swollen and red so I made a cold compress out of paper towels and cold water, stood in one of the toilet stalls, and applied the compress to my face for a while.

After ten minutes of minimalist first aid, my cheek didn't look too bad, and I exited the store onto Lexington Avenue and walked west across 59th Street to Columbus Circle. I surreptitiously checked my back trail from time to time. Still no one following me. At Columbus Circle, I walked to the plaza in the center of the circle and stood near the huge pillar topped by a statue of Christopher Columbus. Everywhere I turned I could see Christmas decorations, and some of the apartment windows featured Chanukah menorahs.

"Harry?" I said softly. "I would like to speak with you—"

He appeared before I finished.

"You turned off the light?" It wasn't a question. More of a frustrated remonstrance. "A light? You couldn't have warned me beforehand?"

"I didn't know beforehand. The Chairman made me aware of your situation after you had been captured."

"Gee, that was big of him."

As usual, Harry did not respond to comments directed at the Chairman.

"Okay, but turning off the light—really? How 'bout stopping them from knocking me out?"

"You received the help you needed. You always receive what you need."

"Since I needed help to escape capture and torture for that matter, why couldn't you have intervened earlier?"

"The Chairman favors as little intervention as possible."

"Why?"

Harry didn't favor me with a reply.

"Why the hell does the Chairman intervene as little as possible? I could have been killed or hurt."

"But you weren't. And hell has nothing to do with this."

"Fine, we'll leave hell out of this." I paused to take a deep breath. "I was scared tonight . . . scared like I haven't been in a long time. When I thought Flynn was going to take the torch to me . . ."

"You thought you were going to break."

"No, I *knew* I was going to break. I have no delusions about how tough I am."

Harry waited for me to say more and when I didn't, he said, "Something more is bothering you."

I sighed, "As frightened as I was of being burned . . . and I *was terrified* to my very soul . . . I was still going to . . . I was still willing to do the same thing to another man."

"But you didn't."

"I was going to."

"But you did *not* do it."

"I was sick to my stomach and—in the exact same moment—absolutely willing to burn whatever I could out of Flynn."

"You thought it was necessary. You hoped he would give in before you burned him, and he did. You didn't torture him."

"What the hell is wrong with me?"

"I'm not sure there's enough time for an adequate discussion about that."

Rage boiled in me as his words sunk in, and I turned on Harry, balling my fists, ready to destroy him, and stopped.

His Mona Lisa smile was in place.

I relaxed my clenched fists and laughed. "Thank you," I said.

"You're welcome."

Snow was still gently falling in the early evening, white specks floating toward the ground under the streetlights, but it was only frosting the streets and the buildings. The snow plows probably wouldn't even have to hit the streets to deal with it. Cars swirled around the center of the circle—and Harry and me. The stores on the ground level of the towering Time Warner Center on the west side of the circle were all done up in Christmas finery, and the Salvation Army volunteers were ringing bells in time with Christmas carols playing on a boom box. Looking north on Broadway, I could see Christmas lights in the median separating the uptown and downtown traffic.

Christmas spirit seemed unattainable to me. Harry's words had taken the hard edge off of my fears about myself, but I was left with the reality that I would have toasted Flynn like a marshmallow to get the information I wanted.

"Harry, do you have a shrink in your . . . network?"

"Do you mean a psychiatrist?"

"Or a psychologist, just someone to talk to."

"My network? Do you think I manage a vast collective—"

"Harry, yes or no. You must be . . . the case manager for more people than me. I can't be the only one."

"Why not?"

"Really? We have to do this Socratic exploration right now?"

He replied with silence.

"Okay. It's almost impossible to believe that I am the only person who has been helped by the Chairman."

Harry's almost-smile made the briefest of appearances. "I have someone."

"Thank you. Could we set something up for tomorrow?"

"Yes."

"What about the NYPD? Are they closer to finding Marissa?"

"The detectives have not updated their lieutenant since this morning's meeting. The police are still canvassing witnesses from the Philharmonic benefit."

"We still have a bit of time."

"Yes."

I watched and listened to the Salvation Army volunteers. *Silent Night* was the carol of the moment. Their bells were quiet, and they sang along softly.

"Did Marissa murder McGill?"

"I thought you felt she was innocent."

"I think . . . I *hope* she is innocent. I hope that the reason she looks good as a suspect is that I haven't developed another theory of the case. Haven't found any evidence to support another theory, another suspect."

"There's more work to do."

I inhaled deeply then exhaled and watched the steam of my breath disappear into the falling snow.

"Right. More work to do." I listened to the Salvation Army folks finish the last verse of *Silent Night*. "Can we please whoosh to Rye, now?"

"I am not a transport service."

"It's an excellent way to ensure I'm not followed."

He looked up into the snowy sky, back at me, and poof! We were standing at the front door of the Selkirks' colonial house in Rye.

* * *

NIGHT – MANHATTAN: Cú Chulainn Tower

SAVANNAH FARINGER AND REZNIK SAT at the table in the conference room, watching video from the under-construction 53rd floor of the MetLife Building as Tyrrell reversed the situation and captured his kidnappers. Reznik leaned forward as Tyrrell threatened Flynn with a blowtorch.

"Huh, I wonder if Tyrrell would have done it," Reznik said.

"Done what?"

"Burned your man to get answers. It's one thing to bluff torture; it's another to do it. Takes an unusual moral quality."

Faringer's eyes narrowed as she considered Reznik. "And you happen to have that quality?"

"Yes." He sat back. "What do you know about this man?"

"John Fitzpatrick Tyrrell, known as 'Jack'," Faringer checked the open file on the table. "He went to Fordham College, where he was enrolled in Army ROTC. He graduated and was commissioned. He applied for and was accepted into Special Forces. Two tours in Afghanistan. He was part of a special operations team that worked with the CIA. Won a Silver Star and a Purple Heart. After the Army, he was a U.S. Deputy Marshal for six years, commended twice, and then left on disability after being shot. His wife was killed in the shooting."

"A decorated Green Beret and a former Marshal. Clearly a serious talent. Physical details?"

"Six foot two, two hundred twenty pounds, brown hair, blue eyes. A small scar over his right eyebrow, two scars on his left forearm, and one scar from a bullet on his lower right ribs. No other distinguishing features." Faringer closed the file. "He's accomplished and taller than average, but he's considerably smaller than you."

"Size isn't everything. Although I'd rather be my size than his."

"Do you anticipate any trouble?"

"Tyrrell will be a welcome challenge." He looked out the conference room window at Manhattan's night skyline. "Is he the man who took your team out at Marissa Carvajal's apartment?"

"Yes."

"Maybe the next time your people kidnap and torture a key player, you should invite me."

"That was an oversight; it won't happen again."

"Don't tell me they taped the interrogation instead of sending a live feed."

"It was a live feed, but as important as Marissa Carvajal is to Cú Chulainn, I can't spend every single moment of my day managing this problem. I was in a meeting when the feed came in. I didn't know they had Tyrrell until after he escaped. There are now standing instructions that if Tyrrell or Carvajal are captured, I'm to be contacted immediately. And I, of course, will contact you immediately."

"Good." Reznik stared at the frozen video image. Tyrrell was very close to Flynn and to the torch's blue flame. "Any news from the police?"

"Not yet. They are doing a very good job of reconstructing Jackson's evening at the Philharmonic. They'll establish that he left Lincoln Center with Marissa Carvajal. After that, it's a matter of time until they—or we—find her. Her DNA will match the physical evidence from the crime scene, and the security video will confirm that she was the only person to enter or exit the building at the approximate time of death."

"And the case will be wrapped tight, without a tiny trace leading back to you."

She nodded. "What's your next step?"

"Learn about the opposition. I'll visit his apartment and get to know Tyrrell up close and personal."

8

Otto, the Selkirks' all-purpose man, answered Harry's knock and let us inside.

"May I take your bag to your room?" he asked, pointing at my backpack.

"No thanks, I've got it."

"Ms. Carvajal is waiting for you in the den." He turned before we could respond and led the way to a wood-paneled room, with bookcases and the same floor-to-ceiling glass doors facing the Sound as the living room. Large upholstered chairs and couches in elegant floral prints filled the room, seemingly placed at random, but with an eye for the flow of traffic in the room, and every piece of furniture had a view out a window or of the fireplace. Marissa was sitting in a chair near a crackling fire. She had a brandy snifter in her right hand. A tray with a bottle of brandy and more glasses was nearby.

She stood as we entered, "Any news?" Before we could answer, she stretched her right hand to my left cheek. "You're hurt."

"Just boys being boys," I replied. "Nothing to worry about."

"Did that happen because of me? Were you hurt for me?"

"It was a minor misunderstanding. It's resolved now." I wished I believed that.

Marissa didn't look as if she believed it, but she also realized that I wasn't going to tell her what happened. "I don't feel good talking in this house. Could we go outside?"

Harry said, "Yes, but you can trust—"

Marissa was gone before he finished, rushing out in the direction of the front door, and, I guessed, the front closet. A few seconds later she came back, shrugging into her winter coat and leading us out through a glass door. The night had grown very cold, but the snow had stopped. Across Long Island Sound, lights sparkled on the north shore of the island.

"What's happened? Are the police closing in on me?"

Harry said, "Not yet."

"The police are still canvassing the guests at the Philharmonic benefit," I said. "Sooner or later, they'll find someone who will say they saw you with McGill."

"Then what happens?"

"NYPD will do everything it can to find you. Fortunately, you're safe here," I glanced at Harry, who gave me the most minuscule of nods. "They can't find you here. But the police will be building a case against you at the same time as they're looking for you. Unless we find the real killer, you'll be in hiding for the rest of your life. But we're not going to let that happen."

Marissa's eyes were watery with tears. Couldn't say I blamed her—a guy she hardly knew claimed he was going to save her. Not the stuff of reassurance.

"I didn't kill him," she murmured, wiping her cheeks with the back of her hand. "I didn't . . . oh my God, I don't know . . . what if I did kill him?"

"You didn't. I'm going to find out who did and serve them up on a silver platter to the NYPD."

Harry's eyebrows rose at my confident reassurances to her. I have to admit I was overdoing it, but the last thing this woman needed was an honest assessment of her chances. A realistic situation report would have gone more like this: Well, maybe you killed him, maybe you didn't. The police will find you eventually. Either you'll go to jail, or Harry will hide you forever. Whatever happens, you will kiss your old life goodbye. Under the circumstances, my approach, confident baloney that it might be, was much better.

"I'm trapped," Marissa said. "There's no way out, is there?"

"There is. We'll find it."

"Are you really as confident as you sound? Or is that for my benefit?

Harry put a hand on her shoulder. "Have faith. You'll be all right."

My turn to have my eyebrows travel upward. I caught myself and relaxed before Marissa saw what I thought of Harry's faith comment.

"I have to go," Harry said. To me, "I'll see you tomorrow."

I almost asked, When? but stopped myself. His answer would have been: When you need me.

"I'll let myself out," he said. He walked through the door into the house before either of us had a chance to say anything else. If I knew Harry, he whooshed out of there and didn't bother to exit through the front door.

"Do you have a plan for tomorrow?" Marissa asked me.

"Actually, I'm meeting with Jackson McGill's No. 2, Savannah Faringer."

"Why?"

Why, indeed? I wasn't going to tell Marissa my suspicions about Cú Chulainn and SHK Dragon because I wasn't exactly sure what I suspected. Admitting that I was clueless and going to Cú Chulainn to stir the pot and see what happened would not bolster her confidence in me.

"I'm following standard investigative procedure. Ask lots of questions, see if a picture forms, see if additional suspects appear."

"You don't know what to do next so you're going to poke the lion to see if it reacts."

"I can see why you've been successful in real estate."

"Don't change the subject."

"You're right: I don't know what to do next so I'm poking the lion. But that's a technique that's worked for me in the past."

"Really?"

"Really," I said as firmly and positively as I could.

"Are you in danger?"

I gave her my best, most disarming smile. "Not more than I can handle."

She wasn't buying my modestly heroic schtick. "Why are you doing this?"

"Beats swimming with jellyfish."

Marissa grabbed my hand and gave me a gentle squeeze. "Stop it. Tell me why." Her tone was urgent, imploring. "Why?"

I was about to offer another flip rejoinder and stopped. The look in Marissa's eyes was too intense for more bad jokes. "My wife," I replied.

"What do you mean?"

"I'm . . . trying to be the man my wife . . ." my throat tightened to the point where I was only capable of uttering in a husky whisper, ". . . believed I could be."

"She was a lucky woman," Marissa said.

"No, I'm the lucky one."

She nodded and looked across the Sound at the sparkling lights on the far shore then turned back to me, "God, I hope you know what you're doing."

That seemed like an appropriate goodnight prayer; I nodded but said nothing.

Marissa sighed and led the way inside. I followed her upstairs to my bedroom. She ushered me to my room and walked down the hallway to hers. I closed my door and told myself to pretend that Marissa was old and ugly.

*   *   *

In the morning, I grabbed a cup of coffee in the kitchen and asked Andrew Selkirk if I could use a computer. He showed me to the den where Harry and I had met Marissa the night before.

I spent a half-hour reading *Forbes*, *The New York Times*, and *The Wall Street Journal* online. Jackson McGill had named his corporation after a warrior of Irish legend: Cú Chulainn. The warrior was famous for defeating all kinds of beasts and foes, but eventually came to a bad end. I wondered if that was an unfortunate piece of foreshadowing—McGill's way of paying homage to his Irish heritage but also saying he was going to live fast, die young, and leave a pretty corpse. Cú Chulainn Enterprises manufactured all kinds of software and hardware, some for the general consumer and some for the U.S. defense industry. SHK Dragon did many of the same things, but its government business was with the Communists in Beijing. From what I could tell reading the different news articles, there were a few highly profitable synergies to be had if the two corporations worked together.

After my brief research, I went to the kitchen, sat at the huge, granite-topped island, and had more coffee. Frieta was kind enough to cook eggs and bacon. There was no sign of Marissa. After breakfast, I walked out to the front drive with Otto—he was going to drive me to the Rye train station. I looked up at the house. Marissa stood at one of the windows, and I may have been mistaken, but she appeared worried. I grinned and gave her a thumbs up. She walked away, out of sight.

Otto didn't say a word on the drive to the station, and I followed his lead. I boarded a Metro North train for Grand Central then a subway to 14th Street and walked downtown a few blocks to Washington Square.

Dr. Dietrich Hoffman's office was west of Washington Square on West 4th Street in a pre-war building. It had been a studio apartment once, but it appeared that the doctor had been seeing patients there for a long time. The studio's walls were cream-colored, and two large water colors hung to my left and right as I entered, both suggestive of the Maine coastline. The paintings were pleasant enough but not of such high quality that you would remember them for two minutes after you departed from the office. The wall directly opposite me was almost entirely window, overlooking West 4th. There was a dark brown couch to my right under one of the water colors, and facing it were a matching dark-brown armchair, desk, and small chair tucked into the desk's leg space. The desk was spotless. The only things on it were a phone and a lamp. The whole place seemed decorated to bore patients into a sense of serenity.

"Mr. Tyrrell?" he asked, not really needing the confirmation. He gestured at the couch, "Please, have a seat."

Dr. Hoffman was of modest height and modest build. His gray hair was long and combed back from his forehead and over his ears. Large brown eyes on either side of a prominent nose. He spoke with a slight, soft German accent.

"Are you from Bavaria?"

"Yes. You have a good ear."

"One of my favorite professors in college was from Bavaria. You sound alike. Is 'Hoffman' Catholic or Jewish?"

"Catholic. Why do you ask? Would it be a problem if I were Jewish?"

"No, not at all. My college girlfriend was Jewish. I introduced her to the ethnic intricacies of Irish Catholic Americans; she returned the favor by showing me the wonders of Jewish tradition and culture."

Hoffman nodded, "You said in college. Am I correct that the relationship ended back then?"

"Yes."

"Why?"

"She outgrew me."

"Are you being succinct or flip?"

"Both."

He allowed the corners of his mouth to rise at that remark. "Let's go back a little farther in your history. Please fill me in on your background."

"Didn't Harry already do that?"

"When the Chairman wants me to help someone, I do it. I don't need a reason other than the Chairman requested it. Besides, it's useful for me to hear you describe your own background."

"Okay, but remember: you asked for it." I paused to assemble my thoughts for a second then launched into the abbreviated version of my life story: "I grew up in Yonkers, but Yonkers with a Bronxville post office address. The real Bronxville is tony. But my mother lovingly described our part of town as 'the Irish Catholic ghetto'."

"Was it an actual ghetto?"

"Not even close. Beautiful neighborhoods, convenient to Bronxville village and the train station into New York. But all the Catholics lived in Yonkers for the lower taxes so they could send their kids to Catholic grade schools and high schools. I went to St. Joseph's in Bronxville, high school was Fordham Prep in the Bronx, and then Fordham College on the same campus as the Prep. I was in Army ROTC, graduated, got my commission, joined Special Forces—that's the Green Berets in case you don't know—and went to Afghanistan, where things got very interesting."

"You're deflecting."

"Excuse me?" I knew what he meant but wanted a moment to think about what to say next. I know I had asked for help, and Harry had led me to Dr. Hoffman, but it was one thing to seek help, and another thing entirely to get it. I might have to get honest if I wanted to feel better. Sheesh.

"You know what I mean," Hoffman said simply.

Oh, I had to work this out myself. "Well . . . I saw a lot of shit, excuse me, awful stuff in Afghanistan. Everyone who served there did. Then I was assigned to work with a CIA team, and things got downright ugly."

"Deflecting again."

Okay, Tyrrell, do you want this process to work for you or against you? Your choice. I took a deep breath and said, "Our team . . . we handled assassinations, kidnapping, rendition—you take some guy you've caught to a third country and interrogate the hell out of him. Some very heavy work."

"Torture?"

"Yes," I said slowly.

"How did you feel about it?"

"Today, now, I wish I hadn't been a part of . . . some of the things I did. I don't believe in torture. That's part of what I want to discuss with you. Back then . . . I was absolutely sure I was serving my country the best way possible."

"You were doing what you believed in, but that hasn't stopped your suffering from PTSD. You seem to think your prior belief should have protected you from the trauma. Is that what you're saying?"

"Well, it's possible to be conflicted, isn't it?"

"Quite right. I wouldn't be in business if it weren't."

We both smiled.

"Did you seek help when you returned to the States?"

"No," I shook my head. "I toughed it out. Drank a lot, too. Joined the Marshals, worked my ass off, and mostly ignored my feelings."

"Ignored your feelings? Easy as that?"

"If it were easy, I wouldn't have been drinking. When I met Maggie, well, I . . . I don't know if this makes any sense to a psychological professional, but . . . without even knowing if, Maggie put a gigantic happy bandaid on my feelings. For a while, I felt wonderful. Afghanistan was behind me."

"But it wasn't, was it?"

"Not really. I hate to sound like a clueless moron who just got a clue, but I guess it's possible to be delighted that you've fallen in love and depressed as hell over what you did in the war."

"Yes, it's possible. No, you're not a clueless moron—the idea that you can simultaneously feel two emotions that are diametrically opposed isn't easy to comprehend."

I grunted in acknowledgement but said nothing more.

"What about your wife? When and how did you meet her?"

"I was attending a panel discussion on criminal psychology at John Jay College. You know, the CUNY school for criminal justice."

"Yes, I do know. Please, go on about your wife. Was criminal psychology her field?"

"No, not at all. Maggie was a last-minute addition to the panel. She was a substitute for a friend of hers. She was a therapist, like you, and she was familiar with her friend's work and the panel needed someone to present. The whole thing was a fluke—a very happy fluke for me. I don't remember a thing she said, but I kept looking at her and thinking I have to go say hello when this is over."

"And you did?"

"Yes."

"What did you say to her?"

"I took a very deep breath, made my way through the small but fervently adoring crowd around her, and said in front of her fans, 'I know you're in the interpretation business so I hope you'll interpret this the right way: could I buy you a cup of coffee?'"

"What was her reply?"

"She said, 'How should I interpret that invitation?' And I replied, 'Have coffee with me and find out.'"

"And did she?"

"She did. We were together from that night until she died."

The mention of Maggie's death had its usual impact on me: It shut me down. Dr. Hoffman did what many therapists do in that situation. He waited me out. He waited so long that I expected him to say, "Our time is up." But he didn't.

"I suppose you want me to talk about Maggie's death."

"Do you want to talk about it?"

"No." The topmost branches of bare trees were visible through the window, and I focused on them as if they were fascinating instead of just December trees with no leaves. "I guess we won't make any progress unless I talk about the things I don't want to talk about."

"Usually the more honest someone can be, the more progress he makes."

"Okay . . . I'll try." I closed my eyes, gathered my thoughts, or maybe it was courage, and plunged in: "Maggie was the best thing that ever happened to me. She was pretty and caring and funny, and she loved me despite my many flaws."

"You're probably not all that bad. Now, could you give me a little more depth?"

"What do you mean?"

"All those things you said about your wife—they're standard lyrics to a love song or words in a Hallmark card. I'm sure you meant every one of them, but you didn't have to dig deep to say them."

"I could really grow to dislike you, Doctor."

He smiled and shrugged. "Not an uncommon feeling in this office. About your wife . . ."

"I loved Maggie. I loved the way I felt when I was with her. I had come back from Afghanistan and nothing seemed right anymore. I was depressed, working my ass off, drinking too much. Nothing was working for me. Until Maggie. She made everything seem . . . better. She made the future seem . . . like it could be . . . happy."

"Did those feelings last?"

"No."

"How did you feel about her when the feelings went away?"

"I loved her, I told you that."

"I know you loved her. What were the other feelings when you realized that she wasn't going to make everything better?"

"Like what kind of feelings? What the hell are you talking about?"

"Why are you getting angry?"

"I don't like your tone toward Maggie."

Hoffman leaned back in his chair and steepled the fingers of both hands in front of him. "I've been a therapist for many years. I've very carefully developed a professional, calm, almost toneless voice. I'd like to suggest that your problem is not with my tone, but with your feelings."

"What the hell is wrong with you—?" I could practically see the words hanging in the air between us in a cartoon speech bubble. The words all in bold with angry exclamation points mixed with jagged question marks. Which naturally led to another speech bubble in my head: What the hell is wrong with you, ***Tyrrell!!??!***

"I'm sorry," my voice soft. I paused, swallowed, and continued in a whisper, "I was . . ." I could feel tears rolling down my cheeks, "I was angry with her."

"She failed you."

"No . . . yes. I thought she did. I mean, I felt that she did. But it wasn't her fault. I never opened up to her. There was nothing she could do."

"But Maggie was a therapist. Shouldn't she have been able to discern what was going on with you? Help you?"

"No, no . . . she couldn't."

"Why not?"

"Because . . ." Why hadn't she been able to help me? "Because . . . it wasn't her job."

"What does that mean?"

"It means . . . I was her husband . . . not her patient."

"Exactly."

"Isn't my time over?" I wiped at my tears.

Hoffman smiled and checked the clock on his desk. "As a matter of fact, yes, it is." He reached for the touchpad on his laptop and clicked. "Would tomorrow at the same time work for you?"

"Tomorrow? Am I that bad?"

"No," he replied, still smiling. "But Harry said to do my best for you. Tomorrow, same time?"

"I need to talk about how . . . I almost tortured a man. I would have hated myself for doing that."

Hoffman said softly but firmly, as if speaking to a restless child, "Tomorrow? Same time?"

I sighed. "Yes. That would be fine."

He stood up to make sure I understood that today's session was complete. I followed him and offered my hand. He shook mine.

"Today was a good start."

"How come I don't feel any better?"

"Therapy doesn't work like a drink or drug. It takes time. But the effects can be much more lasting. You'll see."

I left his office and walked out of his building onto West 4th Street. It was a cold but sunny. Maybe it was just my perception, but the sun seemed half-hearted in its efforts: there was no warmth or brightness to the air. Then again, it was almost Christmas—what did I expect?

Despite my disappointment with the late-morning weather, I felt drained but good. I walked in an east-north zig-zag to the subway station at Union Square, took the 4 train uptown to 59th Street, and walked east toward Sutton Place, toward the home of my own, personal financial experts, Valerie and David Berk.

The Berks were lifelong New Yorkers and retired Wall Streeters. Neither of them bore the slightest resemblance to Gordon Gekko, Michael Douglas's master of the universe in the movie *Wall Street*. Yes, my friends had made lots of money. But then they left the investment grind.

Now, they lived well, supported a number of New York-based charities, and traveled. They were also fanatical armchair detectives, much more interested in my work than I was in theirs.

Valerie, a tall, slender redhead, opened the door to their Sutton Place apartment and gave me a big hug and kiss. Her husband, David, stood at her elbow. He was a inch taller than I was, broad-shouldered with dark-brown hair and a graying beard.

"It's nice to see you," Valerie said. "Are you working?"

"Yes, and as usual, I need your insight and experience."

We walked through their living room with its floor-to-ceiling windows overlooking the East River, Roosevelt Island, and the pagoda-shaped Queensboro Bridge, now called the Ed Koch Bridge, after New York's famously feisty mayor in the 1980s. We settled in the den, a room with bookshelves, a dusky-rose, upholstered couch and matching arm chairs. The TV was off. The last time I had visited, the set was on, but muted, to CNBC. I wondered if the dark TV meant they were more and more happy being away from their old world.

"Would you like a drink?" Valerie asked. "Water? Seltzer? Coffee? Tea?"

"Water, thanks." I sat in one of the chairs.

Valerie left and David and I talked about the off-season prospects for the Mets and Yankees.

"Here you are," she said, handing me a glass of water and settling onto the couch next to David. "What do you need?"

"What do you know about Cú Chulainn Enterprises?"

"Are you working on the Jackson McGill murder?" Valerie asked, startled.

"That's a homicide and strictly an NYPD matter. But McGill's death was a catalyst for the case I'm working, so I need some background. What can you tell me about Cú Chulainn? What industries is it in? Anything special about it other than the charismatic playboy who founded it? Is it in play for a merger? Anything?"

"You do know that you could read this kind of information in *The Wall Street Journal* and *Forbes*," David rumbled.

"I need the inside stuff. The kind of information that a pair of smart, cynical, suspicious financial services veterans would have."

"You don't need to butter us up as if you're here to ask for a loan," David said with a chuckle. "Especially since you're not very good at it."

"Thanks. But about Cú Chulainn? While you're at it, what about SHK Dragon Technology? Is there a tie-in with Cú Chulainn?"

They both looked at me for a long moment, then at each other, then back at me. "Before we tell you," Valerie said, "would you mind telling us why you put two and two together and came up with SHK Dragon Technology and Cú Chulainn?"

"Let's say I've had dealings with both organizations in the last couple of days. I'm pretty sure it's not a coincidence."

"What kind of dealings?" David asked.

"Hey, I came to you for information."

"What kind of dealings?" he repeated.

"Stakeouts. Kidnapping. Violence. Chases. The usual."

"Oh. It almost sounds entertaining."

"Not so much, actually."

Valerie shifted on the couch and surreptitiously put her hand on David's arm as if to restrain him. It was the kind of touch that passes between people who've been a couple for a long time. "Jack, SHK Dragon is a Chinese company. It's impossible to know how deeply involved it is with the Chinese government. That means you can't be sure you're not dealing with—"

"Chinese spies?" I asked.

"Maybe. Do you remember when President Obama visited Manhattan last summer?"

"Yeah, vaguely."

"He didn't stay at the Waldorf, like presidents have for decades," Valerie continued. "He stayed at the Millennium. Why? According to CBS News, the fact that the Chinese now own the building worried the Secret Service who thought the president might be bugged there."

"The Waldorf-Astoria is owned by the Chinese?"

"The building is. The hotel is owned and run by the Hilton organization. But you need to focus on the fact that the President wouldn't stay there because the building is owned, and presumably controlled, by the Chinese."

"Your point is that you can't trust the Chinese?"

"Well, you can trust them," David interjected, "if you don't mind the country's record on human rights, or intellectual property rights, or hacking U.S. computer networks."

"Oh, that."

Valerie said, "You need to be careful. Very careful."

"I'm the one who's been kidnapped by them and threatened with, well . . . never mind, threatened. I know they're dangerous. By the bye, the folks from Cú Chulainn haven't been doling out the Hibernian hospitality. They seem to be working with SHK Dragon in the kidnapping and violence department. What I was hoping to get from you two was a possible reason for all of this."

"You were kidnapped?" Valerie asked, wide-eyed. She pointed at my right cheek, "Did they hurt you?"

"No big deal. The other guys look much worse than I do. And here I am, safe and sound." I gave them a reassuring grin. "Now, could you please give me a reason for these two companies collaborating so profusely in the mischief arena?"

The Berks exchanged knowing glances, and David said, "There've been a lot of rumors that McGill was thinking of dumping his president and COO, Savannah Faringer. She's been with the company since about 10 minutes after it was founded. She has stock and stock options that go out of sight—a billionaire in her own right now. Obviously, you don't amass that kind of cash unless you're very, very good. She's one of the best."

"But McGill wanted to fire her?" I asked.

"That's the rumor."

"A rumor that David and I agree with, by the way," Valerie said.

"Why?"

"You realize," David said, "that when someone like Savannah Faringer is fired, she gets her golden parachute."

"In Ms. Faringer's case, it's more of a platinum-and-diamond-encrusted parachute," Valerie added. "It was set up to be prohibitively expensive."

"But McGill and Faringer disagreed completely and totally, he was willing to eat the parachute's cost, right?" I asked.

"Right."

"I hate to repeat myself, but why?"

"We think," Valerie replied, "that SHK Dragon wants to acquire Cú Chulainn. If that happens, SHK Dragon would buy a large portion of Faringer's stock and options. She might double her wealth."

"But she's already a billionaire."

"Ah, you sweet, naive pauper," Valerie said.

"To people like Savannah Faringer, there's never enough money," David said.

"I am not a pauper," I objected.

Valerie waved my words away, "McGill had no interest in selling the company. It's his baby; he founded it. Reading between the lines of some of his statements to the media, McGill didn't want to see his corporation, which is a U.S.-defense contractor, go to the Chinese. It went against his beliefs."

"Isn't Cú Chulainn doing lots of business with Dragon?"

"Yes, but not in the defense sectors," David responded. "In addition to the defense products it makes, Cú Chulainn manufactures hardware for all kinds of private and corporate security, and a subsidiary of SHK Dragon provides the software that runs the hardware. It's a small jump from corporate security to national security."

"Aren't there laws in this country to stop the acquisition of defense-essential businesses by foreign nationals?"

"If Cú Chulainn spins off the defense-contractor unit and the security unit into independent entities, then SHK Dragon could buy Cú Chulainn. If Dragon really wants both the defense and security units there are a number of ways it could still acquire them. My favorite theory is that the new entities incorporate in a foreign jurisdiction less hostile to the Chinese and *then* Dragon buys both of them."

"I wouldn't have thought it was that easy."

"I did not use the word 'easy.' It would require lots of lawyers and shell companies for Dragon to buy all the parts of Cú Chulainn."

"And McGill wasn't having any."

"Apparently not," David agreed.

"Why not? He probably stood to make even more money than Faringer."

"If I had to guess," David mused, "I'd go with what Valerie said: McGill didn't want to sell the company he'd built from scratch. And/or he's a patriotic American who didn't want to allow the Chinese to acquire a defense contractor."

"That might be why he was murdered," Valerie offered. "Then again, you're not working on his homicide."

"No, I'm not."

"But your case is closely connected to his death."

"Was that a question?" I grinned.

"No matter how closely connected your case is," David said, his low voice giving the words ominous emphasis, "you need to be careful. The Chinese are an obvious threat. But don't assume that the folks at Cú Chulainn won't play very rough, too. Especially now that Savannah Faringer is running the business."

"I'll be very careful. I promise."

"You always say that," Valerie said.

"I always mean it, too."

"But things happen . . ."

"As you say, things happen."

* * *

On an impulse, after leaving the Berks, I went home to West 76th Street. I didn't *need* to go home; I *wanted* to go home. But I couldn't—my internal radar pinged like crazy at the sight of two black Chevy Tahoes parked on the street where I lived. Two people were sitting inside each vehicle. One Tahoe was parked on the uptown side of the street at the eastern end of the block, the other was on the downtown end near the western end of the block. Can't a man pick up his mail and have a fresh cup of coffee in the comfort of his own home? I really wanted to do those things and see what kind of damage had been done to my apartment last night. I stood next to a parked, early model Forest Green Ford Explorer, the car that practically launched the SUV craze in America, and tried to come up with some original antics to get rid of the teams inside those vehicles. I didn't happen to have any paint cans to slam into faces, and shooting the teams would not lead to a leisurely cup of coffee in my apartment. Not to mention it might be hard to justify shooting a bunch of people who weren't doing anything besides the completely legal activity of sitting in their parked SUVs. A devious, imaginative, easy-to-utilize plan was what I needed in this situation, and nothing was occurring to me.

And then it was time to abort and evacuate the area. A yellow cab stopped directly in front of my building, and an enormous man stepped out of it. This guy had me by four or five inches, making him six feet six or seven. He was wearing a heavy winter parka, but I guessed that he outweighed me by fifty pounds. Easy. He moved like an athlete, with smooth power. He wasn't wearing a hat, and I could see brown hair. Along with the dark hair, this guy had a chin and jaw that could have been chiseled out of a block of granite.

It wasn't his size that made me decide to abort the covert entry to my own apartment. It wasn't his easy, athletic grace and strength. Although, to be completely honest, if I never had to see this man again, I would be perfectly happy. He radiated danger. Much as I never wanted to see him, I dug my phone out of my pocket, zoomed the camera, and snapped a couple of quick pictures.

And that's when I decided to get the hell out of Dodge. As I was photographing him, he spotted the two Tahoes. He nodded to each—a barely perceptible movement so small it would have suited my friend Harry. But the nod meant he was the enemy. And this enemy was going up the steps to my front door.

There was nothing in my mail—unless I had won the Publishers' Clearing House sweepstakes—that was worth doing what I would have to do to sneak by all these people. And there were plenty of places on the Upper West Side to get a fresh cup of coffee.

Reversing course, I headed east toward Broadway and the Café Sabatini. The café felt more Old World than Starbucks with its faux-leather couches and arm chairs, wood coffee tables, and ceiling fans with wooden blades. There were contemporary magazines and newspapers on the coffee tables, and the café's sound system was playing *A Charlie Brown Christmas* by Vince Guaraldi.

I ordered a cappuccino and biscotti, and while the barista made my drink, I used my smart phone and the café's WiFi to look up Cú Chulainn's number. I dialed and asked for Savannah Faringer.

A smooth, young-male voice came on the line, "Ms. Faringer's office."

I decided on the direct approach, "My name is Jack Tyrrell. I want to talk with with Ms. Faringer about Jackson McGill's death. Today, please."

The smooth young man stumbled in response. "I'm sorry . . . but . . . I'm sorry, I don't think she's free. I—"

I interrupted him, "Listen, tell her that it's Jack Tyrrell calling. You don't know me, but I promise you, she does. Tell her I represent Marissa Carvajal."

"I'm . . . uh, that was Jack Tyrrell representing Marissa Carvajal?"

"Yes."

"Please hold." He didn't wait for me to say, "okay," before clicking me into the limbo of holding.

The barista passed my cappuccino over the counter, and I took a sip. Heaven.

He came back on the line, "Would you be available at 3:00 P.M. today? At our offices in midtown?"

"That's fine. Thanks." I hung up before he could say anything else. I took another sip of cappuccino and savored it and the satisfaction of having bluffed my way into a meeting Savannah Faringer.

Café Sabatini was crowded with young mothers at tables with their small children in strollers that blocked the café's tiny aisles. I hovered at the edge of a table with my cappuccino and biscotti in hand, looking for a place to sit.

"You can share this table if you like," a woman said.

I turned toward her. Definitely worth turning toward. Definitely. Long red hair, bright blue eyes, and a wide mouth with full lips. The kind of woman whose picture is on the front of hair-color products or magazine covers. Careful, Tyrrell. Isn't every woman an astounding beauty as far as you're concerned? You should probably tell Dr. Hoffman about that during your next visit—oh my God, one visit and I had become one of those neurotic New Yorkers who constantly compile a list of things to discuss with their therapists. I thought Hoffman was going to be able to help me, but I might need to resist the impulse to reduce my entire life to fodder for my sessions with him. In the meantime, I really ought to take advantage of the opportunity to sit with a beautiful woman.

"Thanks, that's very nice," I said, sitting down and placing my cup on the tiny table top. "I'm Jack Tyrrell."

"Kim Gannon."

"I hate to sound like the oldest cliché in the book, but you seem awfully familiar."

She smiled, "I was thinking the same thing about you. You're a regular in here, aren't you? We seem to have the same coffee routine."

"Given how much time I spend in here, it would be easy for us to overlap."

"You like your coffee, I guess."

"I do. What about you?"

"In the morning, then a mid-afternoon jolt, and sometimes in the evening, but that's not a regular thing."

"Want some of my biscotti?"

"Biscotti? I hardly know you." Her smile was a thing of devastating beauty.

"I'll take that as a yes." Using a napkin to ensure that my grubby paws did not touch biscotti, I broke it and put half on her saucer.

"Thank you."

"You're welcome."

We sipped our drinks and ate our biscotti in companionable silence.

"My turn to be a cliché," Kim said, "but what do you do for a living?"

"I'm sort of a security consultant."

"What does 'sort of' mean?"

"Well, I'm really more of a security troubleshooter or maybe . . . a private detective cum troubleshooter."

"You really understand your mission in life don't you? Do you get many customers with a fuzzy business plan like that?"

I grinned, "Enough to get by." I thought about my first meeting with Harry, when he had explained that he was carrying the same message to me that Jacob Marley had spoken to Scrooge: Mankind was my business. I wondered if I should explain to Kim that the ghost of my dead wife had introduced me to an angel, who had told me that my mission was to serve others. It didn't take a lot of careful analysis to know that revealing the origin of my mission statement was a bad idea. Especially if I wanted to see Kim again, and right that minute, seeing her blue eyes and wide smile across the table, I very much wanted to see her again.

"How does one go about becoming a private detective cum troubleshooter?" Her tone was gently mocking. "Do you have some kind of certificate or license?"

"In my case, you go into the Army Special Forces then into the Marshals Service."

"Oh . . . you're a government-trained private detective cum troubleshooter."

"Maybe that should be my mission statement."

She pretended to wince, "Not sure that works . . . it's not really a mission statement. But it's better than what you came in here with."

"Thank you for helping me with my marketing plan. What about you? What's your mission statement? Or would you rather not talk about it with a stranger?"

"You're not a stranger. You're Jack Tyrrell, government-trained—"

"Stop, please," I laughed. "I surrender. If you don't want to talk about you, don't."

"I'm a marketing-and-communications consultant."

"Of course you are. Do you work for a big firm?"

"Once upon a time. Then I set up shop with two other women."

"Got tired of know-it-all men telling you what to do?"

"That was part of it."

"How are the three of you doing?"

"Very well, thank you."

I finished my part of the biscotti and sipped some cappuccino. I wanted to stay and talk, but I really didn't have the time before my meeting with Savannah Faringer.

"This has been really nice," I said awkwardly, "but unfortunately—"

"You're married," she interjected.

"No, no I'm not."

Kim seemed very pleased with that piece of information and volunteered, "I'm not either."

"Well, now that that's out of the way . . . I'm sorry, but much as I would love to stay and talk with you—especially now that we've established we're both available—"

"I didn't say I was available. I said I wasn't married."

"My mistake. That's very different. Please forgive me."

"You're forgiven."

"Are you, by chance, available? Could I call you?"

"Yes, I am." She pulled a business card out of her bag and handed it to me. "And yes, please call."

"Sorry, but I've got an appointment and have to run. I'll talk to you soon."

"I hope so."

9

Cú Chulainn Enterprises had a gleaming new, sixty-something-story building on Seventh Avenue and 55th Street. The exterior was dark-gray granite and black glass, tapering as it climbed. Inside an atrium the full height of the building and let in much more light than you would expect given the dark exterior of the building. I walked to the security desk, gave my name and ID, signed in, and headed to the glass-enclosed elevators. I pressed the button for 58, the doors hissed shut, and the hexagonal-shaped elevator rose smoothly and quickly. The elevator panel with the door was made of metal, as were the two adjacent panels. The outer sides, the panels overlooking the atrium, were all made of glass. I faced out and watched the people at the bottom of the atrium shrink to the size of ants.

I was met at the 58th floor by a young man, wearing an Italian-cut, medium-blue suit and light-brown oxfords. Very fashionable. He spoke in the smooth, youthful tones of the man who had answered Ms. Faringer's phone. "Please, follow me."

He led me to the door of her office and before ushering me into Faringer's presence, asked if I would like something to drink. I declined and went inside.

The office was big enough that you could have parked a small plane in it and still had enough room for a putting green. It was sleek and modern, complete with stunning views of Manhattan to the south. On one side of the room was a glass-topped conference table surrounded by black-leather armchairs. On the other side, Savannah Faringer stood up behind her ultra-modern desk, a large slab of glass with stainless steel legs. She was a tall woman and wore heels, with the result that she could almost look me in the eye. Her eyes were icy blue, and her face was framed by long, straight blonde hair. Her dark-red pant suit emphasized her long, lean frame.

"Have a seat," she said. There was no offer of a hand to shake, no wasted time on introductions.

"Thank you."

She sat down as I did, and it occurred to me that her only reason for standing up had been to make sure I understood she was tall and couldn't be intimidated by height.

"What do you want?" she asked crisply.

"Are you selling this company to SHK Dragon now that McGill is dead?"

Faringer smiled mirthlessly. "If I were, and I told you, it would constitute passing inside information. That's illegal."

"Acting illegaly doesn't seem to bother you very much."

"That's an interesting statement. I wonder if it meets the standard for slander."

"Did you have Jackson McGill murdered so you could sell the company to Dragon?"

"No."

"Why are goons from your security team staking out my apartment?"

"I have no idea."

"Why were they staking out Marissa Carvajal's place?"

"I can't imagine."

"Why did they work with a team from SHK Dragon to kidnap me?"

"You have an active fantasy life, don't you?" Her mirthless smile widened.

I smiled back. "Did I fantasize that you would agree to meet me if I dropped my name and Marissa Carvajal's?"

She didn't have a rebuttal to that.

After waiting a minute to give her the chance to craft a reply, I continued, "You agreed to meet with me because you're afraid that I know something."

"What could you know that would be of any interest to me?"

"Pardon me for going back over ground that we just covered, but you want to know if I figured out that you had McGill killed enabling you to sell Cú Chulainn to SHK Dragon. His stock in the company is frozen in a trust, which leaves you as the shareholder with the largest chunk of equity. I'd wager a large chunk of your money that somewhere in this office is paperwork that allows you to act with full powers in the event of something happening to McGill."

"Absolutely fascinating, but since our company is already in business—very profitable business I might add—with SHK Dragon, why sell? Why would they buy?"

"I'm going to ignore the fact that you deflected my question with a question of your own. Dragon wants to buy because they want ownership of your technology to expand their market share. You want to sell because the amount of money you would collect is ginormous, even by your standards. But Jackson McGill didn't want to sell. Cú Chulainn was his baby, the money didn't mean to him what it does to you, and he was also a patriot. Corny but true."

"Let me repeat this back to you," her tone businesslike, "to ensure full understanding: You're saying that I had Jackson murdered because he opposed the sale of Cú Chulainn. In other words, I killed him for the oldest motive in the world: money."

"Second oldest. The oldest is love."

"So you say." She smiled in a wide, rictus grin. "You have an elaborate theory, quite wonderful in its own perverse way."

"Yeah," I shrugged, "I have my moments."

"It's only a theory. If you had the tiniest bit of evidence you would have taken it to the police."

"Maybe I wanted to offer you the opportunity of buying my silence."

"I don't buy things of no value."

"If what I say is of no value, why did you agree to meet with me?"

"Still the intrepid detective, digging away at the crime."

"Does that mean you aren't going to offer to buy me off?"

"That's what it means."

"What about Marissa Carvajal? Why do your people want her? Did you frame her for McGill's murder? Now you want to deliver her up to the police? That would tidy things up for you very nicely, wouldn't it?"

Her rictus smile was wider than ever. "You never cease to amaze. You must be the life of every party you attend."

"Not much of a partygoer, actually."

"Why am I not surprised?" She reached for her phone and spoke quietly into it. "We're done here. Yes, thank you." To me she said, "My assistant will show you out."

The smooth young man materialized at my elbow almost as effortlessly and silently as possible for a human. Harry could do it better, but the smooth young man wasn't Harry.

"Thanks for your time," I replied as I stood and followed him out of her office. He escorted me to the elevator, probably to make sure I didn't steal any staplers or paper clips. Not that I saw any to steal. The Cú Chulainn Enterprises offices were the most squared-away spaces I had ever seen in civilian life.

I stepped into an elevator, and the young man leaned in and pressed the button for the lobby. "Thanks," I muttered. "Don't know how I would have managed that."

He gave me an icy grin, and the elevator doors rolled shut between us. I faced the glass panel of the elevator and glanced down into the atrium as the elevator descended as smoothly as it had ascended.

* * *

SAVANNAH FARINGER CALLED REZNIK ON HER SMART PHONE. His phone vibrated in his pants pocket. He was inside Jack Tyrrell's apartment, searching through every nook and cranny. He reached into his pocket and pulled out the phone.

"Yes," he said.

"Faringer, here. Tyrrell just left my office."

"I hope you've got a plan for him."

"A team is going to secure him on the elevator. There's a van waiting in the loading dock."

"Let's hope your team is up to the job." Reznik stepped over to Tyrrell's desk. "I'm in Tyrrell's apartment right now. He reads history and thrillers. He listens to jazz and to rock. He's got lots of movies on DVD. There are a bunch of take-out menus in a drawer in the kitchen. His furniture is old, and the décor looks like it was done by a woman and has been touched up here and there by a bachelor."

"Probably his late wife's influence, which is waning as time goes by."

"Probably. My point: There is nothing special about Tyrrell, nothing obvious. But he's given your people plenty of trouble, and his credentials indicate he could be plenty more. I need your people to secure him, then I'll interrogate him and eliminate him. Does that work for you?"

"Yes."

"Have your people hold Tyrrell at the loading dock. I'm on my way."

*   *   *

The elevator stopped on the 52nd floor and two very large men and a woman stepped aboard. They were like a diversity poster for recruiting employees: one white male, one Hispanic male, one African-American female. All young, dressed in suits, all moved like athletes. Like me, they faced the glass wall. I checked out their reflections as surreptitiously as I could—unless I was being paranoid, they were watching me and not the atrium.

We descended a few more floors, and another man and woman stepped aboard. African-American male, Hispanic female. The two newcomers were also part of the

Cú Chulainn diversity quilt. They also faced the glass and watched me.

My internal radar was pinging like mad.

I cleared my throat and said, "I want to go on record as saying I'm very sorry."

"What?" grunted the Hispanic guy at my right elbow.

"I'm sorry—" I stopped as I swung my right elbow up into his Adam's apple. With a half-second delay, I jammed my left elbow into the Adam's apple of the African-American male on my left. Both men crashed backward, knocking the others back against the doors.

The good thing about a five-to-one fight in an elevator is, if you're the one, everyone you hit or kick is an enemy. And you're in an elevator; it's small. No place for your enemy to hide. The bad thing: it's a five-to-one fight, and you're all by your lonesome.

The African-American woman hit the emergency stop button. The alarm rang: a harsh, clanging bell like the one the nuns used to summon us for our next class. The white man lunged for my legs in a tackle, the Hispanic woman came in high with a blackjack. I threw up my right arm to ward off the blow and ducked, but the white guy grabbed my legs and slammed me to the floor. The Hispanic woman stepped close and swung the blackjack at my head. I lurched sideways and caught her blow on my shoulder. It hurt like hell, but at least I was still conscious. As she raised her arm to take another shot at me, I grabbed the white guy's hair and yanked his head up with my right hand and clawed at his face with my left hand. He punched feebly at me, his fist bouncing off my chin. It was painful but not a threat to my consciousness. I continued to claw his face, and he screamed as my fingers gouged his cheeks and eyes. He let go of me and rolled off of me into the woman as she was trying to swing the blackjack again. His rolling momentum pushed her back against the side glass wall.

I jumped to my feet, but the African-American woman had a Beretta M9 in her right hand and was bringing it up to point at me. I backhanded her gun hand with my left. The weapon fired and the back glass wall shattered and rained down hundreds of glass shards into the lobby. Before she had a chance to adjust, I hit her in the face with my right fist, hit her hard enough to knock her through a wormhole in space.

She smashed back against the elevator control panel, her head making a loud thunk as it hit, and she slumped to the floor unconscious. The Beretta clattered to the floor. The Hispanic woman tried to lunge across her injured male colleagues to get it, but I stomped down on her hand before she could grasp the gun. I picked up the pistol and pointed it at them, shifting back and forth from each one, making all of them targets.

"Okay, you all stay where you are," I said, stepping over their prone bodies. "Don't move and you won't get hurt worse than you already are." I pushed the emergency stop button, and the alarm stopped ringing. What a blessed silence that was.

Surveying my enemies, I decided that the Hispanic woman was the most-conscious, least-injured of the lot, although her hand wasn't going to work properly for a while.

"Stand up," I said to her, motioning with the Beretta for emphasis.

She grabbed the railing with her good hand and pulled herself up. I pressed a button—floor twenty-eight. When the elevator stopped on twenty-eight, I waved her out of the elevator, then re-pressed the lobby button and waited for the elevator doors to close.

"Where's the freight elevator?"

"There isn't one, asshole."

"Hey, I said I was sorry before the ruckus began."

"Fuck you."

"Got it out of your system? Now, where's the freight elevator?"

"I told you, there—"

"Stop. No way people are going to take furniture and computer equipment and all that stuff in those nice, fancy glass elevators. Where is the freight elevator?"

She glared at me as if that was an adequate response.

"Do you want me to stomp on your other hand?"

She only had to think that over for a second and then pointed down the hall behind me. We walked past a number of offices, with my left hand on her arm and my right arm holding the gun down near my leg, where it wasn't too obvious. We reached the freight elevator without any shouts or alarms. It seemed to take forever to arrive, but eventually it did, and we stepped inside. I reached up with the barrel of the pistol and pushed the security camera to the side, pointing its lens at the elevator wall. On many freight elevators, the stop button is separate from the alarm button—makes it much easier to load and unload the elevator without driving people nuts with the sound of ringing alarms. This elevator had separate stop and emergency buttons, and I pressed stop. The elevator did as it was told.

"Is there a loading dock? With easy access to the street?"

"Yes." She answered awfully fast and easily.

"Is that where you were supposed to take me?"

"No, why would we—"

I jammed the pistol against the back of her right hand, the hand I had stomped on earlier. She winced in pain. "Don't make me mess your hand up even more. Where were you taking me?"

"To the loading dock!"

I withdrew the gun, and she gently rubbed her hand. "Where were you taking me once I was in the loading dock?"

"Fuck you."

"Please . . . let's not go through the whole threatening thing again. Just tell me." For emphasis I raised the gun toward her hand.

"Okay, okay. There's a van waiting downstairs. A couple of us were supposed to take you away in it."

"Where?" I asked wearily. It was exhausting extracting each tiny detail from her. Or maybe it was my willingness to torture the details out of her that was tiring.

"I don't know. I wasn't assigned to drive."

"Thanks," I said and meant it. Her face went hard, and she was about to hurl more F-bombs at me, but I held up my hand in a stop motion and said, "Please, don't. I get it. Really I do. No need to repeat yourself."

I turned to the buttons of the elevator and pressed the one labeled "Freight Lobby."

"How the hell do you think you'll get out of here? They're waiting for you down there. And your little stunt with the security camera doesn't mean they don't know we're in here. They'll have seen us stepping in. They can monitor what each elevator is doing, what floors it stops at, all of that. You trapped yourself by coming in here."

"Oh, woe is me."

My plan wasn't subtle or brilliant. But many people had used it in the past, and it was very effective. I stood at the back of the elevator, with the woman immediately in front of me, screening a lot of my body. I had to crouch for my head to be level with hers. I was looking over her left shoulder and could smell the floral scent of her shampoo. Her hair smelled very nice. My right hand held the Beretta under her jaw.

The doors rolled open, and I whispered to her, "Press the stop button." She did. The view through the open elevator doors was width-wise across the loading dock. It was exactly what you'd expect, heavy-duty steel doors blocking the entrance to the street, the driveway sloping down, allowing the back end of a truck to meet the front edge of the cement dock. The walls were cinderblock, not fashionable but very functional. A glass booth at the far end of the dock had a desk and a couple of monitors to watch the feeds from the security cameras. A white Ford Econoline cargo van—with no windows along the sides, the better to hide a kidnapped passenger—was parked with its rear doors open to the dock.

A half-dozen men and women were in shooting crouches and/or positioned behind crates on the dock, pointing Berettas at the elevator.

Nobody said anything or made a move for about a minute. I wanted them to appreciate the gravity of the situation for their colleague.

Finally, one of the men spoke loudly, "Drop your weapon and step out of the elevator. We won't shoot you if you cooperate."

"And I won't shoot your colleague here, if you cooperate."

"What did you have in mind?" he replied.

"Your colleague and I are going to exit the elevator. If the keys are in the van, leave them there. If not, whoever has them needs to drop them and everyone of you needs to drop your weapons. Then you step wide around your weapons, walk to the far side of the loading dock."

"I don't think we're going to do that."

"Don't think I'll shoot, huh?"

"Exactly—"

He was interrupted by my shot—I fired at a man who was a little too casual in his sheltering behind a crate. Caught him in the side and spun him to the ground.

"I hope I didn't kill him," the pistol in my hand was underneath the woman's jaw again. "Didn't have time for a precise shot, but I wanted you to understand what I will do to avoid being kidnapped. Drop the keys and weapons, now."

They did as they were told. The man who had been speaking to me placed the van keys next to his Beretta.

I pushed the woman forward, and we slowly stepped to the door of the elevator. I stopped her in the doorframe and leaned forward ever so gently. A man was pressed against the wall, invisible from inside the elevator, gun at the ready. I stepped backward, tugging the woman with me.

"Put your gun down on the floor in front of the elevator where I can see it. Then step back to your buddies."

He didn't comply right away, but the man who had done all the talking growled, "Do what he says."

A Beretta appeared at the edge of the door, and the man walked back to where the others were. He didn't run, but he was moving as if a speedy departure would keep him safe from a bullet in the back.

"Stay where you are until I tell you different."

Now that I didn't need to use the woman as a human shield, I gently shoved her toward the others, scooped up the Beretta from the floor in front of the elevator, and walked toward the van. Pointing one gun at the leader of the security team, the spokesman, and the other in the general vicinity of a couple of others, I reached the van and glanced inside. Steel mesh separated the driver and passenger seats from the cargo area. The rear doors had steel mesh over the windows and no way to be opened from the inside. Neither did the sliding side door.

"Okay, everyone, climb in the back of this van. You," this to the spokesman, "please bring me the keys. And stay away from your damn weapons as you come over here."

A couple of men carried the man I had wounded. They crowded inside. I slammed the door shut and made sure it was locked. It was hard to imagine that I had much time to make a getaway—more Cú Chulainn security were probably bustling toward us at that very second. I quickly grabbed the weapons and dumped all but one into a garbage can on the dock. I rushed inside the security booth, found the button to activate the steel doors to the dock, and raised them. I jumped into the van's front seat, turned on the engine, and gunned the van out of the loading dock, pausing just long enough to make sure I didn't run down any innocent pedestrians.

The enormous, dangerous man I had spotted going into my brownstone was slamming the door of a taxi and bolting toward the van. He was big, but I was pretty damn sure he couldn't stop a van with his bare hands. Silly me, he wasn't planning to use his bare hands.

The big guy pulled a weapon from under his coat. I stomped on the accelerator and careened out of the dock onto 55th Street, bashing into the side of Danger Man's taxi. I raced away and heard pistol shots behind me. Bullets tore through the van's rear doors and shattered both windows. A bullet reached the windshield, and a starburst crack appeared on the passenger side. I kept the gas pedal mashed to the floor and drove west a couple of blocks, crossing Ninth Avenue. The Cú Chulainn people locked in the back of the van were loud and profane. I asked if anyone was hit, but they were too busy cursing me to answer—I assumed that meant no one was wounded. I checked the mirrors, but no taxi with Danger Man appeared to be following me.

I parked near a hydrant west of Ninth, cracked open the front windows, got out, locked the van, and tossed the keys under the vehicle. Then I sprinted around the corner, toward Columbus Circle, scanning in every direction for any sign of my pistol-packing pursuer, and not seeing him, ran down into the circle's subway station. In the station, I went downstairs, hustled along a platform, and double- and triple-checked to be sure no one had followed me. No one had. I took the next A train downtown.

I rode as far south as West 4th Street, where I climbed to the street and walked east to Washington Square Park. I passed Dr. Hoffman's building but thought better of calling him and asking him to hide me. Instead I went into the park, where a Christmas tree about 25-feet tall stood under the Washington Square Arch, the frosting of snow from the night before still visible on the non-paved areas of the park's grounds. The colored lights on the tree glistened on the icy patches on the ground. Beyond the arch and the Christmas tree, the 1800s-era townhouses elegantly lined the northern edge of the park. It was a glorious, urban, yuletide postcard of a view, but I didn't really have the time to appreciate it. I sat down on a bench, which was very cold and sent a shiver up my spine. I checked the photos I had taken outside my apartment of Danger Man on my phone, found one that was clear enough for identification purposes, and sent it to Joanne Agar, a buddy of mine who worked for the FBI. Joanne had been with Army Intelligence in Afghanistan when I had been, how shall I put this, *on loan* to the CIA. We had collaborated on a few special ops. She was convinced I'd saved her life. She might have been correct about that. I called her as soon as the phone signaled that the photo had been sent out.

"Joanne Agar."

"Hey, it's Jack Tyrrell."

"Wow," she said softly, "a welcome blast from the past. How are you?"

"Oh, you know, same old, same old. On the run from some very nasty people with some big honking guns."

"Doesn't that get boring?"

"Yes, yes it does. I'm thinking of retiring right after this gig."

"Oh sure, that sounds like you. I see you sent me a photo of a hunk. Was he one of the people shooting at you?"

"Yes, he was. I'm pretty sure he tossed my apartment this afternoon."

"That's not nice."

"No. Listen, this guy shops in the super tall section of the clothing store: six-six, maybe six-seven, probably 280 pounds. Moves like a large cat. If he's not a pro, I've never seen one."

"If I can find him for you, I will."

"Thank you."

"Jack, I'm . . . I was glad to hear you got back in the game."

"You know how it is: Being of service is kind of addictive."

"Right, you're feeding your jones. Heaven forbid you should have a higher motive."

"That's an interesting phrase: heaven forbid." I had a feeling the Chairman would be fine with my having a higher motive.

There was silence on Joanne's; my guess was she didn't know what to say.

"Listen, Joanne, I'm kind of on the run, send me an ID on that guy as soon as you can, okay?"

"Òkay. Please be careful."

"I'll try." I disconnected and glanced one more time at the tree and Washington's arch, but since I was on the run from a bunch of kidnapping goons, I didn't dawdle to appreciate it. I stood and walked diagonally across the park toward the northeast corner and University Place, where I found a café that wasn't bursting at the seams with NYU students. I ordered a cappuccino and settled into a corner where I could watch the sidewalk through the window.

Okay Tyrrell, what have you discovered with your intrepid sleuthing? Not a single piece of usable evidence. Nothing that I could take to the police. But, I did have a theory of the crime. Savannah Faringer and whoever was in charge of SHK Dragon had wanted Dragon to buy Cú Chulainn. They had conspired to murder Jackson McGill, and with him out of the way, Faringer could sell the company. But how the hell did they manage to set up Marissa Carvajal as their patsy? Maybe they had followed McGill everywhere, waiting for an opportune moment to kill him. But how had they gotten inside his apartment and not been seen on one of the building's many security cameras? The camera feeds showed only one woman—whom the police would know soon was Marissa Carvajal—going in and out of the building. The doorman had seen no one come or go except the woman; computer logs showed no tampering with the security video system and no opening of the freight entrance. Either Marissa had killed McGill, or the ghost of Harry Houdini had done it. Or . . .

As Sherlock Holmes said in *The Sign of the Four*, "when you have eliminated the impossible, whatever remains, *however improbable*, must be the truth." For my exercise in deductive reasoning, I had to assume that Marissa was innocent. In other words, it was impossible for her to have murdered McGill. Eliminating her as a suspect meant someone else had done it—but the security system showed no one else entering the building in the timeframe for committing the crime. Two conflicting impossibilities. But for my purposes, Marissa was the absolute impossibility. Which meant that another suspect was *improbable*, not *impossible*. Which meant . . . the security system was *wrong*. The doorman had to be *mistaken*.

Someone had hacked the building's security. The video feeds had been altered, the computer logs showing entrances and exits from the building had been changed. As for the doorman, my guess was when the killers had hacked into the video system, they blinded it to the freight entrance—the doorman had no clue that the killers had come into the building.

But how the hell did I go about proving this theory of the crime? What kind of evidence could there be that the building's security system had been hacked? It was unlikely that the original video feeds and entryway logs were still intact. The hacker had probably destroyed the files, the same way murderers throw their guns in the river.

And yet . . . ? If I were Savannah Faringer and I wanted to make sure I retained control over the murderous joint enterprise I had launched with the homicial folks at SHK Dragon, I would probably keep the original video feeds, the entrance logs, everything. I'd keep them somewhere very secure, but I'd keep them.

Who'd hacked into the security system and substituted doctored footage? I was pretty sure whoever it was worked for Cú Chulainn Enterprises or SHK Dragon. As I continued to theorize, I became very sure that the killer or killers were probably security goons from Cú Chulainn and/or Dragon. Probably both—that way Savannah Faringer and her opposite numbers at Dragon were all in the murder together. Neither Cú Chulainn nor Dragon were more or less vulnerable to the law if their crime was discovered. They were inextricably linked in guilt.

Which placed me back on square one: How did I prove this theory of the crime? How did I prove Marissa was innocent?

10

LATE AFTERNOON – MANHATTAN: GRAMERCY PARK

DETECTIVES LUKER AND ISLAS CLIMBED OUT of the unmarked police car and looked up at the townhouse that faced north onto Gramercy Park.

Islas said, "I didn't know any of these was still a private residence."

"Now you know."

"Must require serious assets to afford this."

Like many cops, Luker had a seen-it-all attitude. But she had to agree with her partner that it took a fantastic horde of coin to live in one of the remaining private residences on the park. "Maybe we'll get invited inside to see how the other half lives."

The detectives climbed the steps to the front door, pressed a small button on the left side of the door frame, and waited. An immaculately dressed, ultra-thin woman opened the door. Her dark hair was pulled back tightly, and her smile was as welcoming as a tiger shark's.

Both detectives offered her their shields for inspection, and Luker said, "I'm Detective Luker and this is my partner Detective Islas."

"I am Lorraine Plimpton. Please, come in," the woman said, her voice as thin and hard as her body.

The townhouse was immaculately done in a style consistent with the time of its building in the 1890s, but the paint, plasterwork and moldings were all fresh and clean. The furniture appeared too elegant to use. The woman led the detectives into her living room but didn't offer them a seat.

"How may I help you?"

Islas pulled his notebook out of his coat and said, "Ms. Plimpton, we're following up on the canvass that was done after the Philharmonic benefit. You told an—" Islas had to check his notes, "—you told Officer Williams that you recognized this woman from the benefit." He pointed to a photo that Luker was holding out.

"Yes, it's Marissa Carvajal. I don't know her personally, but I *know of* her."

"Oh?" Luker asked. "What do you mean, you *know of* her?"

"Well . . . ," the woman hesitated. Even in the midst of a murder investigation proprieties should be observed. "Ms. Carvajal has quite a reputation."

"A reputation for what?"

"I don't want to cast aspersions on someone else's character. Let's just say that Ms. Carvajal and I don't usually travel in the same circles. I think the Philharmonic is one of the very few organizations that we both support."

"How do you know this is Marissa Carvajal?" Luker asked, extending the picture toward Lorraine Plimpton. "If you only know *of* her?"

"She's a striking woman. Difficult to forget."

"Do her looks have anything to do with her reputation?" Islas asked.

"They enable it."

"What does that mean?"

Plimpton took her time considering that. She inhaled deeply and on the exhale spoke, "Marissa Carvajal attracts men the way flowers attract bees. And from what I've heard, she likes to be chased and she likes to be caught."

"She's a high-class slut," Luker said.

"Your choice of words, not mine, but yes, that's her reputation."

"Did you see the man she was with at the Philharmonic benefit?"

"Yes. Jackson McGill. I don't personally know him either, but I've see him at many benefits and in the news. Given Mr. McGill's reputation, it's something of a minor miracle that he and this woman didn't . . . connect years ago."

Luker suppressed a smile. "I gather you don't approve."

"I believe in the old adage about not casting your pearls before swine."

* * *

In the middle of savoring a cappuccino at the café on University Place, I got a call from Joanne Agar.

"I've got bad news," she said.

"You couldn't find him?"

"Oh no, I found him. That's the bad news. This guy is a first class nightmare. Paul Reznik. American of Czech descent. Six feet seven, 280 pounds, Marine Corps Force Recon for six years, then hired by the CIA. The Agency let him go because he was temperamentally unsuited to their work."

"What the hell does that mean?"

"I talked to a friend at Langley and the word is that Reznik is as tough and dangerous as any man who's ever worked for them. The 'gold-standard of bad-ass,' my friend said. The problem was that Reznik enjoyed the rough stuff too much. Never used a gun if he could use a knife. Never a knife if he could use his bare hands. Liked to indulge in what my contact called, 'extracurricular interrogation techniques.'"

"Torture? Wasn't a lot of that going on after 9/11?"

"Reznik tortured people even when they had given up whatever he needed."

"Oh . . . a sadist."

"To put it mildly. Anyway, the CIA cashiered him, and he worked as a mercenary for a while, then realized he could make more money with much less risk in the corporate security arena."

"Would one of his clients be Cú Chulainn Enterprises? Or SHK Dragon?"

"SHK Dragon . . . how'd you know? Is SHK Dragon after you? Or Cú Chulainn? Is this about the Jackson McGill murder?"

"It could be. I can't prove anything yet."

"If Reznik gets his hands on you, you'll never prove anything."

"Hey!" I said with faux exasperation. "I'm not without skills myself."

"Jack, you're one of the . . . handiest people I've ever met. But you're not in this guy's league. Seriously, you need to stay away from him."

"I'll do my best."

"And, Jack?"

"Yes."

"If you need help on the McGill homicide, let me know."

"You'll be the first."

I disconnected and walked back to Washington Square and stood, appreciating the Christmas tree under the arch. "Harry," I whispered, "could you please talk to me?"

As usual, his appearance was so smooth and swift that describing it as an appearance gives the wrong impression. It was as if he materialized beside me, but the word "materialized" makes it sound as if there had been a process of his becoming visible, and there was none. When I first spoke, there was no Harry. A second later, he was there, visible. But it was not as if he popped suddenly into view like a camera flash going off. Oh, I give up, there's no good way to explain how Harry made his appearances.

"What do you need?" he asked.

"I would like to get inside McGill's building—unseen—and check out the security system. I think someone must have hacked it and eliminated all traces of Jackson McGill's actual murderer."

"Leaving Marissa to take the blame."

"Exactly."

"Why don't you sneak in and take a look?"

"I've had three encounters with the forces of darkness in the last twenty-four hours. I think I'm due a break."

"You consider the security teams at Cú Chulainn Enterprises and SHK Dragon to be the forces of darkness?"

I sighed resignedly, "I was being hyperbolic for the sake of humor."

"It wasn't funny."

"Now that you point that out, I see the error of my ways. Could you please help me check out the security system at McGill's apartment building without being seen?"

Harry glanced up for the tiniest instant, his usual seeking approval from a higher authority, then looked at me and said, "Yes. Are you ready to go?"

"Yes."

Without the slightest sense of time or motion, we went from Washington Square to the desk in the lobby of

McGill's building on Central Park West. Like many desks in lobbys of elegant buildings, this one had a high, marble countertop on the guest side. Below the counter on the doorman side was a shelf with four television monitors displaying the feeds from the various cameras. A laptop computer sat left of the monitors. At the moment, the doorman was several feet away, holding the door open for a middle-aged woman in a bulky coat with a small dog at the end of the leash. The dog had short gray hair, as did its owner, and was one of those designer mixes of breeds. I couldn't tell exactly what this dog was, but it was pretty despite its mixed genes.

Since the doorman was busy, I leaned in close to the monitors to examine them. A cable fed into the laptop and more cables connected the laptop to the monitors.

I pulled out my phone and whispered to Harry, "Does my camera still work?"

"We're invisible. We're not in an alternate reality where phone cameras do not work."

"A simple 'yes' would have sufficed."

"Yes."

I took photos of the setup and of the cables snaking into the laptop and to the monitors. The doorman was still busy chatting with the lady and her dog, so I used the laptop's touchpad to open the security program. A window opened with mini-displays of all the security camera feeds around the building. At the bottom of the window were controls that allowed the user to manage the display, record feeds, delete feeds, and more. I found the "About" link in the software and clicked on it. The software was called "Dragon Secure" and it was manufactured by Celtic Dragon.

"Celtic Dragon," I mused. "As I recall, the cops said that's the security firm that protects this building. I don't suppose it's also the security firm for Marissa's building, is it?"

Usually Harry checked with the Chairman by looking up for the tiniest fraction of a second before giving me information. But this time, he answered without hesitation, "Yes."

"Very interesting."

The doorman had gone from chatting up the woman to crouching low and rubbing the belly of the dog, who had rolled over on its back and was whoofing excitedly.

Since I still had time, I clicked over to an Internet browser and did a search on Celtic Dragon. It was a joint venture of Cú Chulainn Enterprises and SHK Dragon. Just as the detectives had said, Celtic Dragon provided security services for apartment buildings, office buildings, and manufacturing sites. But I didn't find anything that would help me save Marissa.

The doorman stood up, the little dog jumped, and the woman gently tugged the dog's leash and led it outside. I quickly quit my search and minimized the security window, leaving the laptop as I had found it. As the doorman walked around one end of the desk, Harry and I exited from the other.

"Where now?" Harry asked.

"Let's go check the service entrance camera. The one inside."

Harry didn't whoosh me to the service entrance. He did lead the way through a back hallway. The camera, a cylinder about eight-inches long with a lens on one end, was mounted high on the wall near the ceiling about ten feet from the inside of the broad, steel door. I checked a couple of store rooms that opened off the hallway, found a step stool in one of them, carried it to the camera, climbed up, and saw what I expected to see. A tiny red light glowed on the far end of the cylinder and next to the light, a cable snaked away up into the ceiling. On the side of the cylinder was a sticker that read: Celtic Dragon.

I hopped down off the stool and returned it to its original spot.

"What now?" Harry asked.

"Please whoosh me inside Jackson McGill's apartment."

Harry frowned, but before I could give him a hard time about my need to whoosh, we were inside McGill's private office. He pointed at McGill's computer, a sleek MacBook Pro attached to a 34-inch monitor on the desk.

"Is this what you're interested in?"

"Yes, thank you."

An ethernet cable trailed from the MacBook to a router discreetly tucked behind the desk. The router seemed to be run-of-the-mill, but what did I know? It did have a small decal on the side that read Cú Chulainn Enterprises. Not much of a surprise that the Chairman and CEO had a company router in his home office.

"If I power up this laptop, will you give me the password to get in?" I asked.

"I am not a hacker."

"Was that a 'no?' Could you get me a hacker? Right now?"

"No. What are you looking for?"

"I'm not sure . . ." I looked at the metallic shell of the MacBook. "I'm trying to see if there's any connection between this building's security and Savannah Faringer. But to be honest, I'm not sure if I'd know it when I saw it."

Harry gazed up for the briefest moment in time possible then said, "This computer does link directly to one of the networks at Cú Chulainn Enterprises. Very high security, virtual private network, encrypted communications. The cameras outside McGill's front and back doors feed directly to Celtic Dragon, which, as you know, is a security firm jointly owned by Cú Chulainn and SHK Dragon. Does that help?"

"Yes. It connects all the dots. Faringer could have ordered the hit on McGill and set up Marissa Carvajal. Her experts could have hacked their own security system to hide the presence of the real killer."

"Now you know how it was done."

"But I can't prove that Marissa is innocent."

"What do you do next?"

"I haven't got a clue." I stared at the MacBook then out the windows. Just because McGill was no longer able to enjoy his spectacular view of Central Park didn't mean someone shouldn't. There were splotches of white on the ground where yesterday's light snow had not yet melted away. The bare trees were in stark relief to the patches of snow, and people wandered the park's pathways even on this cold day. I imagined they were huddled tightly inside their coats, but they were so small from this height, there was no way to tell.

"Can I ask you a question?"

"You know you can," Harry replied.

"I'm guessing that you're aware I met a woman earlier today, right?"

"Is that your question? You want to know if I know that you met Kim Gannon at Café Sabatini?"

"What's wrong with that question? Were you expecting me to ask about the meaning of life? Knowing that such a question will touch off a long Socratic debate with you leading me to the correct conclusion."

Harry gave me the silent treatment. His silent treatment was very impressive. As a former law-enforcement professional, I had received the silent treatment from some extremely talented people. Harry's version was right up there. I, however, remained unfazed.

"Am I allowed to date Kim, assuming she's interested?"

"Are you *allowed*? You have free will, don't you?"

"I know that I can choose to ask her out and she can choose to say 'yes.' What I want to know is if you're going to zap her and make her forget me?"

"*Zap?*"

"Stop playing semantic games with me. You know what I'm asking."

"I don't play games," he said firmly. "I believe you are asking me if you would be able to pursue a normal relationship with Kim."

"Exactly."

"Is she connected to your work regarding Marissa Carvajal?"

There it was: the Socratic method. I replied calmly, "No, she's not. I met Kim by chance in a neighborhood café."

"In that case, why would there be any need to . . . *zap* her?"

"There wouldn't."

He flashed his tiny, tight smile. "Exactly."

"Thank you. That's what I need to know."

I continued to enjoy the view of Central Park. After a couple of minutes of silence, Harry said, "There is something bothering you."

"I, uh . . . haven't been in a . . . relationship with a woman since Maggie died. I'm . . . scared. It feels . . . disloyal to her."

"But you were interested in Donna Krueger only a few months ago. You didn't seem afraid."

"You may recall that there were bullets flying, her brother had been tricked into working for the Russian mob, there wasn't time to worry about a relationship. Just the intensity of being in a do-or-die situation."

"Is dating easier in a do-or-die situation than under normal circumstances?"

"No, that's not what I meant, it's . . . oh hell, I was distracted, the testosterone was flowing, it was exciting and crazy and you had told me that I couldn't push any kind of relationship with Donna. For crying out loud, she forgot who I was the minute she and her brother were safe."

"That was our . . . arrangement."

"Yes, it was, and I'm not complaining. I have to do good for others for the sake of doing good, not so they'll be eternally grateful to me. Their forgetting is just the clincher. All of the same rules apply to Marissa Carvajal."

"Yes, they do," Harry quietly interjected.

"Thanks for the pointless reinforcement of a concept that I thoroughly understand." I took a deep breath and slowly exhaled. "But Kim is different. No violence. No death. Just the normal emotional dangers of dating. Assuming that is, that she says 'yes.'. . . I'm not sure I'm ready."

"Is your readiness really what troubles you?"

"Damn, you're good," I reluctantly admitted. "Is that your insight or the Chairman's?"

"His. Funneled to me. Is your readiness really the concern?"

I could feel my throat constricting. "No. I . . . I don't think I'm worthy. I did too many bad things; I've got too far to go before. . . ." I couldn't say anymore.

"Do you know what purgatory is?"

"Of course, I'm a Catholic-school kid. Purgatory is where you go to be purged of your sins before you go to heaven. It's like hell, only there's an exit. Right?"

"More or less."

"Are you saying that there is a purgatory? Maybe even that I'm being purged of my sins right now?"

"It's up to you to decide if there is a purgatory. I mentioned it so that we could discuss the theory of atonement. Purgatory is a place of atonement. It's painful, but the concept is that after you've suffered, you are purged or cleaned of sin—you atone for your bad deeds—and can proceed to heaven."

"The suffering I feel now is a form of atoning?"

"What do you think?"

"I think I hate it when you answer my questions with more questions."

"What do you think?" he repeated.

"I like to *think*, no, I *want to believe* that I am atoning. That I'm . . . becoming worthy."

"You seem to understand the concept of atonement."

"Okay, that means I can ask Kim out?"

"You are monomaniacal about some things."

"Is that a 'yes' or a 'no' to asking her out?"

"Do you have free will?"

"That's a 'yes.'"

"But you understand, this is no guarantee of her response."

"Yes, I know how the whole 'ask a girl out and she's free to respond however she wants' thing works."

His brief, mini-smile came and went. "Good luck."

"Harry, sometimes you're almost human."

For once, he was confused.

I turned away from the window. "Let's go check in with the NYPD—see if they've figured out that Marissa is the one they're looking for."

* * *

The NYPD had, in fact, established Marissa Carvajal as the woman who had left the Philharmonic benefit with Jackson McGill. Harry brought me inside Lieutenant Han's office in his usual invisible, seamless, smooth method.

Detectives Luker and Islas were briefing Han. All of them had slept very little. Which, from our point of view, was a bad thing. The NYPD is as relentless a force as exists in nature or law enforcement. These three were exhausted but tenacious and tough.

Islas said, "Yes, we have three definite ID's on Ms. Carvajal as the woman who went with McGill. We have a warrant and are executing a search of her apartment right after we finish this briefing. We'll collect DNA samples off everything we can and see if we can match them to anything we found at the crime scene."

"Good," Han nodded. "Can you confirm she was at Enthousiaste with the victim?"

Luker said, "We're taking a ride over there as soon as it opens this evening, show her and McGill's pictures around, see if we can get an ID."

Han, "Don't wait for the confirmation at the club. Bring her in."

"Yeah, well," Luker said with a bitter grin, "we can't find her."

"Oh, please."

"Sorry, Loo, we tried," Islas said. "She left her apartment yesterday morning, no one knows where. She didn't rent a car, buy a plain or train ticket . . . nothing. Just disappeared."

"Shit," the lieutenant uttered. I thought it was a nifty summary. And I was delighted that even though they now knew who Marissa was, and were on the brink of confirming her presence at the murder scene, they had run into a blank wall in trying to find her.

"Maybe we get out her picture. Say she's being sought as a material witness," Islas suggested.

"Get it out to the Port Authority cops, too," Luker added. "Maybe all local police in the tri-state?"

"Yes to all of those," Han said. "But I think we go bigger. I'm going to see if we can't get this on local news. I think our interest in a material witness to the murder of Jackson McGill is newsworthy, don't you?"

Luker grinned, "If she's gone to ground somewhere in this area, being on the news will make it impossible for her to go anywhere. And sooner or later, people on the run always leave their hiding places and go somewhere."

Harry raised his eyebrows at that.

"She's right," I admitted. "I escorted a bunch of people into Witness Protection, and even though they knew they were in extreme danger, they almost always broke the rules and exposed themselves."

"Why?"

"They felt trapped, even though the program was for their safety, and they had to break free."

"Will Marissa try to break free?"

"Absolutely."

"Then she's still in danger."

"Absolutely."

We listened as Luker said, "We'll do the usual, complete work up on the Carvajal woman. Check out her job, gym, acquaintances, old boyfriends, family, whatever we can find—see if we can track her that way."

What they were planning was predictable, thorough, and usually worked. It was time consuming, but effective. But since Marissa had left without contacting anyone and had gone to a place with no previous connection to her, she was untraceable. As long as she stayed in hiding. As long as she didn't reach out to contact anyone. . . .

I wondered how long she was capable of remaining invisible.

* * *

LATE AFTERNOON – MANHATTAN, NY

FARINGER AND REZNIK STARED AT THE FROZEN PICTURE ON the giant monitor on her office wall. They were looking at the paused video feed from inside Lieutenant Han's office in the 20th Precinct. The camera providing the images was in the computer monitor on Han's desk. Standing like statues were Han and Detectives Luker and Islas.

Faringer said, "As you see: NYPD has identified Marissa Carvajal as the woman wanted in connection with McGill. They are alerting all law enforcement in the metro area. They are also going to inform the media that they are looking for this woman."

"It's a matter of time before they find her," Reznik replied. "Which is exactly what you want, right?"

"Yes, assuming Jack Tyrrell hasn't hidden her away so effectively that they can't get to her. Assuming that he doesn't prove she's innocent."

"He'd need supernatural powers to hide her from us and all the law-enforcement and media heat. And he doesn't have the magical abilities necessary to hide a fugitive while an overpowering number of local law and media search for her."

"It's reassuring to hear that, but we need certainty. Carvajal has to be delivered to the police one way or another. Her arrest will close McGill's homicide investigation."

"I'm aware of that," he said heavily. No matter how tough his clients were when they first began their criminal activities, Reznik always found that he needed to sooth them, encourage them. It was the part of customer service he disliked. "Ms. Faringer, with your team and SHK Dragon's people, and all your lovely technology combing through databases and security cameras for her—in addition to the police and media—Carvajal will be discovered. Tyrrell would need to be Houdini to hide Carvajal from all that. And, as I just told you, there's nothing about him that indicates he's Houdini. He has no special powers. Leave him to me. You have nothing to worry about."

11

LATE AFTERNOON – RYE, NY
MARISSA CARVAJAL WAS IMPRISONED. Although her prison was a waterfront mansion on the Long Island Sound, she had discovered that no matter its size and comfort and beautiful water views, she was trapped. If she left the house and was discovered, she would go to a very real prison. Andrew and Barbara Selkirk were as kind and gracious as it was possible to be. Their staff, Freita and Otto, was hospitable. But Tyrrell's warnings had made her a captive as surely as if she were in police handcuffs.

Marissa desperately wanted to leave the house, even if only a quick trip to fill the gas tank of one of the Selkirks' cars. Even if it were to take garbage to the dump. (Did the residents of Rye take their garbage to a dump?) When Barbara had mentioned that she was going into town, Marissa had pleaded, cajoled, coaxed, and, finally, begged to accompany her. She wrapped her head in an Hermes scarf that completely enveloped her plentiful, dark hair and covered her large, brown eyes with sunglasses. The beautiful, striking Marissa Carvajal disappeared under the disguise.

Reacting to Marissa's new anonymity, Barbara said, "I guess it would be all right."

Andrew Selkirk shook his head in response, "I'm not sure what Harry would say about this."

"Harry's not here," Marissa had replied. "An even if he were, it's my decision to make."

Andrew shrugged. "I've learned not to argue with determined women."

Barbara asked Otto to bring the BMW around front. Marissa followed her out the front door, as Otto parked a 750i xDrive in Dark Graphite at the front steps. Otto stepped out of the car and held the driver's door open for Barbara. Marissa moved quickly to get into the passenger seat, locking the door as soon as she was inside. She was determined to get out of the house for a short time.

In Rye, they found a parking space on Purchase Street, only a few Christmas-bedecked storefronts away from their destination, *Pain et Fromage*.

"You bring good luck," Barbara said as she got out of the BMW.

"Excuse me?"

"It's almost a miraculous occurrence to get parking this close to the store."

Marissa forced a smile, "Glad I could be helpful."

Barbara slipped her right arm through Marissa's left and guided her toward *Pain et Fromage*. As the name indicated, the store was full of fresh-baked bread and a wide array of cheeses (mostly but not exclusively, imported from

France), plus a variety of olive oils, vinegars, spices, and gourmet-cooking utensils, pots and pans. As the women stepped into the shop, Marissa inhaled the wonderful mix of aromas from the cheeses and spices that permeated the space. She pushed her sunglasses back onto the bridge of her nose and pulled down the front edge of the Hermes scarf to insure her disguise was intact. She had nothing to worry about—only someone who knew Marissa very well would have recognized her under the glasses and scarf, and Rye's *Pain et Fromage* was well outside her normal orbit.

The women browsed, dipping small pieces of baguette in samplings of olive oil. Barbara decided on a garlic-infused oil and then led the way to the cheese counter. There was more sampling. The store was warm, and without thinking, Marissa opened her coat and pulled the scarf down, draping it loosely over her shoulders. Barbara chose three different cheeses, and while she was waiting to pay for her purchases, Marissa took off her sunglasses and wandered through the food displays, enjoying her trip outside her luxury prison.

"Marissa?" a woman's voice as thin and reedy as her body. Marissa turned to see the living embodiment of Tom Wolfe's social x-ray approaching her: a tall, thin brunette in a gigantic, fur-trimmed coat and black boots. The woman's bejeweled hand, almost a claw with flesh stretched tight over the bones and knuckles, was stretched out to grasp Marissa. "It is you, isn't it? What are you doing here?"

"Hello, Charlene," Marissa said, her voice tight with fear. "I'm visiting an old friend. Not staying for long." She spotted Barbara, who was making a beeline for the shop door, jerking her head as if to tell Marissa to get the hell out before it was too late. "I have to go, sorry, my friend is leaving."

She was off before Charlene could manage a goodbye.

Barbara hurried back to the BMW with Marissa immediately behind her, and the women were inside and on the move within seconds.

Marissa leaned forward, tugging against her seatbelt, burying her face in her hands. "Oh my God, what have I done?"

*   *   *

Harry whooshed us to the front steps of the Selkirks' house. There were Christmas lights on two small pine trees in the yard, and the lights sparkled especially brightly in the cold, crisp evening air.

"It's hard to believe that Christmas is almost here and that even as I speak, almost all New York law enforcement and news media are hunting for our client."

"Not to mention Savannah Faringer's people."

I stared at the Christmas lights on the nearest tree—the colorful bulbs danced slowly in a gentle, evening breeze. "I'm not sure I'm up to this particular challenge."

"The Chairman will give you everything you need."

"What does he have in mind? The 101st Airborne Division?"

"My understanding of the Chairman is that if you truly need the 101st, then you will receive it."

"You're kidding, right?"

"No. Besides, you seriously underestimate yourself. I am reasonably certain you will not need an entire Army division."

"Well, I am *absolutely* certain it's gonna take a helluva lot more than me to do this job."

"We'll see."

I walked across the drive until I could see inside the Selkirks' immense living room. Andrew and Barbara were sitting on the couch, a fire burning opposite them in the stone hearth, their Christmas tree filling a corner, ornaments shining in the tree's colored lights. Handel's *Messiah* came faintly through the windows. There was no sign of Marissa; I guess she wasn't joining them for this idyllic Christmastime evening. I strolled to the end of the house for a different line of vision into the living room. Still no Marissa. I wandered to the other end of the house, passing the front hallway and two dark, empty rooms, which I guessed were the dining room and Andrew's home office. Looking up, I saw no lights in the bedroom windows on the second floor.

"Is something wrong?" Harry asked.

"I hope not. Let's go inside. Better break the news to Marissa that the police have established her identity as McGill's late-night guest."

We knocked on the front door. Otto opened it quickly; I suspected he'd been sitting inside. He gestured with his right hand, palm up, directing us to the living room. We went into the cheery, Christmasy room and said hello to the Selkirks. They were both holding large tumblers of whiskey. Barbara's was on the rocks; Andrew's was straight up.

"Marissa and I went into town," Barbara said.

"And . . . ?" I refrained from dropping nuclear F-bombs.

"She was wearing a scarf and large sunglasses, barely recognizable—"

"But something went wrong?" My professional, firm but gentle voice.

"We ran into someone she knows. We were in a store; Marissa took off her sunglasses, and . . . well, she's a striking woman, not easily forgotten, and . . . I'm so sorry."

"Did Marissa talk to this woman?"

"Only for a moment. We beat a hasty retreat."

"Did Marissa say anything about where she was staying or about you?"

"No, she said she was visiting friends, that's all."

"You're sure?"

"Yes. Absolutely."

I stared at the Christmas tree as if the solutions to Marissa's problems were gift-wrapped beneath it. "Where is she?"

"In the den, I think. It's at the back of the house," Barbara stood up to lead me there. "Off the kitchen."

"Thanks, I'll find her."

Harry and I walked through the hallway to the kitchen and then into the den. The only light in the room was from a single lamp, which cast a soft, warm glow throughout the room. Perfect if you wanted to sit on the couch and enjoy the nighttime view of the lights on the far side of the Sound. There was a half a tumbler of whiskey on the end table next to the couch. But no Marissa. I turned and looked through the glass doors.

Marissa was outside, standing on the stone seawall that separated the back yard from the water. Even though it was dark outside, I could see that she was facing the water and wasn't wearing a coat, and I knew from having just come inside a few minutes earlier that it was too damn cold to be outside without a coat. I twisted around and looked at the whiskey glass, then back at Marissa.

"Oh, no . . ." I fumbled open the lock on one of the doors and slid it open.

Marissa heard the door's sliding hiss, turned and saw Harry and me walk outside.

"No," she called, turned back to the water and jumped off the wall, disappearing from sight.

I ran full-out, yanking off my coat, kicking off my shoes, and stumbling toward the wall at the water's edge. I halted on top, searched the water below, and spotted her splashing haphazardly about twenty feet out in the Sound. I dove.

The water was frigid, and I gasped in shock as my body sliced under the surface. I forced myself to stroke and kick—I had no idea how long either of us could survive, but I had a very bad feeling that it wasn't long. The air was arctic, the water was almost freezing, and I was panting so hard from the cold that I couldn't breathe in a proper freestyle stroke—I swam as hard as I could with my head up and out of the water. Not very efficient, but I could keep an eye on Marissa, who was bobbing over and under the surface of the Sound.

I was only a few feet away when she disappeared. I ducked underwater, kicked hard in her direction, and prayed that I'd find her. My fingers touched something, and I grabbed her right arm and kicked toward the surface. I twisted her over onto her back on the surface, cradling her upper body in my left arm, careful to keep her nose and mouth above water, and side-stroked back toward the wall. It's really hard to side-stroke with any efficiency when you're semi-frozen and towing another semi-frozen body. I wasn't going to make it. We were both about to drown. . . .

I gasped, "Please help me . . ." Talking was a terrible idea, I needed every last breath. But suddenly I was touching the wall, and by sheer chance I had ended up at the set of stone steps that led down to the water. I was able to put my foot on an underwater step and stand up in water at waist level. I scooped up the unconscious Marissa in both arms and staggered up the steps. I reached the top of the wall, slung her over my shoulder, and hurried toward the the house, hoping my bouncing movements would pump the water out of her lungs. We were only a few yards from the house when I heard and felt her coughing and spitting up water. I didn't stop; I was afraid that if I halted, I wouldn't have the strength to get Marissa into the warmth of the house.

Harry trailed us, carrying my coat and shoes. How considerate, I thought. Andrew and Barbara were at the glass doors, stepping back as I hustled inside.

Barbara pointed across the den and said, "Go to the guest room, I'm running a hot shower."

Doing as I was told, I stumbled through the guest suite, convinced I was going to freeze solid before I ever managed to reach the hot shower. But we made it. I stepped into the large, glass-doored shower, Marissa still in my arms, both of us fully clothed in frigidly wet shirts and pants. The first few seconds were torturous and joyous. The hot water seemed blisteringly hot and then, almost immediately, life-giving.

After a minute, Marissa began to revive, and I was finally able to stand her up on her own feet. Another few minutes and we were warm enough to peel off our sodden apparel. As we dropped our clothing to the bottom of the shower, I was vaguely aware of Barbara ushering her husband and Harry out of the bathroom.

Hot water from multiple jets coursed over both of us. I don't know how long we soaked in the hot water before the realization came to me that we were both naked and standing very close together. I was still in a state of shock from the cold, but not so shocked that I was unaware of this amazingly sexy woman standing naked in the shower with me. The realization that we were nude became a crystal-clear and an exciting reality when she put her arms around my neck, pulled my head down, stood on tiptoe, and kissed me.

It was my first, hungry, lustful kiss in more than five years. It was the first kiss with anyone besides Maggie in much, much longer than that. The hot shower, our wet, naked bodies, her lips touching mine, her full breasts pressed against my chest . . . my hands were on her hips, holding her tightly. I cupped her butt and was going to lift her and make love to her right then, right there—and I thought of Harry. Damn.

In no conceivable way was making love to Marissa part of my mission. I could imagine Harry standing on the other side of the shower door, watching me with a disapproving scowl on his face. Assuming he ever allowed himself to scowl. I let go of Marissa's delectable rear end and gently grabbed her arms and pulled her off of me.

"I'm sorry," I said. "I can't do this."

"No, no, I'm sorry, I shouldn't have . . . I'm sorry—" she pushed through the shower door and stepped out.

"Marissa, wait." I turned off the shower, which took a bit of doing since there were several valves that had to be turned to shut down the multiple shower heads.

Marissa slid into a thick, white terrycloth robe and tied the sash around her waist. The bright white robe contrasted beautifully with her dark coloring. I shuddered at the thought that, much as I wanted to, I couldn't grab her and start kissing and caressing her.

I grabbed a bath towel and wrapped it around my waist. "Listen, you didn't do anything wrong. I did."

"No, no, my response to any man is always sexual. Which is the reason I'm in the situation I'm in and why I need your help. You'd think I'd learn my lesson."

"Marissa," I took her left hand in my right. "You were just expressing your gratitude in an overenthusiastic way. I really, really wish I could respond in kind, but my boss frowns on that kind of thing."

"Is Harry your boss?"

"Uh . . . no, but he's closer to the boss than I am." I pulled another towel off a rack and dried my hair. I rubbed my head with a lot of vigor, avoiding looking at Marissa. Instead, to distract myself from her, I took note of the bathroom—when I first entered, I was only conscious of the shower. Now I could appreciate the size of the room, which was quite large for a bathroom. It even had a nice chair and an end table to one side, in a window nook. For the life of me, I don't know why there was a chair in the bathroom, but there was one in this bathroom, and I was glad of it. I led

Marissa to it, and she sat down. I crouched near her, careful to keep the towel around my waist tight to avoid exposing myself. The nude portion of this evening was finished.

"Why did you try . . . to kill yourself?" I asked.

Her eyes watered up. "They're going to find me. I was terribly stupid. I convinced Barbara to take me into Rye . . . I ran into someone I know . . . I've ruined everything. . . ."

"We don't know that. There's no connection between you and the Selkirks. Even if the woman you ran into guesses that you're staying somewhere in Rye, it doesn't mean the police are going to find you. For that to happen the woman would have to know that law enforcement is looking for you, then she has to contact them, then they have to search Rye, and they're going to have a long slog searching door-to-door."

"Why?"

"It takes immense amounts of manpower to go door-to-door in a town like this. And the police wouldn't even know that you're in Rye. You could be anywhere in this area. Maybe across the border in Connecticut. Or maybe you were up from the city for a few hours. The police would probably use Rye as ground zero and step up surveillance everywhere they can in the hope that you show yourself again. But you're not going to do that."

"You're saying that I'm safe?"

"Yes. You're safe."

My tone wasn't as convincing as it should have been. I could lie with utter sincerity to the lowlifes I had met through my years as a Marshal, but spend a few minutes naked with a woman in a hot shower, and I couldn't get anything past her.

"I don't believe you," she said. "You need to be honest with me."

"If you were in my shoes and had pulled me out of the very cold Long Island Sound, would you feel you could be completely honest with me?"

"I'm not going to attempt suicide."

"Any more?"

She jumped to her feet and pushed me away. I held onto my towel as I toppled, keeping my manhood covered. Marissa paced the bathroom—it was a large room but didn't really provide a premium pacing space.

"I made a mistake. I did something horribly stupid. But—" she stopped and looked down at me. Her voice softened, "but you saved me. At tremendous risk to yourself. I won't throw your gift away. I promise."

"Okay," I said, standing. "Good."

"Now I need you to be honest with me. Am I safe?"

I wished I could give her an ironclad guarantee on that, but there was always the chance that the bad guys would find her. "Look, it's possible that Cú Chulainn and SHK Dragon—"

"Who?" Marissa asked, completely bewildered. "Who are those people?"

"Cú Chulainn was Jackson McGill's company. SHK Dragon is a Chinese corporation. McGill's No. 2 at Cú Chulainn, a woman named Savannah Faringer, wants to merge with SHK Dragon, but McGill wanted no part of that. Harry and I believe that she arranged to have McGill murdered and frame you for it. Now their security teams are looking for you. Their reach could be longer than law enforcement's. They could be tapped into local traffic and private-security cameras. Maybe by cross-checking camera feeds, they'll be able to trace your afternoon excursion and—*maybe*—track your trip all the way back to the gatehouse of this community."

"And then what?"

"Let's just say that, if, and I emphasize *IF*, Cú Chulainn and SHK Dragon track you back to this community, they won't be very careful about protecting your rights in a house-to-house search. But that's not going to happen in the next few minutes or even hours. You're certainly safe here tonight. Probably for another day or two. I'll speak to Harry about moving you again." I could see her lower lip quiver and a tear forming in the corner of her right eye. "Don't worry, we'll keep you safe."

"I'm sorry, but . . ." she was crying, "I can't go to prison. I can't."

"I'm going to do everything I can to make sure that doesn't happen."

"Oh?" her eyes were wide with fear and anger. "You? You're going to protect me? You and Harry? Are you two so powerful you can stop the police and Cú Chulainn and SHK Dragon and everyone else from finding me and locking me away? Are you even sure I didn't kill McGill?"

"Yes, I'm sure you didn't kill him."

"Why?"

"Because. It's what I believe."

"Your belief won't stand up in a court of law."

"True. We'll have to keep you out of court."

"How can you do that? Do you have that kind of power and influence?"

"No, I don't. But . . . my boss does. No one is more powerful than He is."

"I wish I had your faith."

I smiled. Marissa was staring at the floor and missed my expression.

"Let's get dressed and then go to the kitchen and drink something warm. I don't know about you, but even after that shower, I feel chilled right through."

"I'm sor—"

"Stop it, please?" I said. "You gave me a chance to play the hero. I live for that."

She smiled. "You're a bad liar."

I grinned. "I wasn't lying about wanting to get dressed and drink something warm."

There were clothes laid out for us on the bed in the guest room. Women's clothing on the side nearest the bathroom, men's on the far side. I picked up the pants, turned my back to Marissa, and tugged them on. The jeans must have been Andrew Selkirk's, because they were a reasonable fit. Otto's would have been much too small. I wondered if Marissa was watching me or also dressing with her back turned. Odd how modest we had become now. I pulled an off-white, cable-knit cotton sweater over my head.

I said in a soft, unchallenging tone, "Have you remembered any more from the night with McGill?"

"No . . . well, there've been flashes of things."

"Like what?"

"You have to have the details?" her voice was rising.

"It's hard to know what could be important, so yes, I need the details. I'm sorry."

For a long moment the only sound was cloth sliding over skin. I don't think I'd ever been in a situation that was very intimate and very distant at the same time.

Finally, she sighed and said, "When we were coming up in his elevator, Jackson began kissing me. Really kissing. His hands were all over, under my coat, touching me. He began to undo my dress."

"In the elevator?"

"Yes . . . it was . . . exciting."

"Anything else?"

"We arrived on his floor before I was completely undone, and Jackson led the way into his apartment."

"Did you go straight to the bedroom? Or did you stop to grab a drink on the way?"

"I don't remember . . ."

"Hmm, in between the elevator and the bedroom is kind of a blur?"

"It's all like a mirage—I don't know what was real and what's a drunken dream."

"It's okay," I said. "Let's drop it. If anything comes to you, anything at all, whether you think it might be a mirage or you're sure it's cold, hard reality, tell me."

"I will. All dressed?" she asked.

"Yes."

Marissa was in jeans and a light-gray sweater. Her long, wet, dark hair spilled over her shoulders. She took my hand and led me to the kitchen, pointing me to one of the stools. I sat down, and Marissa went about making coffee. Her time with the Selkirks had clearly been spent learning the essentials of existence in their home: where is the coffee and how do you work the pot? Actually, for people as affluent as the Selkirks, the essentials probably included: where did I park my German luxury sedan and will my hedge-fund manager call me before close of market? But since I didn't own a car, never mind a luxury import, and my investment portfolio consisted of a balanced collection of mutual funds, coffee was the absolute essential.

Marissa perched on another stool and we waited in silence for the coffee to finish dripping. She faced me and reached for my right hand, gently cradling my fingers in hers. It was an affectionate gesture not a seductive one. We sat in comfortable silence until the dripping sound petered out. Marissa stepped down from her stool, poured coffee into two mugs, which she placed on the island in front of our stools. Then she filled a small tray with a tiny pitcher of milk, a sugar bowl, and packages of artificial sweetener and set the tray next to our mugs.

"If the real estate career doesn't work out, you have a nice way about you as a food server."

"I was a waitress in a diner in college."

"I bet you were good at it."

She sat down and shrugged, "Well, I always had the most tips. But that probably had as much to do with my looks as with my service."

I grinned. "Could be."

"Did you have a job in college?"

"I had an Army ROTC scholarship at Fordham. I received a stipend. But I did a bit of work here and there. I delivered pizza for this local red-sauce place and cases of liquor for the liquor store. Mowed lawns, raked leaves."

"Army ROTC—I think you said something about being a Green Beret?"

"Yes, Special Forces. Seemed like a good idea at the time."

"That sounds as if it turned out to be a bad idea."

"I was being flip. Special Forces training doesn't build a lot of transferable skills for civilian life. But I felt I was serving in an important way in Afghanistan and got to meet some great people."

"Are transferable skills the reason you became a Marshal?"

I laughed. "Yes, when you become expert at sneaking up on people and subduing or killing them, there's always a use for you in law enforcement."

"What about your wife?'

I parried her question gently, "What about her?"

"Did you meet her in the Army?"

"No, shortly after I joined the Marshals Service."

"You said she was a therapist."

"She was."

"Would you like me to drop the subject?"

"Uh . . . no. Sorry for the short answers. I'm . . . I'm still not over losing her."

"Do you ever get over losing someone you loved?" Marissa asked, looking down into her coffee.

"I don't know. I guess not." I reached for her hand, and she let me hold it. "Did you lose someone?"

She pursed her lips and nodded. It took a long moment for her to summon the ability to answer. "My fiancé." She sipped some coffee, breathed deeply, and went on, "We were hit by a car—the driver had lost control, and the car jumped the curb onto the sidewalk. He was killed instantly. I was in the hospitable for weeks, right past our wedding day."

Something told me that her story wasn't quite finished. As bad as what she had told me was, there was still one more sad thing to relate. I waited, watching her, still holding her hand.

She gave my hand a gentle squeeze then let go, pulling her hand back close to her chest as if to protect herself. "Our baby died. We didn't even know I was pregnant until two days before the accident. I lost everything that day. Everything."

"I'm sorry for you. No one should endure that kind of . . . loss."

"Why do you think that . . . why does that kind of thing happen? I . . . I wasn't always this way . . . I didn't drink to the point of drunkeness, I didn't sleep around . . . but afterward, there didn't seem any point . . ." her voice trailed off.

"And everything hurt. A lot."

"Yes." She stared into her coffee mug for a while then slowly shook her head. "Why? Why did this happen to me?"

"I don't know. Accidents aren't planned; they're random mistakes, not deliberate and malevolent. But they do happen, and . . . I guess they have to happen to someone. I don't mean to sound unfeeling, but maybe the accident was a case of: why not you?"

"Why not me?" Marissa slid off her stool, her eyes glaring. "Why not me? Are you fucking kidding with that? There's no cause and effect, there are random bad things happening, and my fiancé and my baby got killed?" She punched me in the arm "Are you fucking kidding?"

"Marissa—"

She stopped me by the simple expedient of slapping me. It was a helluva slap. To be honest, I saw it coming—my reflexes and training are very good. I could have ducked the slap or parried it. But she was angry and probably entitled to slap someone, and the Chairman wasn't handy. So I let her slap me.

Then she slapped me again. (Yes, I saw it coming the second time, too.) Then she began pounding on my chest, crying and raging. I silently and stoically did my heroic, he-man thing and let her pound and cry. A few seconds later, she collapsed against me and sobbed into my sweater. I gently hugged her close.

After what seemed like an hour but was only a few minutes, her sobbing faded. She stepped away from me, spotted a tissue dispenser, grabbed a few tissues, and wiped her face.

"I'm sorry," she whispered.

"It's okay."

"No, it's not. You didn't deserve that."

"Yeah, but I was handy."

She managed a tiny smile at that remark. "You let me hit you, didn't you?"

"No, of course not—"

"Yes you did. A big, ex-Green Beret and former Marshal doesn't get bitch-slapped by a tiny little woman."

"He does if he was caught by surprise."

"You weren't surprised. Why did you let me hit you?"

"Like I said: I was handy."

She sniffled, used more tissues, then took a deep breath and exhaled very slowly. I almost expected her to assume a yoga pose. Instead, she turned her beautiful if reddened eyes on me and asked, "Do you believe in God?"

"Oh, definitely. I work for Him."

"What does that mean? Are you a priest in addition to being in Special Forces and the Marshals?"

"Uh, well," yeah, go ahead and get yourself out of this, Tyrrell. "I, uh . . . I was speaking figuratively. For Jews and Christians the second great commandment is to love thy neighbor." Marissa was puzzled. I went on: "In *A Christmas Carol*, the ghost of Jacob Marley sums up that commandment by saying that 'Mankind was my business.' And that's kind of how I see myself."

She was, to put it mildly, nonplussed. "Are you telling me that mankind is your business?"

"Sure. It's everybody's, isn't it?"

"What if you don't believe in God? Is it an atheist's business, too?"

"We're all stuck in this life together. Seems to me, we should all be working together."

"Are you going to start singing *Kumbaya*? 'Cause if you are, I need to throw up."

I laughed, "Sorry. I deserved that." At least she had moved on from my "I work for Him" comment. "What about you?" I asked. "Do you believe in God?"

"I want to."

"But you're having a hard time because of what happened to your fiancé and baby?"

"Wouldn't you?"

"Yes. Absolutely."

"Where does that leave me?"

"I think you're looking for God."

"Where? In a bottle? 'Cause that's the only place I look for my answers," she admitted bitterly.

"Probably."

"What? Are you kidding?"

"No, not at all. Have you ever been to England?"

"Yes . . . ?"

"You probably saw lots of pubs over there, right?"

"Yes . . ."

"Over the door, a lot of pubs have a sign that says something like 'Beer, Ale and Spirits'. Spirits referring to harder alcoholic drinks. That term, spirits, is not a coincidence. Alcohol can have a transformative effect on our emotions and psyche, similar to a spiritual experience. And throughout history all kinds of people have used alcohol or drugs to enhance what they thought were spiritual pursuits."

"I don't believe this . . . you are really suggesting that I'm looking for God in a bottle."

"Yes, I am. You're not aware that you're trying to fill a spiritual hole inside you with spirits, but yes, that's exactly what you're doing."

Marissa stared at me for a long time, walked over to the sink, poured the dregs of her coffee out, rinsed the cup and put it in the bottom of the sink. She walked back to me, took my now-empty mug, and repeated the rinsing process. Then she returned to stand in front of me. I was still sitting on the stool; I didn't tower over her the way I did when we both standing.

She whispered, "I don't know if you're crazy or I'm crazy or we're both crazy."

"Maybe neither of us is crazy."

"I hope so." She kissed me tenderly on the mouth, turned, and walked out of the kitchen without another word.

I pushed the coffee pot's power button to off, threw out the grounds and rinsed the pot. Then I went back into the den, sat on the couch, and stared out the window at the sprinkle of lights on the north shore of Long Island. Harry stepped through the door, entering from the kitchen.

"Did you see and hear everything?" I asked.

"No. I am not a spy."

"But you know everything that is essential for you to know."

"I am aware of the facts, yes. You acquitted yourself very well tonight."

"Why did you disappear? You would have done a better job explaining things to Marissa then I did."

He pursed his lips then said, "The Chairman wanted you to deal with her doubts."

"Holy moly. You guys are more messed up than I am. What's the point of *my* telling her anything? Once this is over, she won't remember me—won't she forget everything I said to her?"

"No."

"Oh? How does that work?"

"Marissa won't remember you, but what you said to her tonight may come back to her as a stray thought, maybe when she meditates or takes a long walk or in yoga class. It's possible that a song lyric or something she reads might be similar enough to what you said that she'll react with what she believes is an original thought. But it will actually be something you said."

"Is this how the Chairman inspires people?"

"You tell me."

I waved him off. I was done explaining things for the night.

Instead he repeated, "You acquitted yourself very well tonight."

"Thanks. Does this mean I'm ready to teach Sunday School?"

"I don't know. I doubt that teaching Sunday School is the mission the Chairman had in mind for you."

"I was kidding. We need to work on your sense of humor."

"You continue to deflect my comment. Marissa is alive because of your quick action."

"All I did was keep swimming despite the frozen state of my anatomy. Anyone dumb enough to jump in frigid waters could have done it." I focused on the lights on the Long Island shore. "Will she try it again?"

Harry's head titled up at the tiniest of angles for the briefest of pauses, then he said to me, "No, she won't. Not for a few days anyway." Harry walked to the window and peered into the night. "Are you seeing Dr. Hoffman tomorrow?"

"Yes."

"Good," he replied and whooshed out of sight.

"Whoa," I sighed appreciatively. "Way to drop your punchline and make an exit, Harry."

12

I woke to the smell of coffee. Marissa was standing in front of me, with mugs of steaming hot coffee, one in each hand. I realized I was still on the couch in the Selkirks' den. I stretched and reached out for the coffee.

"Good morning," she smiled, handing me a mug. "Why did you sleep down here? Too exhausted from deep thoughts to make it to the guest room?"

A long sip of coffee was wondrous, and I thought: I didn't need Harry to have a spiritual experience—I just needed hot coffee. "I guess so," I replied.

She sat on the couch next to me but not too close. "What are your plans for today? Are you going back to the city? May I go with you? I'd be safe with you, wouldn't I?"

I shook my head. "Sorry, no. The best way to keep you safe is to keep you hidden. Stay here with Andrew and Barbara—there's no apparent connection between you and them. As I told you last night, it's a very, very long shot that anyone could track you here."

"But with you—"

"Marissa, you can't. I know you're scared, and your fear makes you restless." I grinned, "Do a heavy workout. I bet there's some kind of a gym somewhere in this house."

She grinned, too, but it managed to be a sad expression. "There is, in the basement."

"It's a great way to burn off restless energy."

"But with you . . . after last night, I know that I'm . . . safe with you."

"I'm not a miracle worker. I can't protect you from everything. Please believe me: you're safer here than anywhere else."

"Okay." She was not a happy camper. She stood up and walked out of the room.

There was no sign of her when it was time to leave.

Otto drove me to the train station as he had the day before, and once more I rode the rails to Grand Central

Terminal. I walked through the main concourse and remembered uneasily that less than forty-eight hours earlier, on the 53rd floor of the MetLife Building directly above where I now strolled, I had come very close to burning a man with an acetylene torch. What kind of man had I become that I would do something that hideous to another human being?

"Harry?" I said softly.

"Yes."

As usual with Harry's sudden arrivals, no one on the concourse had any reaction whatsoever—as if men, or in Harry's case, angels—appeared out of nowhere as a matter of routine.

"Could you please take me to the 53rd floor? Invisibly please?"

He nodded and his nod finished as we arrived on the 53rd floor. A quick count showed almost a dozen people, mostly men, all in hard hats, milling around. Definitely construction workers. I walked to the table where Flynn, Bouchard, and the Chinese men had set my personal effects the night we'd had our little party here. Blueprints and wiring diagrams were spread out on the table now. In the bottom right corner of each document was a legend with the name of the architect or the chief electrical engineer and the 53rd floor's tenant: Celtic Dragon, the joint security venture of Cú Chulainn and SHK Dragon.

"Do you need anything else here?" Harry asked.

I looked at the fuel tank, hose, and torch that stood a few feet away from the table. My stomach knotted at the memory of the little get-together in this space. I closed my eyes, breathed deeply, and felt grateful to the Chairman for sparing me the necessity of torturing Flynn.

"No, thank you."

Before I had the chance to request a whooshing to Greenwich Village and Dr. Hoffman's office, I found myself back in the middle of Grand Central. No sign of Harry. I hurried through the concourse, ignored the Christmas season bazaar that filled the Vanderbilt Room, exited through the front doors onto 42nd Street, and turned right to head west. I walked past the Public Library with its stone lions guarding the massively wide front steps, past Bryant Park where Christmas carols were playing over the loudspeakers hung above the ice rink, then descended to the subway and took an F train to West 4th Street.

I walked to Dr. Hoffman's building and found myself sitting on the dark-brown couch under the Maine-looking watercolor in Hoffman's office inside of two minutes.

"How are you today?" Hoffman asked.

"Not cured, yet."

"Maybe by tomorrow," he deadpanned.

"That would be nice."

"If only it were that way," he replied. He waited for a minute for me to say something then gently prodded me, saying "You can begin wherever you like."

"Don't you ask and I answer?"

His smile was so slight he could have been borrowing one of Harry's Mona Lisa expressions. The smile was his only response.

"Okay . . . okay . . ." I said, trying to buy time. "We were talking about Maggie and how she couldn't help me because I was her husband not her patient."

"Yes."

"I said I was angry at her for not helping me, and that's true, but I . . . I think I was really angry with me."

"Why?"

"I couldn't relate to people. I took no pleasure in my job, in fact I was super pissed off that I had to deal with criminal scum, that I was mostly running down fugitives, and occasionally delivering people into witness protection. I'm not talking about nice people who unfortunately witnessed something and then have to go into hiding for testifying; I'm talking about criminals who testify about even worse criminals and are reward with a nice new life."

"That's the way the system works, isn't it?"

"Yes, but . . . I hated it . . ." I thought it over for a moment. "I was transferring my anger, wasn't I?"

"What do you think?"

I grinned, "You and Harry have a real knack for answering questions with questions."

"Do you think you were transferring anger?"

"Probably."

"And whom were you transferring it from?"

"Me. I was transferring it away from me." I thought for a second. "And transferring it to Maggie."

"Yes."

"Not that I was obviously angry with her, but . . . I withheld my real feelings. My real . . . pain."

"Yes."

I noticed a half-full glass of water on his desk, within easy reach for him. Was it half-full or half-empty, I wondered. Looking at the water reminded me of another lovely behavior from my past.

"I drank too much."

"Because you were angry with yourself?"

"Yes. And I wanted to hide from my anger and pain. I wanted to forget some of the things I'd done in the war."

"Like torturing people?"

"Yes." I turned my gaze to the window and stared at the bare treetops outside. The view hadn't changed a bit since yesterday. "When I was in Afghanistan, I could do whatever needed to be done. I didn't like it, but I was convinced it was necessary. I did it."

"Again, not to belabor the point, but you're talking about torture?"

"Yes. But once I came home, had a little time to think about things, I wasn't so sure anymore. I . . . don't believe in torture. I was glad I wouldn't have to do that again. But recently . . . I don't know, there have been a couple of times in the last few days where I thought . . . it seemed like it was . . . necessary. But I don't want to be that man anymore."

Hoffman was nodding, mostly to himself, considering what I'd said. "You feel your experiences in the war drove your drinking?"

"Yes. At least partly. My drinking was an attempt to escape, an attempt at a slow-motion suicide. But it didn't fix anything . . . the drink only stopped the pain for the time I was actually drunk."

We sat quietly for a few minutes.

Dr. Hoffman surprised me by breaking the silence, "Please tell me about the end of your time with the Marshals Service."

My gut twisted at the memory: "I took a bribe."

"Why?"

"My reason doesn't make any sense. I was angry and depressed and I took the bribe. Some mafia mook offered me money. I never intended to give him the information he wanted—in fact, I couldn't give it to him. He wanted info on a protected witness, which I didn't have any access to, so I figured in my drunken, angry way, Hey! Why not take money from this crooked jerk? I'm just screwing over a thug."

"But that rationalization didn't work for you?"

"No."

"Why not?"

"I knew that . . . it was wrong. All of my rationalizations didn't make it . . . right. And—" I was breathing hard as if I had been running, "And . . . I got . . . my wife killed." The tears rolled down my face. "My wife died because her pathetic, angry, loser husband took money from mobsters . . . I practically pulled the trigger myself."

"But you didn't pull the trigger."

"I might as well have—"

"Stop it," Hoffman said softly but very firmly. "You didn't kill her. The man who shot her killed her."

"But I—"

"You're guilty of taking the money. Of lying. Of feeling tragically sorry for yourself. But you didn't kill her."

I grabbed a tissue from a conveniently located box next to the couch and dried my tears. "Aren't you being awfully direct for a therapist? Aren't shrinks supposed to listen and question? Lead the patient to a greater understanding?"

"You're deflecting again. But all right, yes, I'm being more direct than usual. Harry suggested that I might need to be more active with you."

"I think I'm insulted . . ."

We both grinned.

"Tell me how you met Harry," Hoffman instructed.

"My wife intervened for me, and the Chairman sent Harry."

"Your wife intervened?"

"Yes."

"The woman you practically killed?"

"Yes," I replied through gritted teeth.

"The woman who loved you so much that she intervened with the Chairman on your behalf?"

"Yes, but . . . I . . ."

"Don't you think that if your wife intervened for you she has forgiven you for anything and everything you had done? Don't you think her love was deep enough that she would forgive you?"

The tears came again, and I looked at the floor. "Yes . . . she would."

"Many people never experience love like that." He paused, and I realized he was waiting for me to look at him. When I did, he said, "You are very fortunate to have had that kind of love in your life."

"I know. I'm a lucky guy."

* * *

On the sidewalk outside Hoffman's building, I called Harry's name softly. He appeared instantly.

"Yes?" He cocked one eyebrow to demonstrate that he was curious.

"Could you please take me to the 20th Precinct? I'd like to see how the search for Marissa is going."

"A reasonable request. Especially by your standards."

Before I could issue a snappy rejoinder, we were standing in Lieutenant Han's office. "Are we in invisible mode?"

He cocked the eyebrow again; this time the expression struck me as annoyed. It was remarkable how much emotion he could communicate with such limited facial movement.

Detective Luker was saying, "A couple of people at Enthousiaste confirmed Marissa Carvajal was there with McGill."

Islas added, "The case against her is pretty damn tight."

Han grimaced. "Now all we have to do is arrest her. Where are we on notifications to other law enforcement?"

Luker checked her notebook, "The FBI and TSA were notified since McGill's death might have national security implications, and we're not sure how far she might try to run."

"Nice touch," Han said.

"Thanks." She looked down at her notebook again, "We cast a wider net than we discussed with you yesterday: local cops in every state in New England, New Jersey, Pennsylvania, and New York, of course. And we talked to the Port Authority cops."

"What about the media?"

"All the local news shows were talking about the hunt for Marissa Carvajal as a person of interest last night at 11. CNN, Fox News, and MSNBC also picked it up. A bunch of news websites are running it, too."

"It's only a matter of time," Islas said. "She can't stay hidden forever."

I looked at Harry and hitched my thumb over my shoulder in a "let's get out of here" gesture. He obligingly repositioned us on the sidewalk outside the precinct.

"I hate to say it," I said, "but Detective Islas is correct: it's only a matter of time."

"What are you going to do next?"

"I don't know." I shook my head in exasperation. "I don't suppose the Chairman would do his forgetting thing."

"What forgetting thing?"

"Well, he makes everyone I contact on one of these cases forget me, right? Why not have all the police and media forget Marissa?"

"And the thousands of people who've seen the media reports? And should the Chairman—and you—ignore the fact that Jackson McGill's killer is still out there?"

"Okay, sorry. I should leave the cosmic thinking to you and the Chairman."

"It would be best."

"Could you do me a favor and whoosh me to Café Sabatini? The place on the Upper West Side—"

"I know where it is. Why would I do that?"

"I asked as a *favor*; there's no hard and fast reason that you should do it."

"Shouldn't you be pursuing the real killer?"

"I told you, I have no idea what my next step should be. I think the real killer is someone or someones from Cú Chulainn and SHK Dragon, but I can't prove a thing. But

Marissa is safe if she stays at the Selkirks. Maybe if she hides long enough, we can force the hand of the killer."

"In other words, since you have no plan, you are going to wait."

"Yes. Not the worst strategy in the world."

"And while you wait you want to see Kim Gannon at Café Sabatini."

"Yes."

"And you want me to transport you there?"

"Yes, please."

He flashed his Mona Lisa smile and disappeared. I was still standing outside the precinct.

"Well, thank you very much," I said to myself and trudged to the subway.

*   *   *

As I climbed the steps of the Broadway and West 72nd Street subway station to street level, I dug Kim Gannon's card out of my wallet. It was a creamy white, embossed card. Simple and expensive. Exactly what I would have expected from Kim. I carefully rubbed my thumb over her name. What the hell is with you, Tyrrell? Why are you stalling? I looked up away from the card and north up Broadway toward Café Sabatini. I couldn't pick out the café's storefront amongst the other retail establishments. Almost all of them had Christmas lights flashing in their windows, making it impossible to tell them apart. I had a nervous flutter—a sensation I hadn't had since the first time I ever called Maggie for a date. A sensation I first experienced when I was thirteen-years old, calling Alice McDonnell to ask her to a junior-high dance—my first-ever request to a girl for a date. I took a very deep breath and slowly exhaled. The nervous flutter abated but didn't disappear. Oh for crying out loud, Tyrrell, you are—ostensibly—a grown man. Just make the damn call.

I dialed the mobile number listed on the card.

"Hello, this is Kim," came the answer.

"Hi. This is Jack Tyrrell—"

"Government-trained private detective/troubleshooter."

"You remembered me."

"You're hard to forget."

"Thanks. I guess."

She laughed. "What can I do for you?"

"Any chance you'd be free to meet me at Café Sabatini sometime soon? I happen to be in the neighborhood, and I was hoping—"

"Sure, that'd be nice. About twenty minutes?"

"Great, see you there."

To fill the time between now and when my date—was Kim a date?—would arrive at Café Sabatini, I wandered over to the street where I lived. Unfortunately for me, the boys and girls who worked for Cú Chulainn and SHK Dragon still had my place staked out. A Chevy Impala was parked right across the street from the stoop leading to my front door. A bit farther west, a black Tahoe was parked. From my vantage point near the corner, I couldn't see the faces of the occupants of the vehicles. Whoever they were, they were annoying the ever-loving crap out of me. My life had turned into the Thomas Wolfe novel *You Can't Go Home Again*. If I hadn't had a date with Kim in a few minutes, I probably would have done something aggressive and stupid. Instead, I headed to the land of cappuccino and the beautiful redhead.

Kim was at a table when I arrived. "I'm sorry, am I late?" I blurted.

"No, I got here faster than I thought I would. But I haven't ordered yet."

"Allow me."

We both had cappuccinos and biscotti. I ordered and paid, and the barista offered to bring them to the table when the drinks were ready.

"I'm glad you called," Kim said as I sat down opposite her. "But should I take it as a bad sign that you only asked me to coffee and not dinner?"

"Ah . . . no." I paused as the barista placed our drinks and biscotti in front of us. "This was an opportunistic thing, seize the moment."

"In that case, thank you."

"You're welcome."

"How's your mission statement and marketing plan going?" she asked.

"I've been a little too busy to pay much attention to my marketing issues."

"Busy?" she pointed to my cheek. "Or getting beaten up?"

"I extricated myself from a precarious position. Given the givens, a successful outcome."

"Hmmm," she said, pursing her lips as she continued to consider my cheek. "Maybe you don't have marketing issues. How's your health plan?"

"Adequate to my needs."

"Okay, I'm getting the impression this is an aspect of your business you'd rather not discuss." She drank some cappuccino and used her napkin to wipe a little bit of white froth from her lips. "Changing the subject: How do you get the business you get now?"

I thought that over for a moment. "Referrals."

"All of your business is referral?"

"Yup."

"You must be an amazing troubleshooter."

"I work with the best. Makes being amazing easy." I smiled, thinking to myself: You have no idea.

Kim returned my smile, sipped more cappuccino, and said, "Let's not talk business."

"Fine by me. What would you like to talk about?"

"We established that we're both available. How come you're available? Are you divorced? Or recently out of a long-term relationship? Or so impossibly weird that no one can stand to be in a relationship with you?"

"Impossibly weird."

She laughed. She was a gorgeous woman no matter what her expression, but when she smiled or laughed, she was radiant. The kind of woman who made lyricists wax about a heart skipping a beat. I know that's how I felt. Whoa, slow down, Tyrrell.

"Really, what's your problem?" she asked, still laughing.

"Wait, we've gone from the reason I'm available to my problem?"

"Poor choice of words. How 'bout your situation? What's your situation?"

"I hate to dampen the mood, but there's no light-hearted way to answer. I'm . . . a widower."

She was serious. "I'm sorry."

"Thank you."

"Did she . . . die recently?"

"About five-and-a-half years ago."

"Oh."

There was an awkward pause. I had the distinct impression that Kim really wanted to ask more but couldn't think of a polite way to do it. I could have made some kind of weak joke, which she probably would have accepted with relief, and we would change the subject. Or I could be straight with her. But no jokes came to mind, and even though this was only our second time having cappuccino, I wanted to be honest with her.

"I'm guessing that right now, you'd love it if there was a graceful way to change the subject. But you're also probably curious. . . . I'll tell you what happened—"

"You don't have to do that. It's none of my business."

"Thanks, but I want to get to know you. I'd like to tell you what happened, and if you decide you want nothing to do with me after that, well, that's your choice."

"Why do I feel I need something stronger than cappuccino to drink?"

I smiled even though I didn't feel like smiling. "My wife and I were shot on the front steps of our brownstone by someone trying to kill me. She died. I was hit, too, but after a few weeks in the hospital, I was almost as good as new."

"Oh my God," she said slowly, "I remember hearing about that in the news. That was in this neighborhood, wasn't it? Is that right?"

"Yes, we were the lucky winners of free bullets courtesy of the mob."

"I'm so sorry."

"Thanks. I appreciate your feeling, but . . . it was my . . . fault. I took a bribe from a mobbed-up guy, I didn't deliver, and my wife was murdered as a result."

Kim said nothing. How do you reply to a story like that when you're only having your second cappuccino together?

"I, uh . . . I could try and give you a long explanation about what a pathetic shit I was to take the bribe and . . . well, there's no point. My wife helped me to . . . my wife's memory helped me to turn my life around. It seemed the least I could do after I got her killed."

Kim's eyes were large and teary. She stretched her right hand out and gave my left hand a squeeze.

"Look, I, uh . . . I understand if this is all a helluva lot more than you bargained for. If you want me to go—"

"No," she cut me off with a husky whisper. "No, please don't go. I don't think any man has ever been that honest with me."

I shrugged. I wasn't capable of repartee or even a weak grin.

"Your troubleshooting business, do you help people? Is that what you meant by turning your life around?"

"Yup."

"You really loved your wife, didn't you?"

Admitting that I loved my late wife to another woman seemed a poor way to proceed in terms of developing a new relationship, but what choice did I have? "She was the love of my life."

"And you were hers?"

"I think so."

"Lucky guy."

"Very lucky."

"They say that once you've loved someone like that, you've created the ability in yourself to love again. Do you think that's true?"

"I hope so."

Kim gave my hand another squeeze, then let go to wipe a tear from her cheek. "Boy, you are the most unusual date I've ever had."

"I told you: impossibly weird."

She grinned, "Not *impossibly*."

"Thanks for making the distinction."

"Are you going to call me again?"

"I'd like to. May I?"

"Please. I really want you to."

"Good," I said, "because next time it's your turn to reveal all the bizarre details of your past love life."

"We'll see about that."

"Wait a minute, I bare my soul to you, and you give me a conditional commitment to respond in kind?"

"Yes, that's an accurate appraisal of the situation."

"That's not fair."

"I'm not fair. But I am tantalizing. And fun."

"Yes, you are definitely tantalizing."

She treated me to one of her radiant smiles. We'd successfully navigated the rapids of my past and were flirting for the future. Not bad for a second cup of cappuccino.

And that was the moment at which Harry came through the front door of the café, took a step inside, saw me, and beckoned me to come to him.

"Excuse me," I said to Kim, "but one of my, uh, colleagues just stepped in."

She turned in Harry's direction. "Were you expecting him?"

"No, unexpected. And unpleasant." I stood and walked to Harry. "What's up?"

"We need to go to Rye. Now." He spoke with quiet urgency.

"Why?"

"Savannah Faringer's people found Marissa. A team from Cú Chulainn and SHK Dragon is on its way."

"Oh, shit." I glanced over my shoulder at Kim then back at Harry. "I need to say goodbye. Then we'll leave."

I stepped back over to our table. "I'm sorry about this, but—"

"Someone's in trouble. You have to go."

"Yes." I hesitated, awkwardly leaning over the table. She gave me the tiniest of nods, and I leaned in all the way and kissed her softly on the mouth.

"Call me," she said.

"I will." I turned toward Harry, stopped, twisted back to Kim. "Listen, if I . . . If I don't call, please know that I wanted to. If I don't call, it's because I can't."

"You'll call."

"I hope so."

Harry and I walked outside Café Sabatini.

"I need to get into my apartment without anyone noticing."

"Why?"

"I need more weapons. Heavy weapons."

He nodded and in less time than it takes to read this sentence, we were in my living room. During the last case I had worked for Harry, an old friend from my Afghanistan days, a CIA agent named Alex Cranston, had helped me take on a Russian Mafia chief. Among other things, Alex had procured a diverse and lethal set of weapons. Really good stuff if you go in for fire fights with Russian mobsters or private security types like Cú Chulainn and SHK Dragon. My hope was that I wouldn't need this stuff, but I didn't want to be caught needing it and not having it.

The last time I'd been headed to my apartment, I'd spotted Reznik with his cinderblock chin. Cinderblock hands, too. At the time, I'd thought he was trouble and was convinced he was going to search my apartment with dedication and destructiveness. Unfortunately, I had been correct. He'd trashed my place. Books and CDs were scattered all over. The television screen had been smashed and the entertainment system torn up. The front closet was open, and coats had had their linings torn out then had been tossed to the floor. Every pair of shoes had been pulled apart to be sure there was nothing inside the soles. Furniture had been smashed and/or cut open.

But that was all stuff. It could be replaced. Don't get me wrong, I was royally pissed off that cinderblock chin had done this. But the thing that really got to me? He'd smashed the frames of three photos of Maggie and torn the photos to pieces. I leaned over and picked up what was left of one of them—Maggie's left eye looking at me from a chunk of broken frame.

Harry asked softly, "Are you all right?"

"No. This guy wanted to fuck with me. He and I will settle up, and then I'll be fine."

"Are you planning to kill him?"

"No. I'm *hoping* to kill him." I put the shattered photo down and walked into my bedroom. The mattress and pillows were a fluffy disaster area. The photo of Maggie on my night table had received the same treatment as the photos in the living room. The night table was more like kindling than table.

Thanks to the way cinderblock chin had treated my place, he had confirmed something about himself: He took his work personally. He wanted this to be about me and him.

I shook my head at the destruction and stepped to my closet. The door was hanging off the lower hinge, and the top one had been pulled loose. The clothes were all in a heap on the floor. The hanging rod had been broken. The shelf above the clothes had been pulled out and the sweaters and sweatshirts that I'd stored there were now on the bedroom floor.

Harry asked, "Did he find it?"

"No," I grinned. "Mr. Destructo was a wee bit too angry for his own good. He even saved me the trouble of taking all the hanging clothes off the rod and pulling out the rod." I used my phone to send a text to a digital lock, and the right side closet wall popped open about an inch. I had built a false wall, creating a secret cabinet about a foot deep, seven-feet tall, and two-feet wide. I pulled the false wall open, exposing a black duffle-pack of ballistic nylon. The duffle was filled with the lethal tools of my sometime violent trade. I lifted the duffle out and pushed the door shut until it clicked, locking again.

I sorted through the piles of clothing until I found what I wanted: a pair of dark gray cargo pants, loose fitting for action and with huge pockets for ammo, guns, and grenades. I took off the cotton sweater I was wearing courtesy of Andrew Selkirk and pulled on a black T-shirt and a dark gray sweater that matched the pants. A hunter's vest in black went over the sweater, and my ensemble was topped off by my parka. I hefted the duffle over my shoulder and slipped my arms through the pack straps. There was a lot of firepower inside that duffle.

"Why did you come warn me at the café? You've never done that before."

"The Chairman gives people what they need. You needed a warning if you were going to help Marissa, and she *needs* help. *Now.*"

"Okay, then. Where are the bad guys now?"

Harry looked up and then to me. "The team is approaching the Selkirks' community gate in two SUVs."

"Okay." I took a deep breath. "Please take me to the Selkirks' front yard, under the huge pine to the right of the house as you face the door."

And just like that, we were in the front yard, under the pine. The afternoon was cloudy, making it dark under the pine's thick branches. The air felt as if snow was on the way, but I wasn't sure snow was coming. I wish I could have said the same about the imminent arrival of a bunch of heavily armed hostiles.

13

I pulled the duffle off of my back, laid it on the ground, and unzipped it. I pulled out an M16 assault rifle and a couple of extra ammo clips. While I was at it, I added an Uzi submachine gun to my under-the-pine arsenal, two smoke grenades and two concussion grenades. All of the weapons were on the ground, on the side of the tree farthest from the house, virtually invisible in the cloudy-day darkness.

Shrugging into the duffle-pack again, I asked, "How soon?"

Harry replied, "They are inside the main gate."

"We've got two minutes. Maybe." I scanned the yard and ran for the far side, past the Selkirks' BMW parked in the driveway, to some very healthy rhododendrons that would provide a lot of cover despite their leaves being curled by the cold. Nothing that would stop a bullet, mind you, but pretty hard to see through. I again took off the duffle and opened it. I took off my coat and slipped on a shoulder holster, pulled out a Ruger SR9 with a 17-round clip, checked it, and tucked the pistol into the holster. I took another Uzi and more grenades out of the duffle and laid them on the ground. A knife with four-inch blade went into a specially designed pants pocket that functioned as a sheath. Finally I took out a second Ruger and four 17-round clips. I stuffed the clips in various pockets, but kept the pistol in hand. My coat and the duffle were shoved deep into the rhododendron thicket.

There was no sign of anyone in the large yard, but I heard the soft hum of engines. Hard to tell how far away, but I had a feeling my evil playmates were about to show up. I turned to Harry—but there was no Harry. I spun around, looking for him. He was gone.

I whispered into the air, "Really? You don't think I *need* you right now?"

There was no answer. I hadn't expected one.

Then the bad guys arrived. I sensed them before I saw them. They were dressed in black coveralls with black knit ski masks. I'm sure they were unappealing looking under the masks, but there was something eerie about six, all-black figures advancing through the Selkirks' vast front yard. They approached in three teams of two, each team with a leader and a "wingman" protecting his flank. The teams were spread out and staggered; the two pairs on the outside protected the flanks of the leading team, the team on point in the center of the formation. I had to admit it was a nice set-up. They weren't bunched together to provide someone like me with easy targets. And they moved quickly and quietly, each carrying an automatic pistol with a suppressor. Just my luck: They were professionals and ready for some close-quarters combat.

I could be quick and quiet, too, and I was definitely prepared for close-quarters mayhem. I retreated through the bushes and circled behind the wedge of the oncoming teams. The wingman of the trailing team, the last man in the formation, was only a few yards ahead of me. I held my pistol by the barrel, rushed silently behind him as he was looking toward the house and not checking his back trail. He heard me or felt me as I lifted my arm to club him with the pistol butt. He spun around, his left arm high to block my blow, as his right hand raised his gun at me. I slammed his gun down with my left hand. The butt of my gun hammered onto his shoulder and he fired the gun. The bullet tore at my left side.

For the first moment there was no pain, so I acted fast, clubbing the wingman again, which sent him bouncing a the tree to the ground. Unfortunately, the gun shot had attracted the attention of the entire formation. His teammate came back toward us. The other two teams broke for the house in a run, staying focused on their mission.

Another shot, this time from the teammate. It missed. I shot him twice in the chest, dropping him in his tracks. Behind me I heard a groan and turned to see the wingman roll over, take aim, and pull the trigger again. This bullet whined past me. I dove for the ground, rolled to a prone shooting position, steadied my right hand with my left, and fired four times. I only hit the wingman twice, but twice was enough.

I snaked my way through bushes and small trees until I could see the side of the house. There was no sign of the other four men. I crawled back to the wingman and felt for a pulse. Nothing. I pulled off his ski mask. It was Liào, the quiet member of the Chinese team. I checked his teammate to see if he was dead. He was. I tugged off his mask and revealed Wei—the man with the impeccable English.

"Shit," I hissed angrily into the air. "Come on, Harry. I'm glad I don't have to worry about these two, but seriously, is it part of the Chairman's plan that I do all this killing? I'm not the Angel of Death. . . . anyway, I don't want to be."

Once again, there was no sign of Harry, never mind a reply of any sort.

"Harry, you and I need a new way of dealing with this kind of situation," I whispered. "Please put that on the agenda for our next serious conversation, okay?" I stood, using a tree as cover, and checked the house. I didn't hear anything coming from inside. The last thing I wanted to attempt was a frontal assault on a position occupied by an overwhelming force with heavy weapons and holding prisoners. But getting to the house without being seen was going to be tricky—men could be watching from various windows, but they would be invisible to me.

There were smoke grenades under the rhododendron thicket. There was a first-aid kit, too. My left side had begun to burn and hurt like hell. I lifted the hunter's vest, pealed back the torn edges of my sweater and T-shirt, and inspected the wound. It was a ragged trench through the flesh of my love handle, not deep but bleeding and getting more painful by the moment. Since I needed to go get the smoke grenades, it made sense to use the first aid kit and minister to myself at the same time. But quickly. Very quickly. I scrambled to the rhododendrons, crawled underneath the leaves to the duffle, yanked out the first-aid kit, and went to work. I poured peroxide over the wound, not a fun activity, then applied a thick, gooey wad of antiseptic cream to the wound, gently spreading the goo with a fingertip. This was not your run-of-the-mill first-aid kit. It not only contained a can of Xylocaine, which I sprayed all over the wound, and after a few seconds, its numbing kicked in. The kit also contained a surgical stapler I took a deep breath, said "Don't try this at home, kids," to myself, used my left hand to close the wound as much as possible, and then stapled it shut with my right. Each staple was no damn fun at all, and by the sixth I felt woozy. But the wound was tightly closed, and after another deep breath, more Xylocaine spray, and a couple of ibuprofen tabs for pain, I felt better. Almost as good as new. I admit that "almost as good as new" was overstating the case, but I felt good enough to do whatever I was going to have to do next.

I slung one of the Uzis over my right shoulder, sliding a couple of extra clips into the large pockets in my cargo pants. A fresh clip went into the Ruger I'd used to kill the two men I'd killed. I inched my way on my belly toward the yard. I stopped just before I reached the lawn, still under the cover of the branches that drooped over the edge of the brown, winter grass. No one was visible through the windows, and there had been no gunshots since the four surviving members of the assault team had gone inside. I watched and listened for a few minutes, but there were no signs of any activity in the house.

Edging backward, I got off my belly and knelt as soon as there was headroom under the rhododendron. I placed four grenades, three smoke and one concussion, on the ground. I was about to make a lot of noise and set off a small cloud of smoke—which might attract unwanted attention from the neighbors? And the neighbors might summon the police and/or fire departments. I twisted around to find the nearest houses. The closest mansion—there were no Plane Jane houses in this community—was at least three hundred feet away. A very slight breeze was blowing toward the water. Would the distance, the gentle wind, and the walls around the houses, help buffer the sound? Buffer it enough for me to get away with my attack on the Selkirk place? Did I really have a choice?

No choice at all. Time to go.

I pulled the pin on a smoke grenade and tossed it about halfway to the house; the second, closer to the house, hit the ground and exploded in a cloud a couple of seconds later. The third grenade was the concussion baby. I aimed for and hit the side of the house under the living room windows. It exploded with a sharp crack, and the windows shattered. The last smoke grenade followed. All of the smoke and the concussion explosion had occurred within seconds. I hoped it was all confusing enough to get me to the house. I jumped out of the rhododendrons, unslung the Uzi, and strafed the ground floor windows, aiming high enough to make sure I didn't hit any of my friendlies who might be standing on that level. I ran toward the BMW, continuing to fire along the front of the house. Windows shattered, and the front door splintered, the wooden shards hanging askew on the hinges. I crouched behind the BMW, slapped a fresh clip into the Uzi, and carefully peered around the car's front end to see if anyone in the house had decided to shoot into the smoke cloud.

A shadow moved in the billowing smoke around the living room window, and the flat, suppressed crack of an automatic erupted twice. I pulled out my Ruger, very carefully lined up my shot, and took out the shadowy gunman. I would have preferred to use a quick burst from the Uzi, but I couldn't take the chance on hurting the hostages. As soon as I shot the attacker—three down, three to go—I ran behind the BMW. I heard bullets hitting the car and thought that's going to leave a mark. Careful to keep the car between me and the living room window, I ran out into the already dissipating smoke cloud over the front yard, then headed to my left around the corner of the house.

The windows on the side of the house were still intact, but being close, I could see across the dining room and the front hallway into the front part of the living room.

Standing well back from the shattered windows, out of sight from most of the front yard, two of the masked attackers were signaling to each other. Actually only the shorter attacker was gesticulating to the other. If I read their body English correctly, they were my old acquaintances Bouchard and Flynn. Bouchard seemed to want Flynn to go to the back of the house, exit, search, and destroy. Okay, the search and destroy mission was surmise on my part, but I was pretty confident I was right. The attacker I thought was Flynn crept into the front hallway and out of sight toward the back of the house.

I dropped below the window sill and scuttled toward the backyard as fast and quietly as I could. I reached the evergreen hedge that bordered the patio outside the den only seconds before one of the glass doors slid open. I dropped behind the hedge, which was barely tall enough to cover me. My Ruger was in my right hand, my left hand was planted on the ground to help me push up into a kneeling position. Easier to shoot from my knees than through the hedge.

The glass door stopped when it was open about a foot and a half. The attacker, mask still on, stepped through the opening very slowly and silently. If this was Flynn, he was showing more patience and style than I would have given him credit for. Once he was completely outside, he didn't bother to shut the door, instead, he stopped in the center of the patio and scanned all around for sight of his enemy: me. Satisfied that he was alone, the attacker took a step in my direction.

I popped up, but he had lightning reflexes and fired. I shot him twice, even as I felt something hit my left shoulder. His bullet spun me around, and I crashed to the ground, dazed. I wasn't sure how badly hurt I was. There was a lot pain and bleeding.

After what was probably only a minute, I crawled behind the hedge and checked the house. No one had come to see what was going on. Had they not heard the gunfire? Or had they heard and not cared? Maybe they were leaving, which meant they were taking Marissa. I had to get moving. I staggered to my feet, walked to the attacker, checked his pulse, confirmed he was dead, and pulled off his mask. It was Flynn. I straightened up and walked cautiously through the open glass door.

Although confused, I seemed to be capable of putting together a couple of coherent thoughts together. Since I had spotted Bouchard and Flynn in the living room, I assumed that Bouchard and the sixth teammate were still there, probably guarding their hostages. I know it's dangerous to assume, but assuming was about the limit of my cerebral abilities at that moment. Instead of going toward the front door and entering the living room from the hallway, I crossed the kitchen, went through a short hallway to the door at the rear part of the living room. I stood and listened for a minute or two. Nothing. I took a deep breath and kicked the door open.

Bursting into the room, I dove for the floor and rolled, my pistol at the ready. As I rolled, I saw the Selkirks,

Otto, and Frieta spread out on the floor, each in a puddle of blood. Marissa was duct-taped to an over-stuffed, upholstered chair. Her eyes went wide as I made my sudden entrance. The two masked attackers wheeled toward me, guns firing.

Bullets tore into the floor and the furniture, smashed the rear windows, and exploded Christmas tree ornaments. I fired until I was out of ammo. Rolling on the ground, aiming, and shooting is nowhere near as easy as it looks in the movies. But I got lucky. By the time my gun clicked empty, the attackers were no longer firing either. I inserted a new clip into my Ruger and slowly walked toward the masked marauders.

The first thing I noticed is that they were breathing. And both were bleeding from wounds that at a quick glance looked non-lethal: one had been hit in the shoulder and a leg, the other in an arm and a leg.

"Oh, thank God," I said, looking up.

I kicked their weapons away, quickly patted them down to make sure they weren't carrying anything else, and found they were carrying pistols. I tossed their pistols out into the hall—then pulled off the ski masks. Bouchard and the black woman who been one of the attackers in the Cú Chulainn elevator. Both women were unconscious and likely to remain so.

My relief at finding someone who wasn't dead was short-lived. The Selkirks, Otto, and Frieta had all had their throats slashed. Four innocent people doing the Chairman's bidding and trying to help Marissa—all dead for their trouble.

Marissa made some indeterminate noise behind her duct-tape gag.

"Oh, I'm sorry . . ." I stepped toward her, but her eyes went wide. I twisted sideways to see—

Reznik stood behind me. He grinned tightly, his hands empty. I took that as a very bad sign—he didn't need a weapon. I brought my gun up as fast as I could, but I was too slow. Even if I had been in perfect health at that second, I still would have been too slow for Reznik. His right fist slammed into my jaw and sent me careering backward. I tripped over Otto's outstretched arm and went down on one knee. Reznik loomed over me, winding up for another blow and hitting me again. My head felt as if it exploded. And then I felt nothing at all.

* * *

Was I dead? Was I about to float upward and look down and see my corpse on the floor? I had a vague consciousness, but I couldn't tell you if that consciousness was located in my skull or floating in the ether.

But no, I wasn't out-of-body. Something pressed against my neck, about where my pulse would be. The something was three fingers. Three large fingers. Reznik. My killer. The fingers left my throat and I heard a his deep voice muse, "I would have preferred to be more methodical in dealing with you, but. . . ." He sighed as his voice trailed off. Maybe I missed his tone—I have to admit I was not at my perceptive best—but his sigh was not the plaintive moan of a romantic heroine. It was a disappointed groan.

The soft padding of footsteps on the living room carpet made me think he was leaving me for dead. After all, he had been unable to find my pulse. That must mean I had, indeed, expired. I wondered if Harry would be upset. I wondered if I'd get to meet the Chairman face-to-face.

Maybe I could see Maggie again. There were lots of things worse than dying if death would reunite me with Maggie.

A gun fired, but not into me. If I could feel Reznik's fingers on my pulse, I would have felt a bullet, right? More footsteps, another gunshot. Still no bullets in me.

"Let's go," Reznik said. I couldn't hear an answer, but if he was speaking to Marissa, there wouldn't be an answer. Why was he taking her away? I tried to open my eyes, but they didn't seem to work. I couldn't be sure if my eyes were open but unseeing, or the eyelids wouldn't open. Why couldn't I see? Was I dead? My consciousness faded away. . . .

* * *

The smell of burning wood drifted into my nose. I loved the smell of a campfire. Wasn't crazy about the smoky way my clothes smelled afterward, but the aroma of burning wood was fabulous. Yes, definitely a campfire; I could hear the crackling, hissing, and popping of the flames as they consumed the wood. Do they have campfires in heaven? Was this some kind of welcome to my afterlife?

"Jack?" Harry said. His hand was on my good shoulder, my right, and he gently rocked my body. "Jack?"

I opened my eyes. Normally, opening my eyes is not an enormous task, but right that minute, it seemed very hard. My left eyelid rose very slowly, as if it were a heavy door being pulled up and open. My right lid refused to cooperate and stayed closed.

It was dusk, and a light snow was falling. I knew this because I felt the cold, wet flakes touching my face. I was outside the Selkirks' house, lying on the flagstones of their patio. I tried to focus my one eye on Harry.

"Why are we outside?"

He pointed in the direction of the house. I turned toward it—my neck was operating as slowly as my left eyelid—and saw that the Selkirks' beautiful house was engulfed in fire.

"Oh, no," I pushed myself to a kneeling position. "No. . . ." I suddenly remembered, "What about the two women, Bouchard and the other?"

"Reznik killed them before he left."

My mind was beginning to work again, "With my gun?"

Harry pointed to the ground. There sat my Ruger.

"What happened to the members of the assault team that I shot outside the house?"

"They're all inside, along with all of their weapons."

"Reznik wanted this to look like a home invasion gone wrong." I said the words almost without thought, years of experience speaking without being driven by the brain. But as I spoke, the import of what I said struck me. "I was supposed to be inside, too. Did you pull me out?"

Harry shrugged, "You needed help."

"That's for sure." I reached for the Ruger, wiped it off on my sweater, and holding it by the trigger guard, tossed it into the fire. I turned to Harry, "Unregistered weapon."

"Unregistered weapons can be dangerous," he deadpanned.

"Harry, did you just make a joke?"

"It seemed an opportune moment."

"Whoa, two for two. Nice." I smiled and watched as a large chunk of the roof collapsed. I could feel the heat. "Is the fire department on the way?"

"They are rolling now. About three minutes."

"I guess it would be good if we were invisible."

"We are."

"Good . . . good," I slowly stood. "Did Reznik take Marissa back into the city?"

"Yes."

"But he's not handing her over to the police, is he?"

"No."

"So we've got some time before he makes his next move, right?"

"A little."

"You're such a comfort." I concentrated on opening my right eye and failed. "I'm afraid to ask, but what's wrong with my right eye?"

"It's crusted over with blood. That's all."

"My blood?"

"No, Otto's. You fell into the blood from his slashed throat the last time Reznik hit you."

"Guess I'd better wash it off." I turned my back on the burning house and walked to the Sound. I found the stone steps and made my way down to the water. I knelt on the last step above the surface and dipped my head into the bracingly cold salt water. I stayed under as long as I could hold my breath, gently rubbing my right eye, feeling the crusty blood washing away. After about a minute, I rose, gently wiped my face dry with a sweater sleeve, and opened my eye. Worked just fine.

I walked up the steps. Harry waited for me at the top of the steps. We looked out at the water for a moment, and then, almost as if by mutual consent, at the fire that had now consumed the entire house and was actually burning a bit less ferociously now. The fire department would have nothing to do but water the embers of a completely destroyed home.

"Was I dead? Did the Chairman resurrect me?"

"No, you're not Lazarus. The Chairman doesn't perform major miracles when sleight of hand will work."

"What the hell does that mean?"

"It means it was easier to make Reznik think you were dead than to bring you back from the dead."

"Couldn't he have done the same thing for the Selkirks? For Otto and Frieta? Why the hell did he let them die?"

"Maybe it was their time."

"It was *their time*? Are you fucking with me? They were nice people; they were living up to the Mankind Is Our Business motto by taking care of Marissa—and they were killed for doing something nice?"

"There are two things you might want to remember: The Chairman didn't let them be killed—Reznik made a choice to kill them. And maybe their service helping Marissa was the completion of their mission. They were ready to go home."

"I thought they were home."

"This?" Harry pointed at the house. "That was not their home."

"Okay, enough. How much time before Reznik gets Marissa wherever he's taking her?"

"Fifteen or twenty minutes."

"Let's get my stuff and get out of here."

We walked around the right side of the house, and as we came around to the front of the house, we could see the burned out, smoldering BMW in the driveway. A bit of fiery debris must have exploded out of the house and touched off the BMW. Maybe sparks had landed in the gas that leaked when the bad guys shot it up.

Four fire trucks roared down the driveway and fire fighters hopped down and began deploying hoses. A fire fighter sprayed down the BMW with an extinguisher. A red-and-white SUV rolled onto the lawn near the trucks and two older men stepped out and assumed command roles.

The first thing I did when we reached the equipment still sitting under the rhododendron was find the first aid kit,. I peeled off the hunter's vest, sweater, and T-shirt, and sprayed Xylocaine all over my left shoulder. I had Harry hold a flashlight from the duffle on the wound, and I got to work with the antiseptic cream, gauze pads and surgical tape. This one was not even as deep as the one in my love handle.

As I attended to my medical needs, I said, "Are these shallow wounds your handiwork?"

"I don't understand you."

"I got shot twice tonight, and neither bullet caused much damage. That's an awful lot of luck. Although, if you were giving me some luck, how 'bout having the bullets miss completely?"

He turned away and watched the fire fighters. I carefully repacked the weapons and grenades in the duffle.

"Let's go," I pointed across the dark yard toward the pine tree where the other weapons were stashed. We gave the fire vehicles a wide berth; our voices raised to carry over the rushing sound of water spewing out of the fire hoses, the crackling and hissing flames, and the occasional deep crunch as more of the house collapsed. Looking over the burning wreckage of what had been the living room, I saw lights on Long Island's north shore. It had been a beautiful home with nice people living in it.

I wondered if the Selkirks had realized they were in danger. Did they think the Chairman would save them? Were they disappointed when He didn't? Were they angry? I was furious, lost in an absolute fucking rage. I stopped walking and stared as the last of the burning structure collapsed into itself.

"Anger won't help," Harry said.

"I don't want to hear it."

"What do you want?'

"I want to tell the Chairman to go fuck himself."

Harry didn't blink at my rage or my profanity. "Go ahead."

"Go ahead what?"

"Tell the Chairman how you feel. He can take it."

I looked at the fire and felt the rage surging. I leaned back and screamed "Fuck You!" at the night sky.

"There's room for anger in your relationship with the Chairman."

"Yeah? Well fuck Him and fuck you, too."

Harry stood quietly, waiting patiently on me.

"I guess I should direct my anger at Reznik."

"That might be more appropriate."

"Why am I angry with the Chairman if Reznik is to blame?"

"Why do—"

"Stop it. Don't answer my question with a question."

"You're angry with the Chairman because you want him to be in control and to protect you and the people you like from bad things."

"But if the Chairman's in control, it means no free will, right?"

"Yes."

"Oh . . . crap."

"And . . . please don't become angrier when I say this, but it won't help to let rage drive your behavior toward Reznik."

"I need to stay focused on saving Marissa."

"Exactly."

"Okay, let's get going." I resumed walking toward the other stash of weapons. Once under the pine, I carefully packed the guns into the duffle. I paused in the middle of packing, looking at the guns in my hands and considering how easy it was to kill for some people. Reznik had murdered his own assault group and killed innocent bystanders like the Selkirks, Otto and Freita. But not Marissa. At least, not yet . . .

"Why did they kidnap Marissa?" I asked.

"I don't know. Was that a rhetorical question?"

"Yes, it was. They could have confirmed her location and ratted her out to the police, no messy shooting and killing. Much cleaner, but they didn't handle it that way."

"They must need her for something."

"Yup." I slid the last gun into the duffle, zipped it up, and slipped my arms through the straps to carry it on my back. "Reznik's going to kill her but make it look like suicide. Probably have her write a note taking the blame for McGill's murder and saying her guilt has driven her to this final action. When the police find her and the note, they'll close the case."

"Leaving Savannah Faringer free to merge Cú Chulainn and SHK Dragon." Harry paused, and I would have sworn I saw him frowning in confusion. As with all of Harry's facial expressions, this was minimal. I couldn't be sure I'd even seen it. "Where do you think Reznik will fake her suicide?"

"That's a good question. I don't suppose you could ask . . .?" I pointed a finger skyward.

He shook his head, looked skyward, then at me almost immediately, "No."

"You mean 'no' you can't ask? Or you asked, and the answer was 'no'?"

"The answer was 'no.'"

"But how the hell am I—wait a minute, is this one of those *need* things? I don't need this answer and that's why it's not being given to me."

"That's correct."

"You must be kidding—I don't need this?"

"Don't confuse urgency with need."

"What the hell does that mean?"

"You feel that this is imperative for you to know where Reznik is taking Marissa. But that does not make it a necessity."

I sighed, "When this is over, I'm going to give you such a beating . . . okay, I don't need this information, which means I can figure it out on my own, right?"

"Right."

"Since I don't know where Reznik is taking Marissa, I *need* to talk with someone who does know."

"Yes."

"Savannah Faringer?"

"Yes."

"Do I have enough time to get to Ms. Faringer, persuade her to tell me what I need to know, and save Marissa?"

"I hope so."

"You're not funny. Do I or don't I?"

Harry consulted the night sky and said, "Reznik won't reach his destination for another twenty minutes approximately. Once there, he'll have to coax Marissa into producing the note. Then he has to prepare the faux suicide and finally kill her."

"Which means . . .?"

"It's possible that you have forty minutes."

"Let's not dally then. Please whoosh me to Savannah Faringer."

14

Before I could make a joke or perceive a change in location, I was standing on the northeast corner of 57th Street and Park Avenue. Diagonally across the intersection, set back from both 57th Street and Park Avenue, on the southwest corner was a white and blue tower—the tallest residential building in all of New York. I had read about this incredibly thin, tall, and bland building in *The New York Times*. Its rooftop was even higher than that of One World Trade Center, but the building itself was dishwater-dull for every one of its almost fourteen hundred feet. I had read that the architect had been inspired by the design of a trash can. Who the hell would build something that tall and give it the look of a trash can? Despite my architectural misgivings, apartments in this building sold for tens of millions of dollars each.

"Does Ms. Faringer live there?" I asked.

"Yes. Sixty-seventh floor."

"Can you whoosh me inside her apartment?"

Harry quick-checked with the sky, "No."

"Oh, come on! Time is of the essence. And . . . I'm not exactly at my best."

"I'm sorry, but I believe the Chairman feels that it is not necessary."

"You believe? Don't you know? Don't you have the inside track?"

"All creatures with free will have to discern what the Chairman wants of them."

"Hmm. Not sure what I find most surprising about that statement: that you're a creature or that you have free will."

"Are we finished here?"

"Almost, are you telling me I don't need to be whooshed all the way to Savannah to accomplish my mission for Marissa?"

"That is my belief. Or . . ." he let his voice trail off.

"Or . . . maybe the Chairman doesn't intend for me to finish the mission. Maybe I've done my bit, and my death is . . . imminent."

"That could be the case."

"You're such a comfort. How far in can you whoosh me?"

Another quick check, and Harry replied, "To the freight elevator. I will override the security cameras and alarms, and you will be able to reach the sixty-seventh floor undetected."

"Just like the folks who murdered Jackson McGill."

"Turnabout is fair play."

I grinned, "Wow, a creature with free will and a budding sense of humor." I glanced upward. "Can you tell me what's waiting for me on sixty-seven?"

"Aside from Savannah Faringer?"

"Yes, aside from her."

"She has traveled with a four-person security team ever since McGill was killed."

"Do you know where they are in the apartment?"

"No."

The people on the sidewalk were passing us by as if we weren't there. "Are we invisible right now?"

"Yes."

I swung the duffle pack off of my shoulder and set it on the sidewalk. I yanked out a couple of smoke grenades and extra clips for my Rugers and stuffed them into the cargo pants pockets. I checked the two automatics, both held close-to-full clips.

"I'm not asking this to yank your chain, but . . ." I ignored Harry's raised eyebrows, ". . . would you please whoosh this duffle back into its hiding place in my apartment? I can't be lugging it around. And it's not the kind of thing you want to leave on a Park Avenue sidewalk."

"That makes good sense."

The duffle disappeared.

"Thank you. Okay, one or two more questions and then I'm ready to go. Are you coming with me?"

"No."

"Will you whoosh me out of there once I find out where Marissa is?"

"No."

"All right then. I guess I'll see you outside. Assuming I make it."

"Yes. Assuming."

I took a deep breath and said on the exhale, "Let's go."

And . . . I was standing in a cement hallway. Lots of cables and pipes were suspended on steel brackets just under the ceiling. There was a soft hum of machinery, maybe from a buildng generator, maybe from the elevators. I decided to walk toward the increasingly loud hum. Coming around a corner, I found a loading bay to my right and a large freight elevator to my left. The loading bay was empty, and the corrugated steel door to the street was closed tight. The elevator was open, ready, and waiting. A stack of neatly folded, quilted pads, the kind of thing you wrapped furniture in when moving, were in the corner of the elevator floor diagonally opposite the control panel. Next to the pads were a few coils of common clothesline. Very convenient if you needed to move a large china cabinet or a couch. Not much use to me in my current circumstances. I stepped in and pressed the button for the sixty-sixth floor.

The door clanked shut, as freight-elevator doors always seem to do, and the elevator rose slowly and steadily toward sixty-six. When the car stopped, I waited at the rear, Ruger at the ready, until the door had rolled open. I saw no one waiting for me, and when the door began to close, I stepped to the control panel, pushed the open-door button and walked off into an empty, cement corridor much like the one on the ground floor.

There were two doors. I tiptoed to the extra-wide one directly opposite the elevator, pulled it open, and confirmed that it led to the apartment. The other door was a standard-width affair, with a small window about five feet from the floor, and led to the building's fire stairs. I checked the stairwell through the window, then pushed the door open very, very slowly. I didn't want a creaky door alerting Savannah Faringer's security team on the floor above. One of the advantages of sneaking around a brand-new building is that it hasn't had time to develop the creaks and noises so common to older buildings. The fire stairs door had opened without the tiniest sound.

I checked my watch and realized I only had about thirty-two minutes to save Marissa. Thirty-two minutes in which to disable a security team of four, persuade Ms. Faringer to tell me where Marissa was, and finally stop Reznik from killing Marissa in a faux suicide. Much as I wanted to hustle up the stairs, kick in the door, and blast my way in, I had been very well trained and knew that being steady and stealthy was much more likely to accomplish my goal. Time for one last deep breath and then up the stairs as fast as I could silently climb them.

On the sixty-seventh floor, I delicately pulled the wide door open about a quarter-inch, peered through the slender opening, and spotted my first obstacle. The Hispanic woman from the attack in the Cú Chulainn elevator was sitting on a folding metal chair immediately outside the apartment door. I couldn't get a good look at her weapon, but if forced to make a guess, I would have said it was a Heckler & Koch submachine gun. Regardless of which HK model it was, it was a very nasty piece of business. With her right hand resting on the trigger guard, there was no possible way I could get to her before she sprayed me with most or all of the 30 rounds in the clip. She was an immovable object, and I was *not* an irresistible force.

Then again, was she immovable? I thought about that for a few seconds, turned away from the door, and hurried down the stairs to sixty-six and the freight elevator. I grabbed two of the packing pads along with a hunk of the clothesline and moved as fast as I could back up the stairs to sixty-seven.

Stainless steel grommets edged two sides of the approximately eight by eight foot square packing pads. Using my knife, I cut a pair of two-foot pieces of clothesline and knotted them into the grommets at the far end of one side of the pad. Then I climbed the standpipe behind the stairwell door and tied the pad to a pipe that ran above the door.

I climbed down, crouched below the level of the window, crossed to the other side of the door, and climbed a few stairs leading to sixty-eight. Leaning back toward the door, I grabbed the pipe. Holding myself at arm's length, I checked the Hispanic woman through the window. She was looking away from the door so I pulled the pad along the pipe like a curtain on its rod, covering the window. I froze for a long moment but heard nothing from the far side of the door. I walked down the stairs to the now-covered door. I unfolded the second pad and spread it over the lower steps leading to 68 to keep it handy. Then I slid my hand under the pad, found the door handle, and rattled it up and down.

The woman's metal chair scraped on the cement floor. I quickly went up three steps and held up the second pad with my arms spread wide to create a dark screen for myself. When the security woman came though the door, there would be nothing but darkness in front of her and to her side.

The door opened slowly; pulling the covering pad aside. I watched around one edge of the pad I held and could see the HK's barrel poke out from the door. There was the tiniest hesitation, then the woman lunged into the stairwell. Well, she tried to lunge. She would have made it, except I dropped my pad like a net on her.

We crashed to the floor. She grunted in pain as I landed on top of her. My arms were clamped around her, pinning her arms—and more importantly, her submachine gun—to her side. She tried desperately to wriggle free, but I used my legs to keep her helplessly pinned, then used the butt of one of my pistols to thump her on the head and knock her unconscious. I didn't feel too good about doing that, but her odds of surviving this encounter had skyrocketed, so I didn't feel too badly, either. I pulled back the pad and took the submachine gun from her fingers, patted her down, and grabbed two extra clips from her security-uniform coveralls. I also found and took a single key out of another pocket. I put the Heckler & Koch's safety on, placed the weapon and clips on the floor, and leaving her wrapped in the packing pad, I trussed her up with the clothesline. She was very slender for which I gave sincere thanks as I carried her down to sixty-six, and laid her inside the freight elevator.

Returning to sixty-seven, I slung the submachine gun over my right shoulder and carefully pulled a smoke grenade from one of my pants pockets. I slid under the packing pad that covered the still open door to the sixty-seventh floor into a small hallway leading to a steel door with a folding metal chair next to it. It was the apartment's service entrance, probably at the rear.

A doorbell button on one side of the door frame sat under a small, neat sign that read: 67A. I had a feeling there was no B—Savannah Faringer didn't seem to me to be the sharing type. Since the door also had security peephole, I kept very close to the wall as I walked toward it.

The door was formidable. The steel frame overlaid the edges of the door; there was no way to jimmy the door. There were no hinges on this side, which meant I didn't have the option of yanking the door out of place. If, by chance, there was a security on the other side of the door, I couldn't easily smash in the door. I could try using the HK to shoot my way into the apartment, but I was pretty sure that, when I finally got through the door, I would be shot up into teeny weeny pieces by the bad guys inside.

I dug into my pocket and found the key I'd taken off the security woman. "Oh, please," I whispered to myself. In the slowest (and quietest) of slow-motion, I inserted the key and gently turned it. The tumbler obligingly and almost silently fell into place.

Okay, Tyrrell, it gets really tricky from here on in: there are three armed security people somewhere on the far side of this door, and Faringer struck me as the type who wouldn't be adverse to wielding a weapon of her own. Toss a smoke grenade and go in firing? Toss a grenade and go in crawling under the smoke? Or attempt a stealth entry and save the smoke once I was deeper in the apartment? I have to admit that the idea of smoke and bullets seemed the safest play. Then again, it was also the play least likely to yield Savannah Faringer into my custody in one piece.

Before launching my incursion, I did a situation analysis. This is a great way to think things through and come up with an estimate of enemy forces and their locations. In all honesty, it is also a great way to procrastinate when you really don't want to get killed in the next minute or so . . .

Think, Tyrrell: Where was the first security guard? *Outside* the rear entrance. Since you deployed one of your four people that way, how do you think you'd deploy the other three? When I considered the situation in that way, the answer seemed simple: another guard *inside* the rear entrance, and probably the same outside/inside deployment at the front door. Both entrances would have redundant defenses. This arrangement also kept the hired muscle out of Ms. Faringer's sight, leaving her to enjoy the splendor of her ridiculously lavish apartment. Like any normal, non-homicidal billionaire.

I slipped the key into a pocket and wrapped my finger around the HK's trigger, ready to fire. My left hand held the grenade. With the fingertips of that hand, I pushed the door open a millimeter. Maybe two millimeters. No shooting from inside. I pushed a little farther and stopped. Was I crazy, or did I hear a soft foot fall? I backed up, dropped to the floor of the hallway, and used my right thumb to pull the ring on the smoke grenade—

Gunfire from the apartment's interior ripped apart the quiet. Bullets smashed the door shut, tearing through mere inches above my body. The shooting stopped. I rolled, my feet next to the apartment door. I was on my left side, the HK aimed upward. Footsteps moved closer to the other side of the door. The door opened a fraction of an inch, and there was a thirty-second pause when nothing happened, and then an eye was visible in the crack of the door. I kicked hard with my right leg, slamming the door open into the guard.

I was on my feet and shoving my way into the apartment instantly. The security man, a white guy of medium height and very bloody nose, was sprawled on the floor, groping for his HK. I cracked him on the head with the barrel of mine, and he collapsed unconscious. He was going to wake up with one helluva headache, but I felt good about the progress of my incursion into enemy territory. I had neutralized half of the opposing force and managed to do it without killing anyone. So far . . .

More footsteps came pounding my way. I tossed the smoke grenade deep into the apartment, where it popped and gushed smoke. Whoever was coming hesitated; the only noise now was the smoke hissing from the grenade.

I knelt and put my HK on the floor near the unconscious guard, inches from his own submachine gun. I pulled one of my Rugers, a much more maneuverable weapon in tight quarters, then wriggled on my belly under the security man's body. He was nowhere near big enough to cover all of me, but I didn't think the approaching team would be able to figure that out through the smoke.

The grenade was done spewing smoke, leaving a dense fog. I waited, forcing myself to be patient, very aware that the time to save Marissa was quickly disappearing. Within seconds, my patience was rewarded. The soft padding noise of footfalls reached me. After a few seconds, I could see feet coming toward me. The figure was crouched over, holding a submachine gun in both hands, ready to let me have it.

"Drop your weapon," I said. "Now."

The figure straightened and fired toward the sound of my voice; his aim close enough that I heard the bullets whiz past. I pulled the trigger three times, each round catching the figure in the chest, spinning it all the way around, and sending it face down to the floor. There was no other noise after the sound of my shots. I waited to see if the fourth member of the security team would make an appearance, but no one came forward. The gunfire must have driven Savannah Faringer to some very interesting emotions at that point in time. But that was her problem. Mine was what to do next.

I crawled out from under my human shield and, staying on my belly, moved to the security guard I'd shot three times. He was stunned, bleeding from a wound on his upper right arm. Two slugs had gone to his chest, but he was alive thanks to a Kevlar vest. I tapped him none too gently with the butt of my Ruger and knocked him cold. Three for three, and no deaths.

"Thank God," I whispered to myself.

Where was No. 4 on the security team? When the rear entrance was compromised, all other team members could have coalesced at that entrance . . . or one of the front-door team could have gone to the rear as a backup, while the final member covered Savannah. That seemed like the high-percentage play to me. It was similar to an army retreating and forming shorter, tighter defensive lines. It was easier to defend a small space than a large apartment—if an attacker breached the perimeter, sooner or later that attacker would have to go for Faringer, and the best place to protect her would be close to her. No. 4 and Faringer were probably in the same place. But where?

A check of my watch showed that I had about thirty minutes before Reznik murdered Marissa—no time for dawdling. I had to find Faringer, disable her last guard, and not get hurt or killed in the process—I wouldn't be much use to Marissa if I were unable to go to her aid—and do it all in five or six minutes. Simplicity itself. I took my last two smoke grenades, pulled the rings, and tossed them deep into the apartment. They thunked as they hit the floor, then popped and hissed smoke. I picked up my HK, and crouching low next to the wall, made my way to a corner in the apartment's hallway. It was hard to tell with all the smoke, but it seemed as if the right hand wall continued on, but the left fell away into some large, open space.

I grabbed the HK, held it at shoulder height and fired high, toward the ceiling. All I wanted was a distraction, not a death. I stopped and waited, but there was no return fire. For one of the rare times in my life I wanted someone to shoot at me so I could figure out their location, and what did I get? Nothing. Whoever the final security guard was, he or she was not a shopping mall's rent-a-cop. Gunfire and grenades were not enough to spook this one into doing something stupid.

Ugh, I thought. I dropped to my knees then to my belly and wriggled along the floor. The smoke was still too thick for me to get a good idea of what this room was, but judging by the upholstered couch and chairs, I guessed it was a den. Seemed a bit too casual for a living room, but I have to admit that snaking through a smoke-filled room watching for an attacker is hardly the best way to assess the décor. I passed behind the couch and poked my head around its corner. The smoke was a little less dense; maybe it was wafting into another part of the apartment. In my line of crawl were gigantic windows with the night sky visible through the glass and to my right, the upholstered bulk of another arm chair. I couldn't see anything to my left through the smoke. I fired into the ceiling again, waited, again, and heard nothing, again. I hated to expose my blind flank, but I turned right and began moving across the floor. There was a tiny scratching noise behind me. A teeny, weeny noise that terrified the ever-loving crap out of me. Moving as fast as a top, I rolled toward the windows, knocking over a very tall floor lamp.

Behind me, diving through the air, was a horrifically squat man with a very long knife. His body slammed to the floor in the space I had just occupied, the knifepoint where my gut had been a second before. I clubbed him with the HK, catching his arm and knocking the knife loose. The blade skittered across the floor and disappeared under the far end of the couch. From the floor, he kicked at me, and sent the HK flying.

Both Mr. Squat and I jumped to our feet and circled each other, ready to grapple, but neither making the first move. He was Asian and only about five-and-a-half feet tall, but he had ridiculously wide shoulders, a deep barrel chest, and hands the size of a gorilla's. His eyes were dull, but he was grinning. I had two pistols on me, and he was probably armed as well, but neither of us wanted to waste time going for a weapon. Well, he probably didn't want to waste time going for a weapon—those hands were all he'd need to do a job on me. I didn't want to go for a weapon because I was afraid of what he'd do to me in the single second I spent reaching for a pistol.

After what seemed like an eternity, I side-stepped to my right. It was a very small step, more to keep me loose than to create any kind of advantage. Mr. Squat took an equally small step to his right, maintaining the distance between us, but as soon as he finished the side-step, he rushed me like an express train. He tucked his shoulder into my chest and rammed me over the couch, the two of us crashing through a glass-topped coffee table and slamming down to the floor. Between his initial rush and his landing on top of me, he had knocked the wind out of me. I was on my back, gasping for air, when his tremendous paws found my throat and began squeezing. Great, I thought, in a few more seconds, my life will pass before my eyes . . .

Mr. Squat was very confident of his abilities to squelch me with his bare hands—and he had very good reason to be confident. But he was *too* confident. I knew this because he got careless. Half-lying, half-kneeling on top of my chest, he hadn't pinned my legs down with his own.

I kneed him in the groin with the strength of one desperate to survive. It was one helluva knee job. The blow buckled him in half, groaning. Let's see you grin now, Mr. Squat, I thought as I caught his jaw with my right fist. It wasn't the best punch I'd ever thrown, but it was more than sufficient as a follow-up to the superlative knee job. He flopped to the floor, and I rolled clear of him and stood up.

He was still groaning when I kicked him in the head. That shut him up.

"That's enough of that shit for one night," I said to no one in particular. I stood over him, panting and noticed the smoke had mostly dissipated. I stared out the window in the direction of Central Park, but it was too far below to be seen in the dark. However, the taller apartment buildings that marched up Central Park West to my left and Fifth Avenue to my right presented a wonderful view. Whatever the price tag for this apartment was, it was almost worth it for this view—a reflection in the window moved behind me. I jumped back from the reflected image but way too slowly. Savannah Faringer stabbed me with Mr. Squat's knife, tearing through my parka and sweater, slicing open my right tricep.

It hurt like hell. Since I'm as macho as the next guy, all right probably not as macho as Mr. Squat, but since I have normal testosterone levels, I didn't scream like a stuck pig. I grunted manfully and immediately lashed backhandedly toward Faringer. My movement drove the knife farther down to the outside of my elbow, but it also caught her by surprise. I hit her on her Scandinavian chin and sent her reeling backward. She tripped over the broken remains of her coffee table and fell to the floor.

I pulled out the knife, and, holding the handle in my left hand, advanced toward her. She kicked at me when I got in range, which she quickly discovered was a mistake as I slipped past her kick and slashed through the leg of her slacks with the knife she'd used to try to murder me. She screamed in pain and grabbed her calf with both hands, blood instantly oozing through her fingers. After the briefest second, she glared at me, and her screams turned to a stream of profanity. She cursed with the same lack of imagination that her security team did. Although, to give credit where it's due, she cursed much more fervently than they did.

Reaching her head without further incident, I knelt, grabbed a handful of her hair with my right hand and tugged. Fortunately for her, since my right arm was severely damaged, it wasn't the most forceful tug I was capable of. She grimaced in pain, but kept her hands on her wounded leg.

"You fucking—"

"Shut up," I said and tugged again to reinforce my point.

Savannah winced but was quiet.

"There are only two things I want from you: Marissa Carvajal's location and the unedited video from McGill's building the night he was killed."

"No."

"I'm in a hurry, please don't waste my time. I could threaten you, you could act tough, I'll threaten some more, you'll continue to be tough and uncooperative, I'll torture you, and you'll cooperate. Instead, why don't you consider yourself threatened and tortured and now it's time to cooperate."

"I don't think so."

Here you are again, Tyrrell: To torture or not to torture? Savannah's Nordically pretty face was contorted with anger. She was going to be damn uncooperative. And my arm hurt like hell.

"Do you have a first aid kit?" I asked.

"Yes . . ." she was puzzled, "in the guest bathroom."

"Show me the way."

I helped her to her feet, keeping the knife close enough to use but not close enough for her to easily knock or kick it away. Right then I wasn't sure I could handle another tussle with her. She led the way through her apartment, which was spartan yet lavish: minimalist furniture that cost a fortune. The guest room was simple but expensive, and the bathroom was big enough that you could have parked a Ferrari in it, with every surface either marble or glass. The extravagant nature of the bathroom gave me hope that her first aid kit would be a good one, and I was not disappointed.

Using soap and warm water, I cleaned her leg wound with soap and water, then salved it with topical antiseptic, and taped some gauze pads over it. Her slacks were probably past saving, but her cream-colored silk blouse was intact. I waved the knife at her and told her to sit on the edge of the jetted tub, where I could watch her in the mirror over the sink, and where she'd be too far away to surprise me while I tended to my wound. I felt much better after doing that, and I popped a couple of ibuprofen tabs as the finale to my medical act. I offered Faringer some ibuprofen, but she refused. I shrugged.

"Harry?" I said as I dropped onto the toilet lid. "Harry, I could use a little guidance."

Faringer arched her eyebrows. She wondered if I were playing her in some bizarre fashion. I smiled and called Harry again.

"This is against my better judgment," he said as he appeared.

"Look, I don't know what to do next, I don't know how much time I have, I'm not sure I am capable of torturing Savannah here even though I really need her information. In other words, I need help."

"You have 27 minutes remaining to do whatever you need to do."

"I need to do what I need to do," I said, registering Faringer's completely bewildered look. "She can't see or hear you, can she?"

"No."

I replied to Harry but glanced at Savannah as I said, "She thinks I'm speaking to the air."

"Yes."

I grinned and returned my attention to Harry. "Look, I know the Bible is full of violence and death, and it seems like violence is a tool that God uses to achieve His ends, but . . . *really*? Can that really be what the Chairman wants? That people like me produce results by using violence? By threatening and torturing people? By killing them if the torture doesn't work? That's beyond belief."

"Do you mean that literally?"

"What?" I couldn't believe Harry was playing word games with me. "Oh, 'beyond belief' – do I mean that literally? Yes, I do."

"Why?"

"Stop! I don't have time for your God-damn questions. I need answers. Now."

"The phrase 'God-damn' is ill-advised in this conversation."

"Harry, I have no idea if I could punch you out, but if you don't give me a straight answer right this minute, I'm going to give it a shot. I have—what?—26 minutes left?"

"You will have all the time you need."

"I don't have time for your fucking evasions—tell me what I need to know or so help me I'll—"

He cut me off, "You are willing to use violence to get the answers you seek regarding the Chairman using violence."

"Oh," I exhaled resignedly. "Okay, I won't punch you out. I won't attempt it, no matter how annoying you are. But please, help me understand. Why does the Chairman use violence and death?"

Harry stared at me for a long moment. Usually the opportunity to get into a staring contest with Harry was more than I could pass up, but at that moment, I was exhausted right down into my soul. Assuming I had one.

Out of the corner of my eye, I could see that Faringer was looking first at me and then to a space in front of me, looking for Harry. Yeah, good luck finding him, sweetheart.

Harry said, "Human beings are imperfect. Sometimes the methods and the tools that work best with them are imperfect. Have you ever heard the theory of a 'just war'?"

"Yes," I nodded. "Hitler, for instance. There was no way that bastard was going to respond reasonably to a polite request to cease and desist killing people. It took a major war to put an end to him. That's a 'just war'."

"Exactly. It was first brought up by St. Augustine and elaborated on much later by St. Thomas Aquinas."

"Fascinating. Not really the time for this kind of discussion."

"More recently, the Roman Catholic Church held a conference that rejected the theory of a 'just war.' The conference participants felt that modern war has become so destructive that it cannot possibly be just."

"How the hell does that help me?"

"It helps you to exercise free will in an informed manner."

"Is there any way that killing you could be construed as a 'just war'?" I paused and took a deep breath, considering what Harry had told me. "Since I'm only one man, I can't wage a war of total destruction. I think that in this instance I'm probably fighting a one-man version of a just war."

"That is one possible way to look at your situation."

"Why do I have to fight this war? Why me?" Even though I was still addressing the air as far as Savannah was concerned, my angry tone made her pull away from me. She was worried.

"Why *not* you?" Harry replied.

"Why not *me*? Is that all you have? Throw it back to me with the word 'not' thrown in?"

Harry inhaled deeply before replying, "You're falsely assuming that the question 'why not you?' is merely a rhetorical device. It's not. It's every bit as profound as 'why me?'—but you don't like what 'why not you?' might mean."

"Oh, like it means the Chairman picked me for this ugly, violent job because I have a set of ugly, violent credentials?"

Faringer was growing more uncomfortable by the second. She edged along the hot tub, slinking her way toward the bathroom door.

He nodded, considering my words. "That's probably a part of it."

"Probably? Don't you know?" I snapped at Faringer, "Savannah, sit the fuck still."

She sat still. Very still.

"You're making another false assumption," Harry replied.

"What?"

"You're assuming that because I work directly for the Chairman, I know his thoughts and motives."

"Don't you?"

"No. I'm like you—I have to exercise free will—I have to make choices without having all the facts or complete disclosure from the Chairman."

"Wouldn't you be able to follow orders better with all of the facts?"

"I don't follow orders. I make choices. As you do."

"Sorry, but you aren't actually . . . actually . . . uh, human. Right?"

"No. But I *am* a being of faith. And faith requires that free will be exercised."

I shook my head. "Are you trying to educate me or baffle me?"

Harry's trademark Mona Lisa smile flitted across his face, "I'm trying to do both."

"I set that one up."

"Yes."

"Enough about you, let's talk some more about me. Is my nasty track record the only reason the Chairman gives me these violent jobs?"

"I can't speak for Him, but that's probably not the only reason. These jobs, violent as they are, do help other people. And your wife did appeal to the Chairman on your behalf. His response is to give you these opportunities."

I grinned, "Oh, this is all for my benefit."

"No, it's for the benefit of others."

"Mankind is my business."

"Yes."

Faringer was eying the door, wondering about making a break for it.

"Savannah, don't make me warn you again," I said.

Her eyes locked onto my face. To Harry I said, "I don't understand why the Chairman would make me torture someone to help someone else."

"The Chairman didn't make you torture anyone."

"It's not that I didn't have to do it, it's that I was *willing* to do it. I hated being willing."

"Maybe your willingness to do whatever the job required was all that the Chairman wanted."

"That's bullshit. My willingness to do a job is all that mattered? My willingness to hurt people? Are you kidding me? I was ready to torture someone, and I hated myself for that."

There was a long pause, then Harry said, "The Chairman will never ask you to do anything you cannot do, will never give you a challenge you can't handle."

"That sounds like Theology 101 boiled down into a Hallmark card. More fine-sounding bullshit. I almost tortured a man. I almost did the most degrading, humiliating, painful thing one person can do to another. And I was ready to do it even though I don't believe it works, even though I think it's morally wrong." I forced a huge, insincere grin on my face: "But it's okay! The Chairman will never ask me to do what I can't do." I stopped grinning, "That's—Not—Good—Enough."

"The Chairman won't ask you to do what you cannot do—that does not mean he will ask you only to do easy things. He will not give you challenges you cannot handle, but that doesn't guarantee simple challenges, resulting in happy endings."

I shook my head and stared at the floor. "Shit."

Faringer's feet shifted as if she was going to make a dash for it. I said, "Don't." I stared at Savannah but spoke to Harry, "If I want to free Marissa Carvajal, I have to torture this woman."

"You have to decide," Harry replied.

My eyes were still locked on Faringer's, which were wide with confusion. Maybe they were wide with fear. Or both. If I had overheard me speaking torture to the air, I probably would have been utterly bewildered and horrified. I stood up, shifted the knife to my left hand and pulled one of my Rugers from its holster with my right. I stepped close to her and put the barrel of my gun to her left kneecap. I held the knife to her throat.

"I'm sorry about this." I ignored Harry as I continued, "But I need your cooperation, and I don't have the time to persuade you. You have to tell me where Reznik took Marissa. You have to give me the original video from McGill's apartment building's security. Please believe me: I really don't want to do this, but I will."

Her face was white with terror as I spoke.

"I absolutely will cause you more pain than you ever imagined. I'll leave you alive, but you'll never walk without a limp, never wear a short skirt to show off your legs, never—"

"Stop! Stop, please," she was babbling, sobbing in her terror. "I'll do what you want. I will. Reznik has the

Carvajal woman at the Manhattan Majestic building downtown, near South Street. In apartment 27A—no one lives in it, it's for sale."

I mulled that one over. "Clever. I bet her real estate company is listing it for sale, right? Which will explain how she got in and was able to jump. Is that the plan?"

"Yes."

"Good, thank you." I lifted the knife until the flat side of the blade brushed underneath her chin. "Get up slowly."

She did as instructed.

"Where are the original videos?"

Her eyes scanned my face side to side; she was calculating how helpful she needed to be to comply with my wishes.

"If you think you can stall me and prevent me from saving Marissa Carvajal, think again." I pressed the knife into her throat. I didn't slash or slice, and the pressure wasn't enough to break the skin, but I made my point.

She swallowed, which was difficult with my knife at her throat, and said, "In my office at Cú Chulainn."

"Bullshit."

"No, no, I wouldn't lie to you, they're in my office."

"Nice try. You said that with just the right touch of desperation to make me think you're being sincere."

"No, I'm telling the truth."

"Yeah, well, the videos are probably on some encrypted server at Cú Chulainn. But you're not the kind of person who would let it out of her control. You have copies here."

"No, no, I don't."

"Maybe you should sit down again." My voice was flat, without affect. "When I shoot you in the knee, it'll be easier for you if you're sitting down."

"It's on my computer," she gasped.

"Lead the way," I pulled the knife away from her throat and followed her out of bathroom, deliberately avoiding Harry. I wasn't sure I could pull this off if I saw his face.

Faringer led me back into the den. The smoke was all but gone, and the room was a mess. Mr. Squat was still an unconscious lump on the floor, which was fine by me. I nudged him with my toe to confirm his status. He didn't move or moan. He was out. Faringer went through a door I hadn't seen before; the smoke had obscured it. Inside was the smallest room I had seen in the place, even smaller than the bathroom. Which isn't to say it was a tiny room—it had plenty of space for a desk, bookshelves, and a chair facing the desk. The desk held a phone, a very large computer monitor, a keyboard, and a mouse.

"Sit down," I gestured with the knife, and as she moved to the chair behind the desk, I held the blade against her throat again. She sat very carefully, and I placed the gun barrel on her knee again and pulled away the knife. She reached for the keyboard.

"Pull up the videos."

"Yes, sir." Those two little syllables were packed with anger. But she clicked and typed, and multiple windows opened, each with different views of the interior of McGill's building.

"Fast forward through the front lobby and service entrance videos," I directed.

Faringer did as I told her, and the images flashed by in herky-jerky high-speed motion. I saw McGill and Marissa enter the lobby, and a few seconds later, a team of four black-coveralled, ski-masked intruders came through the service entrance.

I had Faringer show me the elevator video and then the video from the hallway outside McGill's front door. What sped by was the same parade we'd seen in the lobby and at the service entrance: first McGill and Marissa, then the black-covered intruders. The timestamp on the hallway video showed the intruders entering the apartment immediately prior to the time of death. Harry watched it all from behind me.

Turning to him, I said, "I feel like there must be something else. The unedited video isn't enough, is it?"

"No, it's not." He looked up for guidance and received it very quickly, "Get the working files used to create the cleaned-up videos. The program Ms. Faringer's people used saved multiple copies as they progressed through the changes to eliminate all traces of the Cú Chulainn and SHK Dragon people sneaking into Jackson McGill's building. You should also get the keystroke log from the computer used to change the video. It won't show every single thing that was done, but there should be enough on the log to prove that the videos were modified."

"Wow," I whispered appreciatively. "I had no idea you were such an expert in this kind of thing. I don't mean to doubt you in any way at all, but why would she have all those files and the log?"

"Because she doesn't trust anyone and would want to hold all the evidence herself."

"Holy moly. You are on a hot streak," I removed the gun from Savannah's knee and pointed the barrel at the computer. "Give me all the versions of the videos as they were being edited. And the keystroke log from the computer they were edited on."

"I don't have—" she grunted in surprise as I pressed the Ruger to her knee.

"I haven't got the time for your bullshit. Give me the damn files. Now."

There was more clicking and typing and many files began popping up.

"Ah, the motherlode," I said. "Go sit in the other chair."

Faringer moved around the desk to the chair on the opposite side. I placed my Ruger on the desk within easy reach and gave Faringer my version of the Evil Eye. I didn't have to say anything because I knew from experience that my Evil Eye is impressive. After intimidating the woman into behaving herself, I opened a browser, logged into my email, and typed a brief note to Joanne Agar at the FBI, saying I was sending her a large number of video files and a keystroke log from Savannah Faringer's personal computer. I told Joanne that the files would prove that the security videos for Jackson McGill's building had been altered and that a team of masked invaders had murdered McGill. Marissa Carvajal was innocent. I suggested that Joanne share this evidence with the NYPD and also with the CIA and anyone else in the national security business who might want to know about the conspiracy of Cú Chulainn and SHK Dragon to force a merger that was probably not in America's best interests.

Because of the number and size of the files, I had to send them in multiple e-mails to Joanne. It probably took about ten minutes, which, under the circumstances, seemed like forever. But I forced myself to wait and make sure all the e-mails cleared my outbox. I gave Savannah another dose of the Evil Eye, leaned over and popped the laptop out of the docking station, grabbed my Ruger, and stood up.

To Harry I said, "How much time?"

"Four minutes."

"Yikes. Please whoosh Ms. Faringer and me to the apartment where Reznik is taking Marissa? And please make it somewhere safe in the apartment, someplace where I'll have a chance to surprise Reznik."

Savannah said, "You realize that he'll kill you. He's not like you; there won't be any hesitation about hurting people or killing them. No moral scruples whatsoever. He's been paid; there's a bonus waiting for a job well done. He'll collect that bonus. You and Marissa Carvajal will be dead."

"And you'll be in jail—those e-mails I sent? They went to the FBI."

"What?"

"Did you think I was e-mailing them to myself?" I grinned. "After all, I'm practically a dead man, according to you."

"I can get you money . . ."

"It's a little late for that, but thanks for the offer. Now, when we get inside that apartment, you better keep quiet until I tell you to say something. Got it?"

"Yes. But can't we come to an arrangement?"

"Like you pay me lots of money, and I let you leave the country? No thanks. Remember: keep your damn mouth shut." To Harry I said, "Please whoosh us?"

"As you wish."

15

Savannah Faringer, Harry, and I found ourselves standing in an unfinished room on the southeastern corner of the Manhattan Majestic building. The southern wall was all windows overlooking the skyscrapers of Wall Street, One World Trade Center, and New York harbor. The eastern wall was mostly windows, overlooking the South Street Seaport and the Brooklyn Bridge. At the end of each wall of windows were tall, slender windows that opened out. The better for faking a suicide, my dear.

Faringer wasn't appreciating the view; she was confused.

I said to Harry, "She doesn't know . . . ?"

He shook his head; she stepped back from me. I guess my speaking to the air seemed much more menacing in a dark, empty apartment. Ambient light spilled in from some of the neighboring buildings that were close enough and tall enough to throw a bit of illumination our way.

I gestured at the southern windows with my Ruger. "Well . . . if you're going to murder someone, you might as well do it in a room with a view."

"You won't be cracking jokes when Reznik gets here," she said.

"Speaking of your lethal friend . . ." I spoke to

Harry, "How much time?"

"He's on his way up right now. You have about thirty seconds."

I grabbed my phone from my pants pocket and turned on the flashlight app, swinging the light left and right. In this empty room with a view, there was a work light on a long extension cord hanging from a nail in the wall. There were a few two by fours and pieces of plywood leaning against the same wall. But no construction seemed to be going on, the room must have been used as a staging area for whatever work was being done in the apartment. I flashed light around the apartment. Behind us, a small hall led to a door.

"The front door?" I asked.

Harry nodded.

"Any rooms open off of this hall?"

He pointed to the right side, "There's a kitchen."

I grabbed Savannah by the arm and tugged her along. Harry stayed in place.

"Come on, we gotta go," I said.

"This is where I leave you."

"Are you shitting me?"

"You don't need me." He was gone before I could say anything else.

Faringer continued to look confused. "Come on," I repeated softly, turned off the flashlight, and pulled her toward the kitchen. "Don't say a word. No matter what, keep quiet or I'll kill you." In the darkness, I couldn't tell if she was acquiescent or too dazed to defy me. I didn't care, as long as she did as she was told.

The kitchen was a black hole. We stepped gingerly inside and took a cautious step deeper in. I doubted that anyone would find us there.

A key slid into the door lock, and the tumblers clicked over. Shadows backlit from a light in the foyer between the elevator and the front door spilled onto the hallway floor.

Reznik led the way, flashlight in one hand, an automatic pistol in the other. His chin was as cinderblock-like as ever in the back glow from the flash. He'd barely stepped past the open arch of the kitchen doorway when a man and a woman, both in the black coveralls that were popular with Cú Chulainn employees, moved into view, with Marissa between them. She was frightened and bedraggled, her wool coat, fashionable sweater and slacks very much the worse for wear, but her beauty was evident even in the dark, even in this moment of stress and danger.

Each black-clad figure grasped one of Marissa's arms and held pistols in their free hands. As soon as they walked past the kitchen, I followed them, pistol-whipping the back of the man's head. He crashed forward, bounced off the wall, and dropped to the floor. Not that I wasted any time watching his collapse, I was too busy backhanding the woman with my left hand. I snapped her head back as she fired her weapon. Fortunately my blow must have knocked her aim off. She missed me, and I have to say I have always enjoyed it when someone missed me with a gun or a knife. I pistol-whipped the side of her head and she dropped unconscious to the floor. I wheeled toward the room with a view, but Marissa was no longer in the hallway. There was no sign of Reznik. Damn, he was fast.

"Don't kill Marissa!" I shouted. "I have Savannah Faringer here. You kill Marissa, I'll kill Savannah, and you lose half a payday."

"That's interesting. I'm listening." His voice was a steady purr, as if he was deciding which fine wine to order with dinner. "What makes you think I'll lose half my payday?"

"Standard arrangement: half up front, half upon completion." My voice was calm and steady—I could play it cool, too.

I went to the kitchen, shook Savannah, made her stand up, pushed her in front of me, and marched toward Reznik and Marissa. I wasn't ashamed of hiding behind a woman—without her as a shield I'd be dead.

Turned out Reznik wasn't ashamed to hide behind a woman either. He stood behind Marissa, her mouth agape with fear. Given the huge disparity in their relative dimensions, she was a less successful shield for him than the tall Ms. Faringer was for me. But I wasn't going to point that out.

"What now?" he asked. "We can't stand here all night."

"Well, how 'bout you give me Marissa, and the

ladies and I will leave?"

"You don't really think I'll play it that way, do you?"

"No, but I thought I'd give you the option to get out alive."

He grunted derisively. "You have a mighty high opinion of yourself."

"No, I have an excellent team backing me up." I thought to myself, please let that be true, Harry. Please. "If you give up Marissa now, you leave alive. Otherwise you'll depart in a body bag."

"That sounds like a challenge."

"Only a macho fool would think so."

"Now you're insulting me." Another grunt. "Have to say I am curious. I'm going to stick around and see how you handle this situation."

I had to admit that I was curious, too. How the hell did I think I could break the stalemate of two big, dangerous men hiding behind two women. Threatening each other because that was the only thing we could do to avoid getting killed. How was I supposed to save Marissa and not get killed in the process? That may sound selfish, but if I died, Marissa would die, too. At least my death would be quick. Hers would be a long, terrifying plunge out of one of the windows . . .

After a long silence, Reznik said, "I don't suppose I could interest you in splitting the money. You let me do what I need to do with Ms. Carvajal, and I'll split the completion fee with you. Then you and I, and Ms. Faringer of course, all leave."

Marissa was whimpering. I didn't blame her; I probably would have been sobbing if I were in her shoes. I pushed my worries for her aside and asked, "How much money are we talking about? What's my share?"

"A cool million," he said and grunted again, "tax free."

"I'll double that," Faringer said. "Two million if you let us deal with Ms. Carvajal, and let me walk away."

"Really? You seemed awfully quick to double the money. A couple of million is a lot of money to me, but it's peanuts to you. Make it five million."

Faringer was breathing hard, not from exertion but emotion. "All right, I'll pay five. Now let me go." But I didn't let go; I continued to hide behind her.

"Please don't," Marissa begged. "Please?"

"Here's how this is going to work," I said in a husky whisper. "You, Savannah, are going to call whomever you have to call and transfer the money into a bank account that you'll set up for me. Once that's done, I'll let you go, and Reznik can have as much fun as he wants."

"I don't have a phone," she hissed angrily.

"Ah . . . Mr. Reznik, could you be of some assistance here?"

"Sure, why not?" He stretched the arm of his gun hand around Marissa's shoulders, tightly cocking his wrist back to point his pistol Marissa's jaw. His left hand released her arm, dug into his pants pocket, and pulled a phone out.

"Ready?" he asked.

"Yes," I replied.

He tossed the phone, and I fired my Ruger. I wish I could tell you it was one of those amazing shots you see in the movies where the hero clips the only visible square inch of the villain's body. But I didn't even try to hit Reznik—not in a dark room with his human shield in front of him. I'm not a good enough shot for that kind of thing.

I shot his human shield—I shot Marissa Carvajal in the leg.

I aimed for and hit the outside of her thigh. If I missed, the shot would have gone wide to my right and through the window. But I grazed her, because she screamed and immediately fell.

For a tiny fraction of a second, Reznik was confused and vulnerable. I fired again.

I fired twice as quickly as I could. One bullet exploded the window to my left. The other hit Reznik up high somewhere. But unless it found a lethal spot—one bullet would never be enough to stop a man as big and strong and nasty as Reznik. A half-second after I shot Marissa, and she had fallen to the floor, Reznik was charging me and Faringer. The bullet hadn't even slowed him down. He barreled into us and all three of us went sprawling on the floor.

My gun was jarred loose and clattered across the floor, out of sight in the dark. I pushed myself to my feet, spun to meet Reznik, and grabbed for my second pistol all at the same time.

But Reznik was on his feet, too, leaping over Faringer and slamming into me before I could take aim. He crushed me against the wall with such impact that my body cracked the drywall. Which was not much fun at all. He hammered the side of my head with his left elbow and brought his right knee up into my gut. Dazed as I was from the blow to my head, I had seen the knee-to-my-gut move coming, so I pushed off the wall and tucked my shoulder into his solar plexus. It wasn't a killer body block, but it forced him off of me. Reznik was still on his feet, still swinging. This time a roundhouse right, which I parried, stepped inside his incredibly long reach, and chopped at his Adam's apple. I only connected with a bit of his throat, but enough to make him gag and retreat.

I'd never fought anyone as gigantic as Reznik, never faced such a size disadvantage. I knew I couldn't go toe-to-toe with him; I needed to stay inside his reach and pummel him in the gut. I feinted a kick to his left knee, and when he pulled his left side back to protect himself, I stepped inside his right arm and hit him in the gut with everything I had. Experience told me that most guys hit that squarely would double over, gasping for air, but Reznik barely hesitated before clubbing the back of my head with a left hand as thick and hard as a 36-inch Louisville Slugger. I buckled under the blow, dropping to my knees. Reznik's right hand swooped toward my chin, and I could shift only a tiny bit out of the way. His fist caught my jaw and snapped me backward, laying me out on the floor. I was barely conscious.

A voice in my head shouted: Move, Tyrrell! Move or he'll stomp you to death. Or snap your neck. Move!

Marissa was screaming, "No . . . no!"

Reznik's dark mass towered over me; it would be over in seconds. To be precise and accurate: I would be over. Reznik's bulk leaned toward me—I rolled onto my right side and kicked out and up with my left foot, catching him behind his right knee and sweeping his leg out from under him. He went down like a redwood. I used my hands to push off the floor and staggered to an upright position. I reached again for my second pistol, but the holster was empty. My knife, however, was still in its sheath; I pulled it and held it low in front of me.

With a groan, Reznik got to his feet, faced me, and grinned at the sight of my knife. "You're good," he said. "Not sure I've had this much trouble before."

"Gee, thanks. Wanna call it a draw?"

"I can't live with that. I want the rest of my money, and the only way to get it is to kill you and then her." He jerked his thumb at Marissa. "You should put that knife down before I take it and stab you with it."

"You're good," I said, forcing a smile, "but not *that* good—"

He rushed me as I said "good." Unfortunately for him, I knew he was going to make a move because he thought he had me distracted. I sidestepped him and slashed at his shoulder. He spun quickly, cursing and backhanding me. I rolled with the blow, moving away from him, still holding the knife.

"I tried to warn you," I said. "You're not quite *that* good—"

Reznik charged again with his arms outstretched and his hands splayed wide open to catch me. He must have thought I was overconfident. Instead, I was playing him for the sucker. I ducked and sliced at his other shoulder. There was a grunt of pain. But in the same instant, he grabbed me with his left arm, swept me off my feet, and threw me at the wall. I smashed against it. The impact all but drove the air from my lungs. I dropped the knife and slid to the floor.

He stomped across the floor, wrapped his fingers in my hair, yanked my head back, and hit me with one of his huge fists. Hit me two or three times. Maybe four. Then he let go, and I collapsed into a lump.

Marissa was moaning, holding onto her leg where I had shot her.

Faringer said to Reznik, "Kill them both. Let's get out of here."

"First things first," he replied. I heard his footsteps receding, then a faucet running, and then his walking back slowly. "Just needed a drink of water. Damn place doesn't even have a glass."

While he was in the kitchen getting a drink, I had struggled to my knees. That was as far as I could go. In the last few hours I'd been shot and stabbed and pummeled to within an inch of my life—I don't think I'd ever been in such bad shape and not been on my way to a hospital. Or already in a hospital.

Reznik stood directly in front of me. "What do you think, Tyrrell? Am I *that* good after all?"

When I was in training for Special Forces, one of the sergeants in charge had said, "You're a big boy, sir, and you're pretty damn tough. You'll be even tougher when we get finished with you. But you gotta remember one thing: no matter how big and tough you are, there's always some damn sumbitch who's bigger, stronger, faster, and tougher than you. If you ain't met him yet, it only means you haven't met enough damn sumbitches. And there's only one way to beat a man like that. Only one. You have to refuse to be beaten. Refuse to lose. Reach deep inside yourself and find some reserve that lets you take that damn sumbitch."

Right then and there, on my hands and knees, gasping for breath, blood trickling down my face, the toes of Reznik's boots only a foot away, I didn't think I had what it takes to refuse to be beaten. I was used up. Nothing left. But I couldn't let Reznik get away with destroying pictures of my wife. Get away with corrupting the best, most important thing I had ever done—love Maggie. Maggie, who had interceded for me with the Chairman. I whispered, "Please help me, Mr. Chairman. Please?"

"What?" Reznik demanded. "What did you say? No one's coming to help you. It's just you and me."

"Pretty soon, it'll just be me," I replied.

"Big talk for a guy on his knees."

"You're the toughest man I ever had the misfortune to run into, no two ways about it. But you're an arrogant asshole."

"What?"

"You should have kicked my lights out. But you waited, probably 'cause you want to go face to face and end me. But the smart play was to kick my lights out and be done with it, not go for this macho shit." I sat back on my heels and grinned. "You're too arrogant to do the smart thing—"

He kicked at my head—at least, he tried to. But I saw it coming. I saw in Reznik's eyes that I had insulted him. He had moved like lightning, but this time he was too slow. I ducked to my left, grabbed his leg by the ankle, and pushed up. He flipped backward and crashed headfirst into the wall then slid into a lump on the floor.

I staggered to my feet. Amidst the lumber in the staging area of the room, I saw a three-foot long 2x4. I stumbled over to it as fast as I could, picked it up, and returned in a rush to Reznik. I didn't like hitting a man when he was down, but I was damned if I was going to make the mistake of arrogance that I had accused Reznik of. He blinked at me as he tried to focus and push himself upright.

"Sorry about this, but I've had enough," I said and swung the 2x4 at his head. I connected like Mickey Mantle slamming one into the upper deck of the old Yankee Stadium. Reznik dropped to the floor like a sack of cement mix, thudding heavily. I've seen plenty of dead men and women through the years, and Reznik certainly appeared to be pretty damn dead. But I held the 2x4 at the ready in my right hand, leaned in close, and felt for his carotid pulse with the fingers of my left hand. Absolutely nothing. To quote Shakespeare, Reznik "was as dead as a doornail."

I straightened up and turned toward the two women. Marissa was still sitting on the floor, clutching her leg where I had shot her. Savannah Faringer was standing where I had released her, an automatic in her right hand pointed at my mid-section and a phone in her left. The automatic was a Glock; I carried a Ruger, so the gun in her hand must have been Reznik's. Like the phone, which she was speaking into at that moment.

"Ten minutes?" she asked. Listened to the response and uttered, "Good." She disconnected, slid the phone into a pocket in her slacks, placed her left hand under her right hand, and adjusted the Glock's aim right for my heart. I had no idea how good a shot she was, or even if she had ever shot someone—the first time you pull the trigger when aiming at a human being is a lot harder than you might imagine—but I really didn't want to find out.

"Drop the 2x4," she said, "and go stand next to Ms. Carvajal."

I did as I was told. "May I help Marissa to her feet?"

Savannah waved her gun at Marissa in what I took to be a gesture of permission. I turned to Marissa, my back to Savannah, and gently grabbed her right arm to help her up.

Marissa glared at me as I reached to help her up. "You shot me you bastard. It hurts like hell, what were you thinking?"

"I'm sorry, I really am, but I had to get you out of the way."

"By shooting me?" she sounded very angry. As I helped her to her feet, my body screened her from Savannah's sight, and Marissa handed me my Ruger. She whispered, "It landed next to me."

I winked at her.

"All right, Tyrrell, now you can shove her out the window."

"What? Are you crazy?" I carefully kept my Ruger down by my hip, hidden from Savannah in the dark room. "You know, I already e-mailed all your hacked videos to the FBI. You're going to prison. Don't add Marissa's death to that."

"What have I got to lose. Besides, you don't know what kind of contacts I may have in the FBI—your e-mailed evidence will never be used against me. Now, my security team will be here in a few minutes, which means there's no point in discussing this further. Throw her out the window, and I'll pay you the money we agreed to."

"Five million dollars?"

"Yes," she responded through clenched jaws.

"That's very decent of you," I said, spinning and aiming my Ruger directly at her eyes—even though shooting someone in the head is incredibly easy to screw up, there's something awesomely intimidating about looking right into a gun barrel. I hoped to incentivize her into cooperating. "Put your gun down and your hands on your head."

"No," she said, smiled, and fired.

As she smiled I pushed Marissa out of the way, heard a bullet whine past my head, and shot Savannah. She flopped backward and landed on the floor, her head only a foot away from Reznik's. Her eyes were wide open and glassy. My shot had missed her head but torn her throat open.

Marissa limped over to me and stared down at her. "Why did they do this to me?"

"Money." I holstered my weapon.

"That's all? Money?"

"Well . . . billions is a helluva lot of money." I knelt beside Savannah's body as I replied and patted her down, pulling Reznik's smart phone from her pocket. I stepped over her corpse to Reznik and patted him down, pulling a sheet of paper from a pocket in his leather jacket pocket. I unfolded enough of it to see it was Marissa's suicide note, which I tucked away in my cargo pants.

"Shouldn't we destroy that?" she asked.

"Right now, we should get out of here before Savannah's security team gets here."

"I'm not sure I can go anywhere, I'm bleeding like crazy." She was pale and frazzled. Not surprising considering how she'd spent her evening. I lifted her in my arms and carried her to the bathroom, where I hoped I'd find a first-aid kit. Most contractors have first-aid kits on building sites, and this one had left a kit in the bathroom. I worked very fast, ripping open her pants leg, cleaning the wound, gently dabbing antiseptic cream onto it, and taping a thick wad of gauze over it. There was Tylenol in the kit, and she took a couple of tablets and washed them down by drinking straight from the grime-encrusted faucet.

A glance in the mirror showed me the effects of Reznik's work. I cleaned off most of the blood, dabbed more antiseptic into the biggest cuts and used a couple of butterfly closures to fix up the worst of them.

My mental clock was sounding an alarm. I figured we had a minute, maybe two, if we were extremely fortunate, to get out of this place.

I took Marissa's hand and said, "I know you're hurt and tired, but if we don't get out now, we're going to die."

"I prefer getting out," she replied. She was resilient. Maybe she had turned a corner when I pulled her out of Long Island Sound. Now all I had to do was make sure she survived the next few minutes.

We walked out of the empty, dark apartment into the hallway.

"Harry," I said to the air, "please whoosh us out of here. Now, please?"

Marissa wasn't looking at me with as strange an expression as Savannah had, but she was pretty damn bewildered. "Are you all right?"

I laughed, "Yeah, I'm fine. A little wishful thinking spoken out loud. Sorry, didn't mean to freak you out."

"You're sure you're okay?"

"I'm sure."

There were two sets of elevator doors in front of us, and I pressed the call button in between the doors. We heard the elevator hoist as a car moved up toward our floor. I pulled my Ruger out of it holster and pointed it in between the doors, ready to cover whichever one opened.

"Do you think they're coming up in the elevator?" She was very anxious.

I smiled, at least I tried to smile, "They might be. I want to be sure." I jerked my thumb over my shoulder at the apartment, "Given all the goings on in this place, do you think you could get me a deal on it?"

Her eyes went wide with surprise, then she grinned. "Probably, but my guess is that you wouldn't want to live here. There's been a lot of crime in this neighborhood recently."

"Oh, in that case, forget it." I shifted my aim to cover the elevator on my left, where the sounds of an arriving car were obvious.

The elevator doors rolled open. It was empty.

"After you," I said, waving her in. I pressed "2", the doors closed, and the elevator descended.

"You pressed two. Are you trying to avoid someone?"

"I'm hoping to. We'll get off at two and take the emergency stairs down. Assuming you know where they are."

"I do. I'm the listing agent for the apartment." She stepped to the back of the elevator. As if that would help . . .

16

The elevator stopped on the second floor. No one was waiting on the other side when the door opened. We stepped into the hallway, and Marissa led the way to the fire stairs. I slowly opened the door to the stairwell, stepped in, and surveyed the stairs up and down. No one there but us escapees. I took Marissa's hand and pulled her inside the stairwell.

I whispered, "The bad guys will be here any second, assuming they're not here already. They will try to kill us. My guess is they won't be subtle about it."

"You think they'll shoot at us in the street?"

"If we're lucky enough to reach the street. First, give me the low down on the lobby and the exterior of the front entrance."

"It's a lobby. This stairwell goes down to a cement hallway that leads in two directions: into the lobby and directly to the plaza outside. I think we probably want to use that door."

"You got that right. What's the plaza like? Any cover?"

Marissa shook her head, "There are trees and some small planted areas, but nothing big enough to hide both of us."

"How is the building positioned on the street?"

"This building is on Pearl Street. There's a parking lot directly across from the front entrance, and Beekman Street runs alongside the parking lot toward the South Street Seaport."

"Is Beekman to the right or left of the parking lot?"

"The right."

I reached into a pocket and pulled out the remains of my phone. Even though my phone was in a padded case, I guess there's only so much shooting and slamming and kicking a digital device can handle. In any event, it was useless. I showed the crunched touchscreen to Marissa.

"I don't suppose you have a phone?"

"It's still at the Selkirks' house. Why?"

"I thought we'd use an app to order a car. When it arrives, we could run out to the curb and minimize our exposure big time."

"Maybe the doorman would let us use his phone?"

"Faringer's security team could walk into the lobby any time now. We can't risk it." I said. I glanced down at her leg, "I know you're hurting and that doing a lot of running isn't going to be easy." To be honest, I felt as if I needed a visit to the emergency room, myself. But I had to play the hero a little longer. Or die trying. If I managed to survive, I was going to have it out with Harry on his lack of whooshing Marissa and me out of this danger zone we were trapped in. "Do you think you can make it to the Seaport? We'll go into the first restaurant we can find, borrow the phone, and call a car service."

"But we'd have to go out to Water Street to meet the car. Fulton and Front Streets are both pedestrian malls. There's no place for a car to come and get us."

"Oh, shit," I sighed. "You're right. But . . . I haven't got a better idea. Have you?'

After a pause, she replied, "Sorry, no."

"Are you ready to go?"

"Not really, but let's do this."

We descended the stairs, me first, pistol at the ready. When we reached the bottom of the stairs, Marissa pointed to the right down the hallway. About twenty feet down the hallway, we came to a "T." There was a door to our left, and more stairs descended to our right.

"Basement?" I asked, pointing.

"Yes."

"Any way out through there?"

"No."

I gripped the handle on the door, turned it slowly in the hope of avoiding any noise, and pushed the door open to the plazaa. The trees had tiny white Christmas lights strung throughout their branches. The lights illuminated the plaza softly but completely. There was no place to hide.

And . . . there was no one in sight.

"Let's hustle," I said. We walked as briskly as we were capable of walking, me supporting Marissa with my left hand, while my right held the Ruger. I wasn't going to waste any time digging it out of its holster if anyone nasty appeared.

The front of the lobby was mostly glass, and we could see that only the doorman was in the lobby. No bad guys. We reached the sidewalk and turned right, heading for Beekman Street, which opened across from us on the other side of Pearl Street. We crossed Pearl and had reached the corner of Beekman, when a black Tahoe, the vehicle of choice for the employees of Cú Chulainn and SHK Dragon, raced downtown on Pearl and jerked to a stop at the curb directly in front of the building we'd just left. A woman climbed out on the driver's side, and a man got out from the passenger side. Two men stepped out the rear doors, including my old friend Mr. Squat.

Neither of us was capable of a great burst of speed, but we began running down Beekman. A silenced pistol burped a couple of shots that ricocheted off the building on our right. I twisted around, saw that the woman was firing while Mr. Squat and the other two men were rushing across the street toward us. I took a deep breath, aimed carefully, and fired. The woman slammed back into the Tahoe and dropped to the street. We took off and ran another few yards when another bullet whizzed past. We ducked into a doorway, and I turned to see that now it was Mr. Squat's turn to shoot at us. I fired quickly, but he ducked behind a parked car on Pearl and the only thing I did was succeed in breaking the window.

As Mr. Squat hid behind a car, one of the other men fired, and the third member of the team ran for Mr. Squat's position. It didn't take a military genius to see that if the team provided covering fire while taking turns running after us, they were going to catch us.

"Can't you stop them? Shoot them?" Marissa asked.

"I don't think so," I said. But I had to do something. Taking turns firing and running to new places of cover, Savannah's team was moving much closer.

"Mr. Chairman," I muttered, "please help me." I ignored the terrified look on Marissa's face, stepped out of the doorway, stood on the sidewalk, forced myself to aim with deliberation and precision, and fired at the tiny bit of one man's shoulder I could poking out from behind a parked truck. My bullet caught him and flung his body backward out of sight. His gun made a metal clacking sound as it skittered on the pavement.

I grabbed Marissa's hand and ran. She grunted in pain but kept running. I could hear the pounding feet of Mr. Squat and his partner behind us. We rounded the corner at Water Street and tucked in close to the short building that stood there. I checked around the corner, hoping to shoot our pursuers, but they were way too smart to stay in the open. I didn't know if they were taking cover in a building doorway or hiding behind a parked car, but we couldn't stay where we were.

I thought about sending Marissa to safety in the crowds of the Seaport with all its shops and restaurants and tourists, but I didn't know how far she could go without physical support. I couldn't linger and take on Mr. Squat for the simple reason that I didn't think I could handle him. I was too far gone. If I ambushed him and failed, he would kill Marissa at his leisure.

You know what, Tyrrell, if you had killed these guys in Faringer's apartment when you had the chance, you wouldn't have this problem right now. Serves you right for being a do-gooder. You should have shot the bastards.

Marissa tugged at my sleeve and whispered, "Come on, let's get out of here!"

We hurried down Water Street, which had very few people and not much activity, toward Fulton, the main drag of the South Street Seaport and chock-full of life-saving tourists. As we rushed toward Fulton, I looked over my shoulder to see if I could fire at Mr. Squat and his partner. I didn't think I'd stop them—the spin and shoot move that is popular in movies isn't very easy—but gunshots might have forced them to slow down. However, they were doing a good job of keeping to cover. There was no sign of them.

Marissa and I reached Fulton and turned left. Fulton Street is a bit of old New York, but spruced up for the tourists. On the north side was a large market building, with restaurants, food stores, coffee stores, and cafes. On the other side was a row of two- and three-story buildings, completely refurbished, mostly hosting upscale retail. Christmas lights were strung over the cobblestoned street, and Christmas carols wafted over the speakers hung throughout the Seaport. The stores and restaurants were brightly lit and decorated for the Yuletide season. In the middle of Fulton, a pair of street performers, dressed in bright red coveralls with white trim, were juggling bowling pins that had been painted to look like elves. I think they were elves; they had pointed ears. It was too cold to juggle if you asked me, but then again, no one asked me.

We edged through the crowd and were about to step into a seafood restaurant when I heard the flat burp of a silenced pistol and the restaurant's glass door broke into thousands of tiny pieces. The jugglers glanced around nervously but continued their act without missing a beat; the crowd shifted anxiously, and Marissa and I ducked low and crept toward the East River about three hundred feet away. Another shot, another window disintegrated. The jugglers stopped as most of their audience ran here and there, leaving Fulton Street. Marissa and I ran for South Street at the far end of Fulton. Her leg must have hurt like hell, but she made no complaints. We ran across South Street under the elevated FDR Drive and hid on the far side of one of the metal pillars that supported the roadway. The sound of highway traffic hissed by overhead.

From one side of the FDR pillar, I sneaked a glance

back toward Fulton. There was no sign of our pursuers.

"There's no one there!" Marissa whispered, very hopefully.

"Yeah, but that's probably bad news for us."

"Why?"

"If I were those guys, I'd circle around the market building to Beekman and attack from the north."

"Should we go back up Fulton?"

"Nowhere to hide if they find us. And we know they'll shoot, even with innocent people around."

I turned and scanned the riverfront. "Come on, we'll head for the pier."

We ran out onto Pier 17, which adjoined Pier 16 where the S.S. *Peking*, a four-masted ship as long as a football field, was moored on the southern side. The *Peking*'s masts and rigging were festooned with Christmas lights, and more Christmas carols were playing here. Pier 17 consisted of a wide open space with a few vans parked near the edge of Pier 16 and a building on the north side called "Pier 17," housing yet *more* shops and restaurants, as if you couldn't have enough of them in the Seaport district. There were a few people outside, but almost everyone was inside the building.

Marissa and I ran directly toward the nearest door—a restaurant's—when Mr. Squat stepped out from the front of one of the parked vans, while his partner stepped out from its rear. They were smart: not grouping themselves as a nice tight target for me. Unfortunately, I wasn't fast enough to shoot one and then the other.

"Stop right there," Mr. Squat grunted. "You can go. Leave the woman."

"You got here fast. Faster than I thought."

His lips separated, which I supposed was a grin. "Go now. Leave the woman."

"Can I have a few seconds to think that over?"

He shrugged. Assuming the up-and-down movement of those massive shoulders was a shrug.

Without turning away, I whispered to Marissa, "In a second, I want you to run for the restaurant. Don't stop until you get inside. No matter what, you don't stop. Got it?"

"But what about—?"

"You don't stop." I turned back to the bad guys and said, "Okay, she'll come over, and I walk away?"

"Yes."

"Okay," I said to them. To her I gasped, "Run!"

I ran, too, straight at Mr. Squat. The other guy hesitated, then aimed at me. He was too late; still running, I shot him in the gut. Twice. I twisted and fired at Mr. Squat, who was ducking behind the van. I stopped on the side of the van opposite him, dropping to the ground, and looked under the van. There he was, his big honking work boots a few feet from where I lay. Shooting someone in the foot or leg is as much a matter of luck as skill, even at a short distance. I braced my right arm on the ground, carefully targeted his shoes, had a random thought about what this might do to any ingrown toenails he had, and squeezed off the shot.

He screamed. His gun bounced off the thick wooden boards of the pier, stopping several feet away, well out of his reach. But he hadn't fallen to the ground. He must have been hanging onto a door handle. The scream dwindled into a pained groan.

Go ahead, Tyrrell. Finish him. I stood up with my trusty Ruger in my right hand and walked around the front of the van.

Four feet from me was Mr. Squat, holding onto the front door handle of the van, his body sagging against the van, his left shoulder on the door frame. His left work boot was dripping blood between the thick planks of the peir to the East River below. When he saw me, his eyes went wide and a feral grin spread across his face. He lunged at me, hands wide to encircle me.

I fired almost the second he began moving and hit his left leg. But his lunge carried him into me; his weight smashed me to the pier. His left hand clamped on my right, and he banged down my gun hand on the boards until I released my pistol and it slid out of sight under the van. He punched at me repeatedly with his right hand. I parried the blows as best I could, and when opportunity presented itself, I hit him. My fist bounced off his chin like a dull axe off of an oak tree. He wasn't as powerful as Reznik, but he was equally vicious. Then again, I had shot him twice. But to be fair to me, I'd been shot twice, stabbed once, and beaten to a pulp. In a stand-up fight, both of us in good health, I think I could have taken him. But he was on top of me, his anger more than compensating for his wounds, and he was making an excellent effort to pound the life out of me. I rolled to my left and pushed up against his left hand.

The roll maneuver didn't work. But it didn't have to; it was a feint. Mr. Squat braced himself against my rolling by extending his right leg, shifting his balance. I rolled hard and fast to my right. He scrambled to shift his center of gravity back, and our joint movements gave me the momentum to heave him off of me into the lower side of the van. He grunted in pain.

I reversed direction, spun away from him, and jumped to my feet. He stood very slowly, pulling himself up by the van's door handle. The feral grin returned as his hand went inside his coat and emerged with a six-inch blade that glistened in the Christmas lights. I was too far away for him to reach me with one or two steps, I didn't think he was capable of charging me. As I tried to figure my next move—

A New York City cop stepped around the van. He checked me out then Mr. Squat. The officer's right hand cradled his service weapon, but he didn't pull it from its holster. His held out his left hand, palm up as if trying to stop anything from happening.

"Okay, let's not anyone get hurt, okay? Put the knife down, and we'll talk this out. Okay?"

Mr. Squat grinned more widely then dove at the cop, the blade slashing at the officer's unprotected neck . . . the cop was pulling his weapon as fast as he could, but he didn't have a chance of saving himself . . .

I jumped in between them.

Mr. Squat stabbed me below my right collarbone. The blade slid down past my upper ribs deep into my chest. I dropped to my knees, pulling Mr. Squat's knife hand down with me. There were gunshots. My body twisted, and I slammed face first onto the pier. Everything went dark gray. Everything went black.

17

My first impression—drug-addled though I was thanks to a massive load of pain killers—was that I was in a very nice hospital. Unlike my previous hospital experiences, someone hadn't awakened me every five minutes to take my temperature, check my meds, or change the bedpan. I was able to sleep, and I needed every single second of snoozing I could manage. I was later informed that I had been woken up at regular and annoying intervals, but I was drugged out and didn't notice or remember. Wow. Good drugs.

That blissful, drug-induced first impression didn't last long. I was fuzzy about the passage of time, but I had probably not been asleep in the hospital for more than twenty-four hours. Once the twenty-fifth hour arrived, I was aware of every doctor, nurse, and health aide who stopped into my room for any reason whatsoever. And it appeared that almost every single medical worker in New York City wanted to help make my hospital stay as comfortable and as possible..

"What did I do to warrant all this attention?" I asked on day three. I had a vague, fuzzy notion that it was the third day.

One of my vast team of doctors, an incredibly cute,

young Japanese woman named Rachel Hirota, asked, "You don't remember?"

"Would I be asking if I remembered?"

She smiled—and I thought she really is damn pretty, then realized that I must be in reasonably good shape since my affliction of thinking that every woman was intensely attractive was in full force. She's too young, Tyrrell. *And she's your doctor.*

My too young, too cute physician said, "You saved a cop's life. And you almost died doing it. You're a hero."

"Oh, my. You'd think I'd remember something like that."

"It may come back to you," she said, sounding crisply professional. "The trauma of your wounds and the heavy drugs of the last couple of days are enough to crimp anyone's memory."

"I apologize if you've already told me, but what is my medical condition?"

"You're in amazingly good shape. You came into the ER with two gunshot wounds, two stab wounds, and dozens of blunt-force traumas over most of your body. One of the stab wounds was very deep—it's a miracle you're alive never mind in good health."

"That's me: Mr. Miracle."

She bestowed a dazzling grin upon me, checked her chart and her watch, and said, "I have rounds now. I'll see you later."

Lunch was served a little bit later, and I will refrain

from making jello jokes. The food wasn't good—it wasn't terrible either, and I surprised myself by cleaning my plate in a fashion that I hadn't since I was six or seven years old. Not knowing if I was supposed to or not, I climbed out of bed unaided and unsupervised, clutched the rear-opening hospital gown to keep it closed, and scurried to the bathroom, pulling the bottle containing my intravenous drip along on its wheeled stand. I was surprised at how easy it was to walk.

Once in the bathroom, I was sorry that, like all bathrooms, this one had a mirror. I had a couple of stitches near the center of my forehead, a couple more on the left cheek bone, and six stitches above my right jawline. My left eye wasn't a full-blown shiner, but the skin around it was dark and puffy.

"Yikes," I said to my reflection. Then I brushed my teeth and was pleased that all of them seemed to be in place.

A few minutes after I settled back in bed, just long enough to get my breath back after an exertion that should not have winded me, there was a knock on my door, and in walked Kim Gannon. She was every bit as beautiful as I remembered. Maybe I was under the influence of my every-woman-is-gorgeous syndrome. Maybe it was the any-woman-looks fantastic-when-you've-had-a-near-death experience. But, in reality, it was because Kim was truly beautiful.

"Wow," I said appreciatively.

She smiled, walked over to the bed, leaned over, and

kissed me softly on the lips. "Hello, there. It's good to see you."

"It's amazing to see you." I returned her smile. "How did you know that I was here?'

"Your friend came to see me at Café Sabatini." She walked around my bed to avoid all the medical equipment was on that side and the intravenous drip was inserted into the back of my left hand.

"My friend—?" I was puzzled.

"Your colleague? Harry?"

"Oh, Harry. Uh . . . yeah, my colleague."

"I wish my colleagues talked about me the way Harry talks about you," she said as she took my hand in hers. "He said you saved a cop's life and almost died in the process. He told me you were the anonymous hero the media's going on about. Are you?"

"Wait a minute, *what* was in the news?"

"An anonymous man jumped between a police officer and his attacker. The man was stabbed. According to the news reports, it's a miracle he lived."

"What did Harry say about all that?"

"He said it was all true—you were the man who was stabbed."

"Well, I was the guy, but I think the hero thing is the media selling a story—"

"Stop it," she said sharply and squeezed my hand for emphasis. "Stop it. You're great."

I took a deep breath, "Thank you."

"You're welcome." She gave my hand another squeeze. A much gentler and more affectionate sort of pressure.

"Were there any other details in the news about the incident?" I worried how much trouble I could be in. I had been carrying an unregistered pistol and a second pistol, with my fingerprints would have been retrieved from under the van. Ballistics would match my gun to the shootings at the Manhattan Majestic apartments. Things could get very uncomfortable for me.

"Nothing. Not that I heard anyway . . ."

I grunted in response. I wondered if Harry had sanitized things for me.

She looked at our intertwined hands. "Is your work . . . is what you do legal?"

"Absolutely. Believe me, my boss . . . and Harry, there's no way they'd ever be involved in anything illegal."

"Sorry to ask, but . . . the anonymity . . . it's hard to make sense of it."

"Unless I did something illegal, and the cops are withholding information? Then it makes sense to you?"

She laughed, "Well, Harry did tell me the NYPD is going to give you a medal, but . . . because of the nature of your work, it will be done anonymously. What kind of honor is it if it's a secret?" she asked.

"Well . . . it's like the CIA, when one of their agents is doing a classified mission and is given any kind of medal, the medal is classified, too. Has to be in secret."

"But you don't work for the CIA."

"No, but my employer would want me to remain unknown. Better for my work. Safer for me personally."

Kim grinned and pointed at my face, "You call that being safe?"

"Geez Louise . . . I was so happy to see you I forgot to be embarrassed about my battered looks. Sorry you have to see me like this."

"I'm just happy to see you, period." She leaned over to kiss me again. "You'll look handsome again in no time."

There was another knock on the door, and two uniformed NYPD patrolmen walked in. The taller one had what my mother would have called "a map of Ireland" face, reddish brown hair, blue eyes, freckles. The officer with him was slightly shorter and Hispanic with large dark eyes and close-cropped dark hair.

The map of Ireland extended a hand and said, "I'm officer Michael Muldoon. You saved my life the other night, and I wanted to thank you. That was an incredibly brave thing you did. I'm really grateful."

Kim and I let go of each other's hands, and I reached over the bed to shake Muldoon's hand. The other cop pretended to be perturbed.

"I'm not sure it was a great thing you did," he grinned. "I'm his partner, Javier Gonzaga. Thanks to you, I'm stuck with this guy." Gonzaga reached out to shake my hand.

I replied, "I'm sorry, but I didn't have enough time to

consider all the ramifications of my actions. Next time I won't save him."

"Thank you," Gonzaga said. "That's all I'm asking." He spoke across the bed to Kim, "I'm sorry, we didn't mean to interrupt your visit. Mrs. Tyrrell?"

I flushed, and Kim laughed, "No, I'm . . . his girlfriend."

"Lucky lady," Muldoon said and jerked his thumb in my direction. "Not many guys like this around."

"Amen," Gonzaga added.

They stayed for a few minutes, and we made awkward jokes, and they repeatedly told me that if I ever needed anything, get in touch. They owed me, they said.

I admit I wasn't really paying attention. I was focused on what Kim had said: she was my "girlfriend."

I was a lucky guy.

*   *   *

That evening, well after visiting hours, Harry stopped by. Rules about visiting hours didn't seem to apply to Harry. The energy level in the hospital had dropped after dinner. Most of the wards didn't allow visitors, and the lights in many rooms were turned down. It was quiet.

"I thought you might like to know what's been going on since you became a hero."

"Was that a compliment or an ironic comment? I can't tell with you."

"Both."

I chuckled, "Yeah, sure, please tell me what's happened. What about all the eyewitnesses at the Seaport who saw Marissa and me pursued by gun-toting thugs?"

"They remember the men running and shooting, but not the people being chased."

"What about my guns? I had one in a holster and there was one under a van."

"You didn't have any guns or any holsters."

"Really?"

"Really. You had no weapons of any kind when you saved Officer Muldoon's life."

"And the apartment where Reznik and Faringer died? There must have been DNA from me all over. Not to mention one of my bullets in Reznik."

"Your injuries have left you confused. There's no DNA or bullets of yours in the apartment. It's as if you were never there."

"What about Marissa? Was she there? What happened with the McGill homicide?"

"Marissa was there. The police theory is that Reznik and Faringer had a falling out, the . . . bad guys, as you would call them, shot each other, and Marissa escaped. When the police asked her if that was how she gotten away, she realized the best way to proceed was to affirm their beliefs."

"How did she explain her gunshot wound?"

"It was blamed on Reznik, and once again, Marissa

affirmed the police theory. In case you were wondering, she has remarkable healing powers. By the time she had arrived at the hospital, her wound seemed to be the most minor gunshot wound possible. Apparently you barely grazed her."

"I'm guessing I owe that to you."

"Not me."

"The Chairman adjusted my aim?"

"That's what I believe."

"Did the Chairman save my life when I was stabbed? The police and the media seem to think it was a miracle. Was it?"

"I believe it was."

"You don't know?"

"I'm like you, Jack, a creature of free will and faith."

I was too tired to have a discussion about faith. I sipped water from a tiny, blue plastic cup, and changed the subject.

"What about Cú Chulainn Enterprises and SHK Dragon?"

"The files you e-mailed to your friend Joanne at the FBI exonerated Marissa, ended the merger talks between the two companies, and moved the Cú Chulainn board of directors to appoint an acting CEO while they look for a long-term replacement. The directors issued a press release committing to following the polices and vision of Jackson McGill."

"Everything neat and tidy," I said.

"You don't sound particularly happy about that."

"I'm grateful, Harry, I really am. I'm glad everything has worked out, but . . ."

"What is it you're worried about?"

"I prayed to the Chairman for help, and He gave it to me. I didn't want to torture anyone, but I caused a lot of pain and used horrible threats. I'm not sure I didn't trip over the line regarding torture."

"You're not perfect. But you did what you could in very difficult circumstances."

My eyebrows arched in disbelief at what I was hearing. "Are you giving me a direct affirmation? Instead of your usual Socratic technique?"

"Yes. It seemed like the best thing to do considering your weakened condition."

"Thank you."

"You're worried about more than the question of torture. What's wrong?"

"I believe the Chairman answered my prayers and helped me. But I used His help to kill several people. Does the Chairman help people to kill other people?"

"What do you think?"

"I think He did this time."

"Maybe you were an instrument of His justice."

"I hope so."

"How do you feel about killing Reznik?"

"He deserved it."

"I think you've answered your own question."

* * *

Harry and Kim came the next day to take me home. The idea that my guardian angel and my girlfriend were managing my life made me a little anxious, but if I had to, I could get used to it.

I was surprised that my apartment was absolutely pristine when we walked in. Surprised because Reznik's visit had been sadistically destructive.

Harry spoke sotto voce, "I arranged to have it cleaned."

Kim glided through the apartment on a self-guided tour and returned to the living room. "I like your apartment."

"Feel free to stop by anytime."

"I may take you up on that." She glanced around. "You need a Christmas tree."

"I've been a little distracted."

"I'll leave you to settle in," Harry said and offered me his hand to shake. This almost warm, almost friendly Harry was strange to me, but I liked him. We shook hands, and he said, "I'll see you later."

"Six o'clock at Park and East 79th," I confirmed.

He nodded and said, "Goodbye, Ms. Gannon."

"Mr. Mitchum." As he exited the apartment, Kim arched her left eyebrow at me. "Why are you meeting Harry at six this evening."

"A final debriefing with the client."

"Care to join me for dinner afterward? Eight o'clock,

my place?"

"That would be very nice."

*   *   *

Because it was late December and daylight disappeared around four-thirty, I walked to my rendezvous with Harry by going around Central Park on its southern end, then turning north at the corner of Fifth Avenue and Central Park South. By the time I reached 79th Street, I was more winded than usual. I had been told multiple times by doctors and nurses, police detectives, and Harry that I was very lucky to be alive. That good luck didn't make my recovery go any faster. The long blocks along 79th Street from Fifth across Madison to Park only seemed to be 100 miles long.

Harry was waiting for me on the northwest corner of Park Avenue and 79th Street. We were surrounded by tall, elegant, pre-war buildings, and the traffic that flowed past on Park Avenue seemed to have a much higher percentage of Audis, BMWs, Jaguars, Lexuses, and Mercedes than the usual Manhattan mix. I even saw a long, silver Rolls Royce glide by. Yes, it was a nice neighborhood.

"How do you feel?" Harry asked.

"I'm a bit more tired than I expected."

"You shouldn't push yourself."

"Thank you, I'll be sure to keep that in mind."

Harry's Mona Lisa smile flitted across his mouth.

"Could you provide me with some answers?" I asked.

"Yes."

"Does Marissa remember me?"

"She does for now. After she's had the chance to say thank you, she won't. But the Chairman felt she needed to be able to express her gratitude."

"And I need the chance to say goodbye."

"I know."

We walked uptown on Park, past the elegant buildings and past the front of the Church of St. Ignatius Loyola, turned left on 84th Street, and walked along the side of the church to the St. Ignatius grade school. We went through the school entrance and downstairs to a cafeteria. Plastic chairs surrounded formica-topped tables. There was a large kitchen diagonally opposite the stairs, with a couple of tall coffee pots, white styrofoam cups, milk and sugar, and plates of cookies set out on the serving counter. On the cafeteria's far wall a pair of white window shades with black type were displayed. One was headlined: The Twelve Steps. The other was: The Twelve Traditions. The room was set up for an A.A. meeting.

Marissa Carvajal was standing near the coffee pots, a cup in her hand, speaking with another woman. She spotted us as we came into the cafeteria, smiled, excused herself from her conversation, put her coffee cup down on the counter, and walked over to us.

A radiant smile lit up her face as she threw her arms

around me and hugged me as if she never wanted to let me go. I hugged her, too. If I was honest with myself, I had to admit I was very glad that Kim had not accompanied me for this debriefing. People walked into the meeting and smiled at the sight of Marissa and me locked in an embrace.

Marissa let go of me after a minute and wiped tears from both eyes. "Thank you so much," she said, squeezing my forearm with her hand. She did the same for Harry with her other hand. "Thank you. I can't say it enough. Thank you."

"You've said it plenty," I responded, grinning. "I'm overjoyed that you've come here."

She beamed at Harry, "Harry brought me to my first meeting a week ago. It's only been seven days, but I feel hope for the first time in a long time."

"One day at a time, you can continue to feel that way," Harry said.

"I haven't had a drink for two weeks, and I've been to a meeting every day. I feel much better. I think I've changed my life."

"I hope so," I said. "Like Harry said, take it one day at a time."

"That's what everyone in A.A. says." She reached out and took my left hand in her right. "Can I . . . take you out to dinner? I'd like to say thank you. I'd like . . . to see you again."

I took a deep breath and replied, "I wish I could, but . . . well," I gestured toward Harry, "that's not the way we work."

"Against policy?" she forced a smile.

"Yes, I'm sorry."

Marissa wiped more tears from her cheek, smiled, and stood on tiptoe to kiss me. She whispered to me, "I won't waste this second chance." She stepped back, still holding my hand, and said, "Maybe I'll see you later . . . sometime."

"You never know."

* * *

Harry and I left as the meeting began. We went down to the corner at Park Avenue and stopped in front of St. Ignatius church.

Harry said, "I thought you were interested in Ms. Gannon."

"I am. That doesn't make saying goodbye to Marissa any easier. Will she make it?"

"She has a good chance."

"You can't tell me one way or the other?"

"It's up to her."

"Won't the Chairman help her?"

"If He's asked."

I sighed.

"You've done everything you could do, Jack."

"And now she doesn't even remember me."

"No, she doesn't."

"I know that's the deal, but. . . ."

"As you say, that's the deal. Will you be ready for our next job?"

"Yes." I watched the traffic flow downtown on Park Avenue for a minute. "Is Kim going to forget things?"

"Right now she doesn't know anything she needs to forget."

"What if she learns something?"

"I don't know."

"Could she forget me?"

"I don't know."

"Am I . . . could I please see Maggie again?"

"That's not for me to decide."

"Will the Chairman let me see her again?"

"I don't know."

Two miles south of us, the elegant Beaux-Arts Helmsley Building at 230 Park Avenue, straddled Park Avenue. The top of the building was lit in an array of Christmas colors that changed and blended into new combinations. Christmas trees were in the median running down the center of Park Avenue. Beautiful, if you like that sort of thing. I liked it very much.

I took a deep breath. "Could you . . . could you ask Maggie if it's all right if I move on?"

"You can do that yourself." Harry disappeared instantly.

I had enough time to walk all the way to Kim's apartment. Cold weather doesn't stop me from hiking all over Manhattan. I walked down Park Avenue until I reached 59th Street, then turned right. The fountain in front of the Plaza Hotel was filled with Christmas trees and lights. A giant menorah stood on the broad sidewalk at the southern corner of Central Park. I crossed over to the fountain and appreciated the lights and trees. There were little groups of people around the fountain, enjoying the Christmas sights, but no one was near me.

"Maggie?" I said softly. "Maggie, can I talk with you?"

She did not appear, did not whoosh into my presence. I missed her so intensely, it caused physical pain in my gut. My eyes were watering. But even as I was overwhelmed with sadness at the loss of Maggie, I felt lighter than I had for a long time. Since Maggie and I had first started dating. That's what occurs at the beginning of a relationship when the possibilities stretch before you: your step quickens, your smile takes up permanent residence on your face. You become ready to release the pain of your past.

"Maggie, I . . . I've met someone. I don't know where we're going to go. But . . . but I wondered if it's okay with you if I take a chance. If I move on. I love you, Maggie. But . . . maybe it's time to move on. Are you okay with that?"

There was no answer. Maggie did not make an

appearance. There was no white light. No inspirational thought that leapt to mind with brilliant clarity. I took a deep breath and stared at the Christmas trees.

And I suddenly realized that the Christmas carol playing over the outdoor sound system was "Hark! The Herald Angels Sing." Maggie's favorite. It could have been chance. A magical coincidence. Maggie had always referred to moments of magical coincidence as God kisses.

"Thank you," I said. "I'll always love you, Maggie."

I blew a kiss to the air above, and began walking toward Kim's place, taking the first steps of the rest of my life.

ABOUT THE AUTHOR

Geoff Loftus is the author of the thrillers *Murderous Spirit* (A Jack Tyrell Novel), *Double Blind, Engaged to Kill*, and *The Dark Saint*.

He is also the author of *Lead Like Ike: Ten Business Strategies from the CEO of D-Day* and was the 2010 Keynote Speaker at the Eisenhower Legacy Dinner at the Eisenhower Presidential Museum and Library. He also blogs for FORBES.com on leadership.

Like many writers, he once dreamed of writing the great American novel but gave that up in an attempt to write the great American screenplay. The closest he came to that lofty achievement was writing *Hero in the Family* with John Drimmer for *The Wonderful World of Disney*. He has been a member of the Writers Guild of America, East for more than twenty-five years.

He lives in Scarsdale, New York with his wife, Margy; son, Gregory; and the family's wonderful little dog, Heidi.

Acknowledgments

Once again, I must acknowledge three amazingly creative men for guiding me in the writing of the Jack Tyrrell novels: Charles Dickens who wrote the best Christmas story (and best ghost story) ever: *A Christmas Carol*; the dazzlingly inventive Philip K. Dick who wrote the short story *Adjustment Team*; and George Nolfi, the writer-director of the terrific movie based on Dick's story: *The Adjustment Bureau*.

Many thanks to my editorial team: Alice Siempelkamp and Ted Berk. They catch many mistakes and suggest many good ideas, but despite all of their help, I still blow it. Tom Seligson has been my editor and publisher at Saugatuck Books, and I'm very grateful for his continuing to keep me on Saugatuck's roster of authors.

And thanks to the many friends who have helped me through the writing of this book and all the other parts of my life: Tom and Judy Galligan, Ted Canellas and Bob Roth, Erica Fross, Gene O'Brien, Steve Pitts, Katie Ryan, Jill Quist, Marcia Menter, Greg Tobin, Sal Vitale, and Lindy Sittenfeld.

Special thanks to my son, Greg, who inspires me to be better in every part of my life—I hope I can be just like him when I grow up.

Finally, thanks to my wife, Margy. As Brian Wilson and Tony Asher wrote for the Beach Boys, "God only knows what I'd be without you."

Made in the USA
Monee, IL
27 June 2023

37817741R00197